STRANGER TIDES

-A ***Stranger World*** Story-

Jack ♖ Castle

Castle Books, Inc.

Jack Castle/Stranger Tides
www.JackCastlebooks.com
www.JackCastle@aol.com

Publisher's Note: This is a work of fiction. Names, characters, places, and incidents are a product of the author's imagination. Locales and public names are sometimes used for atmospheric purposes. Any resemblance to actual people, living or dead, or to businesses, companies, events, institutions, or locales is completely coincidental.

Stranger Tides/ Jack Castle. -- 1st ed.
ISBN: 978-1-0878-5871-5

Praise for

JACK CASTLE

and the #1 best-selling series

Stranger World

★★★★★

"Jack Castle-style' is officially now a thing! The lines of imagination and reality never have been so blurred as they are in the amazing yet sinister theme park so creatively envisioned by Jack Castle!"

-Joe Butler, Spokesman Review

"I've taught literature at several colleges over the last 35 years, and Jack Castle is a harbinger of great adventures to come."

-Dr. J.P. Waller
Editor for Vice-President, Al Gore

Also by Jack Castle:

Europa Journal
Bedlam Lost
White Death
The Revenants

Stranger World (series):

Stranger Origins
Stranger World
Stranger Realm
Stranger Tides
Stranger Desert
Stranger Dream

For the guy who first believed.
My Best Friend,
Chad Bryant

"The Sea is only the embodiment of a supernatural and wonderful existence."

—Jules Verne

• PROLOGUE •

The Factory

"MEAT-WAGON!"

"Coming..."

Henry, a slender teenage boy pushing a rusty, two-wheeled cart, ran as fast as his oversized clodhoppers could carry him. To do otherwise meant punishment in the form of a demotion. If there was one thing Henry did not want out of life, it was to be demoted; because demotion in the "Factory" meant certain death.

He parked his meat-wagon next to the dead body. It was a real fat one. The man's thin mustache was familiar, as were the blood-stains around his mouth and in the palm of his hand.

Aw shoot, I know this one.

The fat guy's name was Barnaby.

Well, it used to be Barnaby.

Despite the fact that he was always complaining about work, Henry kinda liked him.

Barnaby was always telling all those funny stories about fantastical places that obviously never existed like fairy mazes, and dinosaur jungles. Oh, and let's not forget his favorite, rivers teeming with shape-changing water-nymphs and swamps filled with zombie-pirates. Henry wasn't sure if the old dude was pulling his leg or not, but he knew no place like that could possibly be real.

He wasn't stupid.

No. Henry considered himself the practical sort. If he couldn't see it; it didn't exist. As far as he was concerned, only two places did exist: The Factory where he worked and the bunkhouse where he ate, bathed and slept. Other workers had told him about places above, where the masters lived in the lap of luxury, but he had never seen it for himself, ergo, it was just as mythical as ole' man Barnaby's fantasy lands.

"Henry, you gonna stare at the H. R. (Human Remains) all day, or what?" Piotr, a slightly older boy with platinum-white colored hair, suddenly arrived behind him.

Henry didn't care so much for Piotr because among many other things, Piotr thought of himself as a floor-boss, which he was not. Piotr was only a crew chief, which was only one rank above him. Piotr was also a big fat liar. For starters, Piotr said his mother was a woman named Russia, but if memory served (and it really didn't) he was pretty sure that Russia was a place, and not a woman.

Henry wasn't entirely sure how he knew these things. He figured he must have gone to school at some point for he knew other things too, like how the solar system had nine planets and how photosynthesis worked, but he had no memory of actually going to school. Who was to say Russia was any more real than Barnaby's fairy maze, or the leisure palaces up above? He didn't know. Henry's ceiling was literally only as high as the grimy, smoke-stained roof seventy feet above him. The closest he had ever come to seeing anything other than The Factory was the darkened clouds, barely visible through the massive smoke-stained skylights above them. Even this was only when they had to open them periodically throughout the day to let out the excess smoke.

Both boys grunted as they lifted up the HR and loaded the cadaver into the meat wagon. Piotr coughed into his hand from the exertion. They both froze while Piotr checked the palm of his hand. *No blood.* That was good. Piotr didn't have it. The *Black Lung* or what everyone else on the floor called it, the *Red-Hand*. Once you saw blood in your palm, you pretty much knew you were a *Goner.* Sometimes the bigger men would last for a few weeks, but Henry rarely saw any worker live beyond that.

Seeing Henry stare over at his hand, Piotr asked, "Yeah, you'd like that wouldn't you?" His grin broadened like a snake ready to unhinge its jaw for a meal, "Maybe get a promotion?"

Henry shook his head. "No. I wasn't thinking that at all." He didn't know why Piotr was so worried. The head floor boss had once explained that they had nothing to fear. They were young; they were strong like bear. He was very clear when he said that the black lung only took down the old and lazy workers. Even though everybody was coughing up blood and keeling over, they were young and had nothing to worry about.

Piotr lit up a cigarette, and held it there as he said, "Better luck tomorrow, Probie." The platinum-haired boy took a long drag off his cigarette and then commanded Henry, "C'mon, let's dump this HR before he gets stiff."

Henry didn't talk back, instead, with gloved hands he grabbed the handles of the meat-wagon and began to push. Piotr would only offer assistance when the wagon got caught on something, say a mound of dirt or errant piece of coal, or if a pit-boss was watching he might push as briefly as was necessary.

Their job was simple, body disposal. Load body into wagon. Dump body into chute. Chute took bodies down to the furnace. As far as most workers were concerned, a plump body like Barnaby's meant less coal was necessary for the leisure palaces to burn up above, which meant less coal needed to be shoveled into the furnaces. Someone as fat as Barnaby would burn a good long time.

Last week they had a record amount of bodies because there had been an uprising. *What fools!* Those idiots didn't last five minutes against the guards, and certainly not against their guns.

Henry couldn't understand why so many workers had to make trouble. Why couldn't they appreciate what they had? The floor-bosses had explained it to them perfectly. You work hard–you get food, and even a warm place to sleep at night. Without this job, they'd be tossed out on the street and starve to death or be eaten by the packs of wild dogs that roamed the streets at night.

Besides, shoveling coal into furnaces to fuel the steam engines, which powered the city above, it was a good job. A noble one. Sure, the work was hard, molten burned skin and machines crunched bone. It's what kept wagon-runners like him and Piotr so busy. Pushing around a meat-wagon was a lot better than back-breaking labor like shoveling, or fishing glass out of the furnace where you could easily get splashed by molten lava or your lungs set on fire. Why, streams of hot metal poured down on the glass-retrievers all the time.

Machinists sure as heck didn't fare much better. He had once seen an oiler get his clothes entangled in the cog wheels, which dragged him right into the machine. The poor, sap was so mangled out of all semblance of humanity, his flesh was still adhering to the cogs to this day. Such horrific accidents were of little concern to the management above.

Henry was lucky to have survived both jobs with as little burns, scars and broken bones as he had. If you didn't like your job, you could work your way up through the ranks as he did to get a better one, like wagon-runner.

They were about halfway to the chute when Piotr signaled for him to stop. Checking to see if anyone was watching, Piotr commanded, out of the side of his mouth, "Hey Puke, go bring me that shovel."

Henry hated the way Piotr always talked down to him. He was only a few years older. Henry knew Piotr really didn't need the shovel, any more than they needed a machinist's oil can. It was just an excuse to give Henry something to do while Piotr rummaged through Barnaby's clothes for any valuables.

Piotr would remove belts for the leather and anything else salvageable. Barnaby's shoes were worn out and his hat was far too big for Piotr, but he'd stuff both in his tattered coat and barter them off later. Piotr was always pilfering things off dead bodies; sometimes living ones too, when they weren't paying close enough attention.

That wasn't all. There were rumors that Piotr had murdered his last assistant. The official record was the ten-year-old boy had slipped and fallen down the chute into the molten lava.

The other wagon-runners had warned him to never turn his back on Piotr, and he almost never did, especially around the chutes and cog wheels.

While retrieving the shovel, Henry knew enough to take it slow, allowing Piotr plenty of time to pocket anything on poor ole' Barnaby.

I'm sure gonna miss the old man's stories.

Henry wasn't sure exactly how long he had been in The Factory. The days just sort of all ran together. He had to be working at least a year, because Henry remembered when he started, his pants were over his shoes, unlike now. So, he was no probe, like Piotr was always telling everyone.

Henry flinched heavily at the abrupt sound of glass breaking.

As tinkling glass fell from the ceiling, a chrome-plated missile struck the ground with a loud SHRUUMPPPP, and crushed unsuspecting Piotr instantly.

The impact was so close, it knocked Henry to the ground. For a few moments he remained still, lying face down with his hands covering his head. When the dust finally settled, he flipped over to sit up. Where Piotr and his jam-packed meat-wagon had been only seconds ago, there was now a large chrome cylinder, shaped like a giant dart. It must have been what smashed through the roof.

Henry realized, if Piotr hadn't ordered him to fetch the shovel, he would've been crushed too.

Staring at the giant chrome dart, he finally began to wonder, *Is it a bomb?*

If it was, for some reason, it failed to detonate. It just stood there, sticking out of the ground at a slight angle, looking like a miniature Leaning Tower of Pisa with fins on the tail.

He covered his head again when the last of the broken glass dropping down from the ceiling reached him and crashed all around him. Distant alarms began sounding and soon the guards, with their heavy machine guns, began appearing on the upper catwalks.

Staring up through the broken skylights at the sky Henry saw a giant shadow, shaped like a flying boat. It was slowly moving overhead. It began blocking out what little daylight there was.

Is that a ship? How is it floating?

Suddenly Barnaby's ridiculous stories had a bit more credence than Piotr's mother, Russia.

Henry squinted up at the flying boat just in time to see figures leaping off to their deaths and flying toward the ground at high rates of speed.

Why are they killing themselves?

To his surprise, the jumpers didn't go splat on The Factory floor, as Henry suspected they would. Instead they stopped at the last moment before hitting the ground and stepped down from narrow platforms, about the width of a ladder rung. In turn, the narrow rungs were connected to highly-flexible, telescoping pipes that went back up to the floating ship.

Henry had heard stories of resistance fighters, but he had never actually seen one. He had never even spoken to anyone who had seen one with their own eyes either. So again, he thought it was simply hearsay, but he was beginning to wonder if these guys were them.

The nearest of them looked like a young girl, maybe fourteen. She had mounds of curly hair, welder's goggles over her eyes and a thick scarf over her mouth.

Probably can't handle the soot, he thought to himself.

Suddenly, one of the guards on the catwalks opened fire on them. Henry tried to get up but the girl with curly hair and welder's goggles kicked him in the chest. And in a voice muffled by the scarf, she said, "Stay down kid."

She turned, drew a chubby, chrome-plated pistol from a worn, leather holster and squeezed the trigger. To Henry's amazement, a purple beam of light streaked out of the funny-looking ray gun, and with a loud echoing sound, the beam hit one of the guards on the catwalk. The wounded guard bounced off the wall behind him, and then tumbled over the railing to his death.

Henry knew it didn't matter. In seconds, dozens more would take his place. Whoever these people were, Henry could have told them they didn't have a chance. There was no way they were getting out of The Factory alive.

As if confirming these thoughts, nearly fifty more guards quick-time marched onto the catwalks along the walls and above them.

Instinctively, the girl ducked as bullets zinged over her head and ricocheted all around them. In response, she removed a cylindrical device out of one of the leather pouches on her belt. It was about the size of fat pen. She flicked off a clear-plastic safety covering with her thumb and depressed a round-blue button.

The chrome missile that had failed to detonate now bloomed like a flower, and Henry heard a whining noise building in octaves. The girl with mounds of hair and welders goggles hit the floor and covered her ears. Henry figured he should probably do the same. Before he could, there was an explosion of blinding white light accompanied with a loud, deafening noise.

After the light dissipated, Henry was surprised to find he was still alive.

As his vision finally began to clear, he saw the girl standing over him with her hand extended toward him. He could barely make out the words she was shouting to him, “Come on kid, not sure how long that E.M.P. blast is going to keep them off our backs.”

He realized the gunfire had stopped. When he looked to the guards, he could see they were all doubled over, either unconscious or dead. Some of them even appeared to be emitting sparks, a few more on fire.

The guards are Robots?

A few minutes must have passed while he was waiting for his ears to stop ringing and vision to clear, because he could now see the resistance fighters moving through The Factory workers. Each fighter was making little flag symbols over each worker. The flags they drew were stark white and magically floated above each person’s head.

“Check this one,” one of the fighters yelled.

Henry could see all The Factory workers either splayed on the ground or kneeling with their hands held overhead.

"Over here," the young girl cried next to him. She had drawn a flag symbol over his head and when he glimpsed it, floating there as if by magic, he could see that it was also white.

That was when he saw the demon for the first time.

As it bounded over to him like a giant dog, Henry realized it wasn't really a monster. It reminded him of those statues he had seen in a picture once. They were mounted on a church in Paris, France. The Notre Dame.

Gargoyles, that's what they were called.

The gargoyle bounding toward him had lots of pointed teeth and taloned claws. Henry was fairly certain he only had a few seconds to live, which as it turned out, wasn't that much longer than Piotr. The gargoyle stopped just shy of devouring him, kicking up soot and causing Henry to cough. The stone golem, who really wasn't stone, was dressed in a butler's uniform. And, instead of biting him, it began sniffing him.

"Okay, thissthhhpp one's good," the gargoyle shouted gleefully.

Henry had just enough time to notice it spoke with a strong lisp before it bounded away toward another worker with a floating white flag above his head.

The girl with the welder's goggles; the one who was still standing above him, touched the flag above his head again and this time the flag turned from white to a pleasant green.

"Can you stand? Are you hurt?"

Henry didn't answer. He saw the gargoyle sniff other workers and once he gave the all clear, their little flags turned green as well.

Henry wasn't sure he wanted to find out what would happen if the flag did not turn green.

The girl kicked him lightly with the toe of her boot, "Hey, I asked you a question. Are you hurt? Can you stand?"

Henry nodded.

"Okay, let's go. I don't have all day." She leaned forward and helped him to his feet. He found that he could barely walk. Whatever the blooming flower had done to him, he felt sick to his stomach, and he was pretty sure he was going to puke.

"Can you walk by yourself?" she asked, half-holding him.

"I think so," but when she eased up on her grip, he nearly collapsed.

She sighed heavily. "Alright, I'm going to have to walk you."

He had so many questions he wanted to ask, 'Who are you?' and 'What's going on?" but in the end he settled for, "Where are you taking me?"

"Just keep walking, kid. You're not the only one we have to save," she said, and then commanded, "Left foot, right foot, left foot, right foot. C'mon, keep up the pace."

He lifted his chin from his feet and saw gilded, shark cages resting in the middle of The Factory floor.

Where did those come from?

He lifted his gaze skyward and saw chains on top of the cages that extended all the way up to the floating boat. Now that they were closer, he could make out letters written on the side: ***H.M.A.S. DAUNTLESS***

The girl shoved him inside the shark cage to join several other workers, who were already there looking as shocked as he was. She took his hand and placed it on the bars, so he could steady himself if needed, "Okay, stay put, Mr. Chatty-Cathy." She pointed upwards. "We're taking you up. Just hold on tight. You got it?" When he didn't respond right away she repeated, "Do... you... got... it?"

Henry nodded in reply and heard himself say, "Okay, but my name's not Cathy."

The girl chuckled. "Right." Hiking a thumb to her chest, she said, "Maddie." Then she jumped out of the cage, slammed the door, and the cage lifted toward heaven.

It was at this point it occurred to him...

Maybe that missile hit me after all.

CHAPTER 1

Maddie's Berth

"Who are you? Wait a minute, never mind. I don't care. Get out!"

The same girl Henry had seen before, the one with mounds of curly locks, only this time without her goggles matting it down, swung her skinny legs off the top bed of the bunk bed and hopped down. The girl with unruly hair seemed to be studying his meager trappings for a moment, which were little more than a bedroll and change of undergarments given to him by the ship's quartermaster. Before thrusting a gloved finger in his face and telling him in no uncertain tones, "Don't even think about it. This is my room!"

"I'm sorry," he began. Henry heard himself clear his throat and he sputtered nervously, "I was told to come down here, to this specific room."

"Who told you to come to this *specific* room?" Not waiting for an answer, she launched into her supposition. "Did Traxx put you up to this?" Again not waiting for a response, she pushed past him, stepped out into the hallway and shouted down the corridor, "Traxx, I know you did this. You get back here right now!"

Henry heard snickering down the hallway and figured Traxx was probably the kid with the goggles on his forehead who had led him below decks.

When the girl returned to the room he asked, "Do you want me to go?"

"What?" It was as though she already forgot he was there.

"I said, do you want me to go?"

She saw more refugees crowded in the hallway and now lining the walls. He recognized many of them as factory workers.

"No, you're fine. It's not your fault. You can set up over there," she said, gesturing toward an empty bunk bed on the opposite side of the room. When he removed his coat and dropped it on the lower bunk, she added, "But don't touch my stuff."

Henry didn't reply, he just waited and for a few seconds, neither of them spoke.

She sat down at a small desk and asked, "What's your name, kid?"

"Kid? I'm not a *kid*," he protested. "Heck, I'm probably older than you are."

The young girl made a scathing noise, pushed her long locks out of her eyes and said, "Please. Not in this world you're not. I've ridden on the backs of Wooly-Mammoths the size of skyscrapers... I've been on dozens of rescue missions... I even escaped the clutches of the Zombie-Pirate-King himself!"

"I'm sorry, but I don't believe in such things," although he was in a giant, gilded submarine, floating amongst the clouds.

"Trust me; if you stay aboard the Dauntless long enough, you will."

Henry shook his head. "Truth is, I don't remember my real name. But, there was this peculiar man, back before I woke up in The Factory. He used to call me Henry." He didn't tell her that it was his *only* memory before The Factory.

She studied him a moment longer, then as though deciding something, she stretched out her hand toward him in the form of a handshake and offered, "The name's Maddie."

As he shook it, she asked him, "Got any family?"

"I don't know. Before The Factory, my memory's a little fuzzy."

"Oh," she said knowingly, "You're a No-Mem."

"A what?"

Tapping her forefinger against her temple, she said, "A No-Mem. As in... No Memory."

Henry didn't like the sound of that.

Maddie dropped onto a stool next to a considerably cluttered desk situated against the back wall. She removed something from a drawer that looked like a fat, metallic dart and placed it in a vice. Focusing on her task, she pulled forward a large magnifying glass mounted on a swivel, and using tiny watchmaker-like tools, she began tinkering around with it.

Unsure what to do, he started to examine his new quarters a little more closely. For fighting so vehemently over it, there really wasn't much to it. It was only about ten steps long and half that wide. The walls were smooth, and painted a rusted gold. On the wall above her desk was a solitary porthole. Beneath that, Henry saw a few shelves stacked with dozens of books and more electronic junk. There was also one closet on either side of the room, and that was pretty much it.

The wall space that wasn't taken up by the two bunkbeds was adorned with maps and photographs. One map in particular caught his attention. There were various drawings all over it, many of which were labeled: The Fairy Maze, Dino-Land, Portlandia, and Zombie-Pirate Swamp. All seemed to be centered by a crossroads. Circles were drawn around many of these locations with green question marks next to them, where other circles were marked out with giant red Xs.

He moved closer to get a better look.

Before he could however; he felt two hands grab him by his arm, spin him around and shove him across the room.

"You just leave it alone. It doesn't concern you."

Why was she so mad all the time? he wondered.

Henry was about to apologize again, when both of them noticed a family standing out in the hall watching them. They too were refugees from The Factory. Henry didn't recognize them, only their clothes and the black smudges on their faces. They stood outside, huddled together in the hallway; a mom with a handkerchief holding back her hair, a dad with a thick mustache and leather boiler-man cap, and a blond-haired girl, who couldn't have been more than eight years old.

Spotting the young girl in the hallway, Maddie stepped up to the door and asked, "Hey, you, little girl, what's your name?"

"Sorry Miss, she is from Poland and doesn't speak English." The woman's accent was as thick as Piotr's had been. Even though it sounded like they had the same mother (Mother Russia), Henry detected something different about her accent. "We are Ukrainian, but we have been watching over her for almost a year now. Her name is... Natalia."

Maddie seemed to let this sink in, or maybe she was having a memory of her own. Eventually, she waved them inside. "Come in here, come on."

The pint-sized girl waited for her father's approval. When she got it, in the form of a head nod, she hesitantly led the family inside.

Natalia coughed into her hand and Henry instinctively checked for blood in her palm. Thankfully, there was none.

Maddie removed her bedroll from one of the bunks and tied it to a heavily worn, leather backpack. She then began grabbing some of her personal things and began shoving them into the bag. She then stared at one of her maps for a moment, almost like she was in a trance. When she realized he was staring at her, she quickly tore all the maps from the wall, rolled them up and also stuffed them into her pack. Slinging the bag over her shoulder, and patting the bunk, she said to Natalia's guardians, "Tell her, this, is her bed."

The little girl spoke softly, in Polish. When Maddie raised her palms, shrugged and said she didn't understand, Natalia stretched out a finger to the sky.

"What? You want the top bunk?" Maddie asked, patting it.

When Natalia nodded her petite head, the parents scolded her in Ukrainian, but Maddie quickly cut them off by saying, "No, no, it's okay, she can have the top bunk." To the little girl, she leaned forward and whispered into her ear, "Good choice."

Natalia lunged forward and gave her a fierce hug.

"Alright, alright, don't get all emotional on me," is what Maddie said, but Henry could tell she was secretly moved and may have even brushed a tear out of the corner of her eye.

To the parents Maddie said, "You two take the other bunks here. This is your roommate, Harry."

"It's Henry, actually."

Maddie gave him an eye-roll. "No one cares."

As Maddie finished gathering up a few more of her belongings, Henry stepped closer to her. "Wait. Where are you going?"

"It's a bit too crowded in here for my tastes." Marching purposefully out of the room with her stuffed bag, she left only the sound of heavy work boots as she clunked down the hallway.

Henry stood there a moment, too stunned to speak. He turned toward the new arrivals, but they were busy unpacking their things and getting Natalia ready for bed.

Henry ran to the door shouting, "Wait... I thought you said this was your room?"

But by the time he reached the hallway, she was already gone.

Chapter 2

Mad-Maddie

"Ahhhhhhh..."

Engineer Rick enjoyed the sound of creaking leather as he eased himself into the captain's chair. It was mounted on a metallic pole made of solid gold.

Even though he was officially the chief engineer on board, taking his turn at the wheel on the bridge of *H.M.A.S. The Dauntless*, was easily one of his private joys.

Before getting too comfortable, business came first. He checked the bulky navigation console overhead where the destination coordinates were proudly displayed in latitude and longitude. Presently their heading was North, 40 degrees 45' 84" by West 70 degrees 45' 84".

Swiveling in the captain's chair, Rick also checked their position on the large wall chart that dominated the left side of the bridge. Similar to the navigation board over his head, the design was Victorian, but in reality, the chart was as futuristic as it was functional.

To the naked eye it appeared as though the wall chart was a simple map board that would seem more at home in the 19th century, Royal British Geographical Exploration Society. But all you had to do was speak your destination to the map, and it would adjust to the requested location accordingly. That is, if the location was a mapped area. At some point in history, many of the domains of this new world had returned to uncharted territories.

As he settled further into his chair, the departing sun shone in through the large glass-paned windows and warmed his face. Gazing down upon an ocean of clouds, it was easy to imagine they were inside the Beatles' Yellow Submarine, sailing on a sea of pink cotton candy. In this world, he supposed, anything was possible.

The ship's throttle and other controls were all within easy reach of his chair. When The Leftenant was on the bridge, the controls were mostly just for show. He took another sip of his coffee and set it on the console. If The Leftenant had seen him do this, she would've been furious.

Rick leaned forward and spoke into the gramophone-shaped speaker. Even after all this time, he still appreciated how everything was designed to look like something Jules Verne might have crafted, but worked perfectly.

His voice echoing all over the ship he began, "This is your captain speaking...". He meant this only in jest as his official title on board The Dauntless was chief engineer. "We have reached an altitude of seven-thousand feet and are cruising at a steady speed of two-hundred knots per hour." The refugees they rescued would never know this, but this was a big deal. The Dauntless was originally designed to fly at only a maximum altitude of seventy feet, but after all the major modifications they had reworked over the years, she was capable of flying nearly to ten thousand.

Rick examined the refitted bridge once more. Behind every bolt and every deck plate, hid a memory. Over the years George, Traxx and he had completely remodeled the bridge by combining the fake one upstairs, with all its 20,000 leagues aesthetics, with the altruistic modern one below, to form one large bridge that combined both. Even with the futuristic tools and help from The Leftenant and other specialists they had rescued, the refit had still taken over a year. "Just a reminder, the galley will be closing for the evening at 2000 hours, so if you're hungry, I suggest you get something now. Thank you for flying with Engineer Rick Enterprises. We know you could fly with another airline, but we're glad you decided to fly with us."

Pleased with his own comments, he propped his boots up onto the helm controls in front of him and eased back in the comfy leather chair. Interlocking his fingers behind his head, he sighed with pleasure at the view of the clouds melting on the horizon.

He hungered for the quiet, and this was easily the only place on the crowded vessel he could get any piece of…

THUMP!

A leather backpack appeared on the console. It was one Rick knew as well as his own. There was a bedroll hastily tied to the side of it, while the bag was overflowing with rolled up maps.

Not even turning to see who it was, he began by saying, "No, no, no. You can't sleep here. You know the rules, Pumpkin."

"Oh, c'mon Uncle Rick. I've got nowhere else to go."

Maddie wasn't the cute little eight-year old kid he had first met six years ago. She was fast becoming a young lady. *Mad-Maddie*, that's what the rest of the crew called her. She had every right to be that way, especially after what happened to her parents.

"What's wrong with your room?" Even before she replied, Rick knew the answer. They had taken on way too many refuges. Most likely Maddie did what she always did, which was to give up her berth.

"Don't worry about it," she grumped.

He checked to see if The Leftenant was listening; which was ridiculous, because she was always listening. Nope, even if she wasn't, she recording everything that happened on the ship and played it back later.

"Look, kiddo, you know the rules. You're not even supposed to be on the bridge, especially after that stunt you and Traxx pulled last time."

"Awww... c'mon, just for tonight. I'll set up my hammock somewhere tomorrow night."

"No way. Try again."

Maddie stamped her foot and cried out a hearty, "Ughhh!"

He could imagine the wheels turning in her head. "Fine. I guess I'll just have to find somewhere else to sleep tonight."

Rick bolted upright. "Not in the engine room. Say it. Say, Uncle Rick, I won't set up my hammock in the engine room."

She paused, "With that idiot, Traxx, down there to drive me crazy? Yeah, I don't think so. No. I was thinking of stowing away in the Hopper."

This wasn't a bad idea. The Hopper was a land craft he and Traxx had reengineered for scouting expeditions. It's not like she could take one out while they were in mid-air.

Maddie grabbed her backpack but didn't lift it. She spied her rolled up maps sticking out of it and kept staring at them.

Not moving a muscle, she asked quietly, "You don't think they're dead do you?"

What to say? Rick wondered. George had made him promise never to tell what really happened to her mother, Tessa. No one had seen or heard from him in nearly three years. He felt enormously guilty. He never could stomach lying to Maddie about it. Lying about the truth.

Growing impatient, with a little more fervor in her voice, "Uncle Rick, I asked you a question."

It was time for a dose of tough love. He didn't like doing it, but it had been something he had been thinking about telling her for a good long while now. "Listen kiddo, no one has seen or heard from your parents in over three years." Seeing her face, he quickly added, "All I'm saying is your parents wouldn't want you to spend your whole life looking for them, especially if they're not able to be found."

"What do you know? Huh? You're just a big, fat, stupid, engineer." This time she did grab her backpack. "You were supposed to be his best friend. And you stopped looking for him. You all did." She moved to the hatch.

As far as Rick was concerned, she couldn't leave quick enough. She was killing him inside. "And another thing,...you're not my dad, okay?" She wiped a tear from her eye and picked up her bedroll and other belongings. She tried to leave but tripped over her feet and dropped her things. He was about to offer her a hand collecting her things, but when she flashed him a venomous look, he thought better of it. "So, stop acting like it."

Mad-Maddie was gone before he had a chance to tell her that he was sorry.

He grabbed his coffee, instinctively blew over the top of it and thought quietly to himself, *George, where are you? Are you still alive? I miss you, buddy. And, there's a young girl on board who badly who needs her daddy.*

Chapter 3

Jerry Meets the Board

"Floor please."

Jerry from Corporate flicked his hair over to one side, gave it a brief finger-comb and promptly stepped one polished loafer into the gold-plated elevator... and froze.

There was a man standing in the corner of the elevator. He was leaning against a vast array of brightly-lit, numbered buttons. Jerry could see the Imp was dressed in his normal Victorian attire, which included a ridiculously oversized top hat.

"Oh, it's you," Jerry snarled with disdain, "What are you doing here?" He stepped the rest of the way into the elevator, moved to the mirror at the back and straightened his tie.

He gave his hair another flick, before adjusting his suit and turning around.

The Lamppost Man feigned mocked surprise, "Why Jerry, whatever do you mean? I'm merely showing my support. It's not every day someone from mid-management gets called up to see the Board of the Directors." Without even tearing his gaze away from Jerry, he extended a white-gloved finger and pressed a brightly-lit button labeled 1000.

DING.

The doors of the elevator were of the gilded cage variety and rumbled closed on their tracks.

"Top floor..." the Lamppost Man said sardonically, "must be pretty important."

"Wear that stupid grin of yours all you want, but I truly doubt I'm in any serious trouble."

The Lamppost Man tilted his head as he thought about this for a moment. "Well, you don't exactly get called up to the top floor for nothing, do you? I mean you are responsible for the Zombie-Pirate-King and his crew roaming about, pillaging and plundering across *all* the lands." He straightened his head and asked, "How do you mess up a refurbishment anyway? I mean those R-Techs practically run themselves..."

Jerry dismissed him with a flick of his hair, but as they began passing through the 300's he shivered involuntarily.

Human Resources. The array of screams heard within was as varied in octaves as they were numerous.

The Lamppost Man closed his eyes and listened intently. "Oh, listen to them. What sweet music they make."

The elevator soon passed through them and continued to carry them upwards into the 600's. Most of these floors were combined to accommodate one massive hanger for Research and Development. Within the cavernous space, they could see an early space rocket, like the kind used in the Apollo Moon Landings. Presently a lunar module was landing on a very convincing moonscape littered with strange alien artifacts. Seeing this, the Lamppost Man cooed, "Say doesn't this look interesting."

Jerry harrumphed. "Please. That stuff is decades old. That's merely what *they* want you to see. It's an illusion. Who knows what those filthy lab rats are really up to behind closed doors. Nothing good, I can tell you that." Finger-combing his hair he added, "Oh, how I long for the good old days, when I was little more than a hologram and the streets were paved with paying guests."

"Oh, how silly of me," the Lamppost Man said with glee, "I almost forgot."

He snapped his fingers. When nothing happened, his face fell and he frowned. He snapped his fingers several more times, and still nothing happened. As though suddenly remembering, he held up a gloved finger and said, "Oh, right." This time he clicked his heels twice and almost immediately, "The Girl from Ipanema" began to play over the elevator's invisible speakers. Hearing this, the Lamppost Man drew his arms into his body and sighed appreciatively. "I just love this ditty."

Jerry shook his head in condescension and noticed they were now passing 700. Summoning his courage, and flicking his hair over, Jerry stated, "I seriously doubt that Upper Management would resurrect me solely for the purpose of destroying me all over again."

The Lamppost Man smiled that impossibly wide grin of his before asking, "How long have you worked here Jerry?"

Jerry answered, "428 years, six months, four days," and after checking his watch, "and Thirty-eight minutes."

The Lamppost Man raised his eyes at him once more, "So... not long then."

"Longer than most," Jerry shot back.

820, 821, 822...

To pass the monotony, Jerry from Corporate moved to the back of the elevator to fix his tie again in the mirror, (thirteen times by Lamppost Man's last count). It was while gazing in the mirror the man from corporate noticed the large, heavily-used, black leather case. It was sitting on the floor at the Lamppost Man's feet. It resembled the ones the old country doctors used to make house calls with and was big enough to carry a bowling ball.

Exactly 4.8 seconds passed and...

"What's with the carpetbag?" Jerry asked.

The Lamppost Man waggled his eyebrows at him and replied with unrestrained delight, "Oh, you'll see."

DING!

"Oh my, here already?" The Lamppost Man leaned over in front of Jerry to hasten the rumbling cage open for him.

The yellow light emanating from within the top floor was so bright, it was impossible for any mere mortal to gaze inside and see what was actually there.

Jerry was about to step out of the elevator and into the blindness, but hesitated at the threshold. Turning his head toward the Lamppost Man, and dropping his phony corporate smile, he said, "I know you set me up, Lampy. But don't you worry; I am going to tell them everything you have ever done. I'm even going to tell them about your little pet project, Maddie. I don't care how much you think Upper Management needs you, everyone is replaceable, even you."

The Lamppost Man lowered his head, narrowed his eyes and said, "Run along now, Jerry. Mustn't keep the Board of Directors wai-ting."

Jerry swallowed and tore his gaze away from him. Shielding his eyes with his hand, he purposefully put back on his phony smile and stepped into the light.

"Well good afternoon, ladies and gentleman. My, it certainly has been a long time. It is so good to see all of you. First, I want to thank all of you for inviting me here today. I can't even begin to tell you what a special treat this is..."

As Jerry's voice prattled on and continued to move farther and farther away, until it eventually droned out, the Lamppost Man removed his pocket watch and noted the time.

After a few minutes of this, he impatiently put his fist on his waist, hunched over, and still staring at the face of his watch muttered, "This is taking *forever.*"

Jerry screamed. It was a long and loud one, accompanied by no small amount of tearing sounds, like the kind when you tear someone's arms and legs off one at a time. It was a sound the Lamppost Man knew well. After all he'd practically invented that move.

Or did I?

So much to remember. Some days it was difficult to remember where one century finished off and the other began.

Oh well.

Soon Jerry could be heard pleading for his life, begging them not to refurbish him, and listing all the reasons why they shouldn't; blah-blah-blah. This was quickly followed by the sound of a powerful energy building up and Jerry's final scream was cut short by a very precise detonation.

The Lamppost Man closed the lid to his pocket watch and said, "Huh, that took a wee bit longer than expected." He quickly returned the watch to its rightful place, and in a very deft move, spun around, and squatted down like a catcher behind home plate. The major difference however; was instead of a catcher's mitt, he held the large doctor's bag wide open and ready to receive.

Jerry's recently decapitated head bounced a few times and then rolled the rest of the way into the elevator. The Lamppost Man quickly snatched it up into his bag. He promptly flipped the metallic latch over and secured it, as though its occupant might escape at any moment. Releasing the breath he'd been holding, he rose slowly to his feet.

Realizing he was being watched by those in the light, he respectfully tipped his hat at the occupants within and gave them a two-fingered salute.

He rocked back on his heels and waited for the elevator gates to close. When it didn't he said, "Oh, right," leaned over and pressed the #1 button on the elevator panel.

As the doors rumbled closed, he patted the doctor's bag he was hugging in his arms and said softly, "C'mon Jerry. Let's go home."

Chapter 4

The Raft

A bright light assaulted his eyelids.

It was so intense, he wondered how he could have stayed sleeping in the first place. Eyelashes sticky with the slumber of the dead, George Stapleton attempted to open his eyes. The blaring sunlight was so painful, he immediately screwed his eyes shut again and shielded them with his forearm.

It was then he first felt the rocking motion beneath his back. *Am I on a boat?* Now that he was aware of the rocking motion, it was already beginning to make him queasy. Also, from the knee down, something crisp and cool enveloped his right leg. The rest of him felt like a piece of dried-out wood.

Shielding his face from the sun with his hand, he made a second attempt at just opening his eyes. Staring through squinted eyes, he found himself lying on his back atop a very small, wooden raft. The makeshift vessel couldn't have been larger than a queen-sized bed, and the crudely hacksawed logs were so hastily lashed together with thin strips of leather that water was seeping in-between each piece of timber.

Still lying on his back, George turned his head to the side. As far as he could see, all the way to the horizon, was nothing but endless ocean. Nothing. *Look the other way, the other way.* Turning his head, he witnessed the same view in every direction. Panic welled up inside him. *Am I lost at sea? How far out am I?* Fear fueling his dried out body, he managed to pull himself up onto his elbows. Looking down along his barely clad body, he saw he was wearing nothing more than a pair of white shorts haphazardly cut off at the knees, and past his bare feet, he saw nothing but more water.

This can't be. He smelled the salty air and thought, *I'm in the middle of the ocean. This can't be, this can't be. What happened to everyone else?*

Wait. A memory.

He recalled how he, The Leftenant, and Dawson were holding off the R-Techs so Tessa, Maddie, and the other plane passengers could get away aboard The Dauntless. But whether or not they succeeded, he was drawing a complete blank.

Faint at first, he heard the sound of a motorcycle engine... far in the distance. It took him a moment to find it, but when he finally saw it wasn't a motorcycle, but a bright red bi-plane. The really old kind, skimming over the waves, dangerously close to the surface.

Normally he would think, *That's a short-range aircraft, so I must be closer to land than I thought*, but in this world, anything was possible.

Is that really a plane? He knew he had to get up and signal them somehow. This might be his only chance at rescue. He called upon his last ounce of willpower and managed to slowly clamor to his knees. He lifted his hand high overhead and yelled out, "Hey!" but his voice was hoarse, and George doubted the pilot would have heard him at this distance, especially over the engine propeller's angry whine.

The plane suddenly veered off course.

He did hear me!

George's moment of hope vanished in an instant, when the bi-plane flew straight up into the cloudless sky.

What's he doing?

A cloud of smoke suddenly began streaming out of the tail of the plane as though he had been struck by some unseen anti-aircraft fire. George couldn't locate anything on the ocean's surface that could have caused it.

The plane reached its apex altitude, dropped down backward, flipped around, and began spelling out the letters...

S – O –

George read off the big, fat, puffy white letters...

-R – R – Y...

SORRY.

Word completed, the skywriter dropped back down to only a few dozen feet above the surface and flew by his flimsy raft.

George began waving at the man, but then slowed when he saw the pilot was wearing a top hat and a bemused grin upon his face.

The Lamppost Man.

George lowered his arm. The small bi-plane headed off into the sun now lowering itself beyond the horizon.

Still weakened, George collapsed onto his flimsy raft. One of his legs fell into the crisp, cool water as he watched the plane vanish into sunny oblivion.

He's gone. And what did he mean by, 'SORRY'? Maybe I should pull my legs out of the water before something...

The jaws of an enormous Great White shark exploded out of the water. In one violent motion, it clamped down onto his leg and dragged George off the flimsy raft and into the murky depths of the sea.

The raft continued to bob upon the surface of a vast ocean as though George Stapleton had never existed.

Chapter 5

We All Live in the Yellow submarine…
…in the yellow submarine…
…in the yellow submarine…

"Is he dead?"

This first voice was male, a gravely baritone, with a hint of an accent; Russian perhaps, possibly Yugoslavian. The way he spoke to the others, he was obviously someone in a position of authority.

"He should be, but he's not. No thanks to you," judged a female with a different accent, Mediterranean perhaps. "It's been touch and go for a while now, but I managed to save the leg." Her tone became more serious, almost biting, "Did you have to use the shark?"

"You're kidding, right? We shouldn't have come up this close to the surface in the first place."

“We had our orders,” the woman shot back.

“Just keep him alive. I doubt this guy’s worth it, but I hate to think we came all this way for nothing.”

“What do you think I’m doing?” she snapped back.

“Well, why hasn’t he woken up then?”

George Stapleton knew the answer to that one. It was simple. He didn’t want to. George preferred to wallow in darkness for a few minutes more. He was tired of all the fighting, and constant struggling. He had never hit the snooze button on his alarm clock in his life, but today, right now, at this moment, he desperately craved only a few seconds more in the inky blackness. *Leave me alone.*

KER-RANG!!!

A loud noise, like a dump truck running into a wall of steel, reverberated all around him. The shock wave was so violent even his bed shuddered beneath him.

This was soon followed by the sound of a heavy door unlocking and groaning open. Boots hastily clanged on metal, and then, “Captain, we’re under attack!”

The Russian accent again, “Really? No, kidding.”

Nope. No thank you.

Blessed darkness returned.

****

BLEAT!

Pain.

Open your eyes.

BLEAT!

Where am I... this time?

BLEAT!

George Stapleton opened his eyes. It was all he could do for the moment. Still on his back, he moved his head to the side and scanned the room that materialized before him. He was in a metal box about the size of a prison cell; no windows. The walls were riveted steel and when he lifted his head, he saw a door. No. It wasn't a door. It was a hatch, with one of those round submarine wheels in the center of it.

Gazing down his body, he saw that someone had removed his castaway shorts and slipped him into a white, cotton t-shirt and a pair of boxers.

BLEAT!

The bleating sound again. This was followed by a loud rumbling. The floors, walls and ceiling around him tremored slightly in concert.

BLEAT!

Whatever was going on, it was bad enough for someone to have sounded the alarm.

Although still dazed, George gathered his thoughts the best he could. *Did Tessa and Maddie get away?* He seemed to recall that they had escaped in The Dauntless, along with The Leftenant and all of the other passengers that had woken up with him on the plane. *Did Dawson and Tank survive? I can't remember.*

Gotta move, Georgie.

He summoned his strength, groaned as he swung his bare feet over the side of his bed and placed them onto the frigid steel floor. The bed was narrow, barely wider than the width of his shoulders.

"Ow."

George had banged the back of his head on the bunk's bedframe overhead. He rubbed the ouchness out of his scalp gently with the palm of his hand. As he did so, he noticed his right leg was heavily bandaged from the top of the knee down to his shin. It felt stiff. Extremely stiff.

Staring at it, he shuddered at the memory of a multi-toothed, monster of a shark, exploding from the water, clamping down on his leg and dragging him off of the flimsy raft. The water had been freezing, especially after baking in the sun for an indeterminate amount of time. As the Great White shark dragged him down into the murky depths, he had stared skyward and saw the sunlight sparkling on the surface, believing it was the last thing he would ever see.

BLEAT!

The horrific memory was over. The bleating alarm brought him back to the present. *Gotta stand up.*

Using the overhead bunk as support, he grunted as he lifted himself up. *Wow, that really hurts.* He tested out his bandaged leg by slowly putting his weight on it. It felt sore and painful, but at least he could stand on his own.

The walls were bare, and there weren't any photographs or other keepsakes to indicate ownership. A second set of bunks were on the opposite wall with only a scant three feet between them. Eyeballing his own bed sheets, he saw blood-stains and flecks of blood. How he had survived the massive shark attack and came to be here, he hadn't the slightest notion.

George moved toward the steel hatch, dragging his bad leg behind him. He wasn't really sure how to open it. Although similar to The Dauntless in many ways, this ship seemed more modern, more militaristic. He tugged on the handle, but it was locked. He gripped the small round wheel firmly in his hands, tried to turn it clockwise but it didn't budge. Then, turning it counter-clockwise, he was soon rewarded with the sound of a heavy bolt unlocking. *You were turning it the wrong way. Duh.* The door cracked open on its own and fresh air from the hallway washed over him.

George swung open the heavy hatch. A narrow catwalk in a darkened corridor lay outside his room. Before he could exit, he heard another rumbling sound. The walls around him shifted and his shoulder impacted painfully with the doorframe. Doing his best to keep most of his weight off his injured leg, he righted himself and stepped out into the corridor.

It was dark, but not so dark that he couldn't see. When the alarm bleated again he could see a red light bulb in a small cage glow brighter with each bleating of the alarm. He recalled images in his mind of W.W. II submarines but the memory didn't quite match what he was seeing now. The steel grating was painful beneath his bare feet, so before continuing onward he glanced back into his cabin for any clothes or footwear. *Maybe there's something in a closet or in a footlocker tucked beneath the bed?*

Finding nothing, he left the room behind and hobbled down the long narrow corridor. He passed other cabins, some locked and others with doors open. Peering inside the open ones, he leaned heavily on the walls and doorframes as he did so. George scanned the interiors, but found them abandoned. He checked the rooms for clothing or something he might be able to use as a weapon, but again found nothing. *I can't be the only one on board.* He dragged his stiff leg farther down the hallway.

George was about twenty feet down the corridor, when he heard boots clanging on the catwalk behind him. He spun around and saw a young man with blond hair, sprinting directly for him. The man was dressed in a black military uniform and a cap with tassels trailing out the back of it. He would have looked more at home on a Russian, Cold War submarine than any modern-day sub. Muscles slow to commands, George feebly raised his fists, ready to fight.

The young submariner yelled something, in what sounded like Russian, as he charged past him. Fear in the his eyes, urgency in his steps, the young Russian submariner rounded a distant corner at the end of the hallway, and was gone.

George lowered his fists. *That was weird. I guess I'm not the only one on board. Not sure why I would have thought that.* He wondered if he did in fact, want to run into any more people. In this place strangers meant danger.

With little choice, George continued onward and soon reached the same corner the young man had vanished around. Once there, he saw a ladder leading up to a small circular hole in the ceiling. *This was where the young crewman must have gone.* Not sure what else he could possibly do, George gripped the ladder and placed his foot on the first rung. Every step was painful but he pushed upwards.

He found himself wishing he had a weapon... then again, if he had something like a gun he probably would've panicked and instinctively shot the young Russian submariner, who clearly had no intention of harming him.

George reached the top of the ladder, but before he could climb up out of the hole, a pair of large beefy hands reached down, engulfed his face and pulled him skyward.

Chapter 6

Sven

"This is all your fault!"

A large man wearing a sweat-stained tank-top appeared at the opening of the hole and pulled him up through the hatchway. Like the young blond submariner, his accent was clearly Russian.

The giant threw George against a wall and spat, "I told them not to risk it, but they would not listen." The man was so angry, his face was fiery red. Contrary to his substantial potbelly, his arms were heavily muscled. A horrible looking splotch of wound was on the side of his head. George managed to shake Señor Hairy-Knuckles off, only to have the submariner lunge forward at him again.

"I don't know what you're yelling about..." George began, but the giant landed a meaty fist on his jaw that sent him flying back into the steel plated wall.

"If it weren't for you my Saskia would still be alive!" the crazed-seven-footer roared. Blinded by rage, the submariner went to punch him again. But this time, George ducked and the behemoth's fist impacted the bulkhead behind him. George was pretty sure he heard the man's phalanges break. This was confirmed when Mister Pot-Belly cried out in anguish.

You should probably pick only one nickname, Georgie.

Using the only moment of distraction he'd probably ever get, George violently punched the man in the stomach three times. Gasping for breath, the overweight submariner fell to his knees clutching his belly. When the thick man gazed up at him, George socked him in the temple as hard as he could, which knocked the man out cold. *Señor Hairy-Knuckles'* body collapsed and lay still against the wall at an odd angle.

Fists still clenched, George checked both ends of the hallway for further attackers. Seeing none, he was about to press onwards, but feeling sorry for the man he had just cold-cocked, he took a moment to straighten him out and lay him in the recovery position on his side, so he wouldn't choke on his tongue. George still wasn't sure why the submariner had attacked him in the first place, but evidently the man thought this latest predicament was somehow his fault.

George thought about removing the submariner's clothes, but the pain in his leg was excruciating. In the end, he decided it would take too long. Besides, the man easily outweighed him by fifty pounds, so he doubted the clothes would fit, certainly not enough to convince anyone into thinking he was a crewmember. He settled for searching the man's clothes for weapons. The submariner didn't have anything other a pocketknife, which George gladly appropriated.

Still wearing nothing more than a pair of boxers and a white t-shirt, George continued onward until he came to another circular hole in the floor. Before climbing down this ladder, he poked his head down into it. Scanning aft, he saw the corridor was crunched and impassable, but gazing forward, the way seemed clear. The most alarming thing however, was water was leaking in from the damaged hull and already about two inches deep. A vision of him pressing his face to the ceiling of a flooded passageway and then drowning overcame him. He pushed this fear aside for now. If he was going to go down the corridor, he'd have to go now.

By the time he climbed all the way down the ladder, the rising water had already reached his shins. The water was *fuh-reez-ing*. His injured leg still felt like it was being probed with pins and needles. But, he noticed the more he used it, the better it was starting to feel.

As he slogged down the passageway, a bolt suddenly ejected itself from the hull plating behind him, and then another. Each projectile was followed by a powerful stream of water. George spied another ladder at the far end of the corridor. The water level was beginning to rise with greater speed. With little option, he trudged his way toward the ladder. When the water level rose up past his waist, he dove for the ladder and swam down the steel passageway as fast as his stiff body would allow.

As the water overtook him, he drew in a deep breath just before it rose over his head. Beneath the surface, the water was only slightly murky, so he could make out the ladder in front of him. He grasped the rungs, pulled his feet through the water and began climbing upward; hoping against hope the level above would have air. If it didn't, he was finished.

Soaking wet, George popped out of the hatch like a gopher fleeing a flooded putting hole. A quick glance around showed him a large, open, and well-lit space, but that was all he had time for. He climbed the rest of the way out and quickly moved over to the steel hatch attached to an oversized hinge. By the time he grabbed the hatch's handle, the water was already bubbling up out of the hole. George doubted he would be able to seal it in time.

"You idiot, what have you done!" The voice was the same gruff Russian accent he heard earlier when he was semi-conscious. Without gazing up at the voice he focused on closing the hatch before it was too late; which it most likely was.

Two pairs of hands (one thick and, the other slender and feminine) appeared on the hatch next to his own. The three of them grunted as they lifted the lid and swung it closed over the flooding opening. Instinctively working as one, he and the gruff Russian piled their bodies onto the hatch while the third, presumably a female, spun the wheel. The hatch bucked once beneath them and then sealed tight.

"You stupid American, you nearly killed us all."

"It's not his fault," the woman defended. If memory served, and it usually did not, these were the same two people he had heard earlier.

George lifted his eyes to the two people who had helped him secure the hatch. The first wore Captain's bars on his lapels, a black wool sweater, and sported a stark-white goatee and close-cropped hair. The second, a female, was actually quite striking. She appeared Mediterranean, raven haired with salient green eyes. She was the first to introduce herself, "I am Izabella Santerelli, and that's Pieter Strummer."

"Captain Strummer to you," he said, correcting her.

George took Izabella's outstretched hand and she pulled him to his feet. He found himself on a massive bridge encased in glass windows, offering panoramic views. Dials, levers and pressure gauges lined every available space on the walls. The windows had riveted steel struts between them, and outside them. He could see where the nose of the black submarine had crashed into a man-made and futuristic underwater base.

"Thanks to you," Captain Strummer began, "if the sub shifts again, the bridge will flood and drown us all like rats in a sewer pipe." George could see a bubbling pool of water forming over a jagged hole in the ship's deck.

Izabella made a face which suggested she didn't quite agree with Strummer's assigned blame, but settled for saying, "If we can swim to that entry point over there," she pointed out the windows at a short ladder beneath one of the structures of the underwater base. "We can go up through that access point."

George bit his lower lip, examining the short swim over to where she was pointing. "It doesn't seem that far."

"Be my guest," Strummer said, lowering his hand to indicate the jagged hole in the floor.

"Shhhh... shhh..." shushed a third crewman. It was the same young blond submariner George had seen earlier. He had been so quiet that George hadn't even realized he was there. At the moment, the young man was near one of the large paned windows and hiding behind one of the thick-steel struts, as though concealing himself from an outside sniper. He whispered to no one in particular, "It's coming back!"

George was about to ask, 'Who's coming back' when he saw the impossible. A large marine reptile (about the size of a school bus) that resembled a crocodile only with flippers suddenly swam past the windows.

"That's impossible," George heard himself mutter.

But, it was possible because of where they were; because they were in Stranger World, where literally anything is possible, even that which was not.

"What is that thing?" George asked.

"A kronosaurus, the scourge of the early Cretaceous period," Izabella answered with a sense of awe and trepidation.

George suddenly recalled the unconscious crewman he had knocked out and left in the corridor below decks. "I left one of your men back there."

"Who?" the Captain demanded.

"A big balding guy, wearing a tank top." George thought about it for a second more. "I've got to go back for him."

"No you don't, look!" the young submariner cried. "It's Sven, he's wearing a breather."

"He's not gonna make it with that thing out there," Captain Strummer predicted. Leveling a finger at George he added, "This is your fault. You might as well have killed Sven yourself."

"That's not true," Izabella interrupted. "Sven could have easily stayed inside the ship with his breather on for hours."

George glanced outside the window panes again. *Sven* was about halfway to the access point. Even though the hairy-knuckled man had tried to beat the snot out of him, he did feel responsible for the man.

George scanned the interior of the bridge. "Does this vessel have any sort of offensive weapons?"

"She's a submarine left over from the Cold War," Strummer explained. "She has torpedo bays and deck guns, neither of which we can reach right now. Even if we could, it wouldn't have any effect on that leviathan out there."

George spied a locker labeled in Russian, but he was fairly certain of its contents. Pulling it open he found shelves of tools. He selected a heavy pipe wrench.

"What are you going to do with that?" Strummer asked, "Wrench him to death?"

The terrified crewman closest to the window cried nervously, "I think… I think the krono spotted Sven!"

"You might want to start passing those out," George struggled for the word he had heard Izabella use earlier, "uh... the breathers."

He then moved to the window. Sven was nearly to the ladder beneath the steel structure. The cantankerous Russian was going to make it. The Krono saw this too, changed course and headed right for him.

BANG!

Everyone turned toward George still holding the wrench in his hand, where he'd struck the thick pipe running along the wall.

BANG-BANG-BANG!

"What are you doing?" Strummer asked, his voice incredulous.

"He's trying to save Sven," Izabella answered for him, and then picked up a smaller wrench and began banging on the pipe too.

Just when George thought it wasn't going to work, the creature veered off of Sven at the last possible second and turned back toward them.

"Everybody get down," George shouted and dove for the center of the room as the leviathan slammed into the outer hull.

The creature's blow had moved the entire submarine. George rolled over on his back and surveyed the damage, surprised the ship was still intact from such a massive blow. Multiple leaks sprang from where the creature had slammed into the outer hull, but thus far, the bulkheads held.

George went to get up. His mind may have forgotten his body was still in recovery, but his muscles hadn't. It was a struggle for him to regain his feet. Seeing this, the olive-skinned woman came over to his aid and helped him stand. "Here, let me help you."

He was too weak to argue. As he stood up, George glimpsed Sven's boot vanishing into the structure above the ladder.

"I can't believe it," the young submariner cried. "He made it. He actually..."

Izabella suddenly screamed. When George looked to where she was pointing, he saw the kronosaurus through the glass pane (behind the smiling submariner) hurtling toward them like a missile.

Upon impact, the wall folded in on itself, but somehow, impossibly, it still held.

The young, blond haired submariner was the first to climb to his feet. "We have to get out of here! We have to get out of here!" He sprinted to the wall, grabbed a re-breather and began opening a hatch marked emergency.

George moved over to the open hatch and stared down into it. He saw a short ladder lead down into the water.

Izabella grabbed the young submariner's arm as he put one foot down into the hatch. "You can't," she cried. "We don't know where he is!"

The young submariner shook Izabella violently off him, causing her to fly backwards and skid the last few feet across the floor. The submariner seemed distraught by this, but only for a second; fear soon overtook him once more. "You can stay here if you like. But if that thing hits us one more time..." he began, but never finished his sentence.

There was a loud rendering of metal as the leviathan swam up underneath and forced its gaping maw inside the sub through the hatch.

It swallowed the submariner in one loud CHOMP, and retreated back down into the depths from which it came.

The bridge immediately flooded with seawater.

George knew if the rising water didn't get them, the leviathan surely would.

Chapter 7

Ship's Galley

Henry fell against the wall.

He gripped the steel railing running along the bulkhead to steady himself.

Whoa, where did that come from?

The ship hadn't experienced any turbulence. Other than navigating around a few storm clouds, H.M.A.S. The Dauntless flew so smoothly amongst the clouds, it was easy to forget they were soaring high above the earth.

So, if not turbulence, what then?

Henry realized he was no longer in his quarters. *Wait a minute. How did I get here? The last thing I remember was I was in my room. The blackouts... they're getting worse. No wait. I remember now. I heard the announcement about dinner, and I was headed to the galley to get some food.*

Two passengers walked past him without as much as a second glance. *Judging by their thick overalls and heavy work gloves, they must be part of the crew.*

He followed the two burly men, deep in conversation, as they passed beneath a sign that read: *Ship's Galley*. Henry's stomach groaned at savory smells beckoning to him from within the galley.

This wasn't Henry's first time getting food, but it was his first time going to the galley to get it. Normally, some nice lady named Sue would drop off a sacked lunch from her hovering cart in the hall. Sue would ask him how he was faring, but he still wasn't very good socializing with other people outside The Factory. She was the first one who had told him that he was allowed to leave his room anytime he liked, and if he got hungry, he should find the ship's galley for some food.

See, you haven't lost your memory.

Henry adjusted his new clothes as best as he could and went inside.

The interior was crowded with people. Every table and chair was occupied. Henry would have turned right back around and left, except for the fact he was starving. It was all coming back to him now. His roommates, the couple from Ukraine and their adopted daughter, Isabella, were already gone when he had woken up. Following placard signs written in gold lettering, which Henry knew really couldn't be real gold, he made his way to the galley.

He expected more steel walls, and much of the galley's hull was riveted with nuts and bolts, but there were also beautiful paintings of old sailing ships on the walls, and red velvety table cloths draping the tables. Despite the throngs of people, the place was impossibly clean. Henry didn't see a single smudge mark or drop of black coal anywhere.

When the ship shuddered again, Henry leaned against the steel hull to maintain his balance. This time he managed to keep his feet more easily, but he still hadn't gotten used to the idea of flying inside a boat that looked like something Jules Verne might've dreamt up.

How is it possible that I can remember something as unimportant as "20,000 Leagues Under the Sea," and not my own family, or where I'm from, or anything before I arrived at The Factory?

A disembodied voice, a British female by the sound of it, echoed within the hall, "Your attention. Your attention, please. Passengers may experience some slight turbulence over the next few hours as we attempt to circumnavigate a very heavy storm. Rest assured, you are all in capable hands. But, we may ask you to return to your cabins very soon. Thank you."

Now you tell me.

As Henry carefully navigated the room he spotted someone he knew. It was nice to see a familiar face, even one as mean and annoying as Maddie's. She was sitting at a table with another boy of about the same age. They were laughing. He didn't think Maddie was capable of laughing. There was something else too. He couldn't put his finger on it, and it confused him.

Henry had been around female workers before, but he'd never seen a girl like Maddie. Maybe it was the way she smiled, or played with her hair. *She should smile more often*, he thought to himself. When she smiled, it lit up her whole face, and those around her.

His stomach growled in protest at the delay.

Maddie spotted him and waved him over, "Hey, Harry! Over here."

Henry pointed to himself and raised his eyebrows in question.

She nodded and yelled, "Yes, you. Who did you think I was talking too?"

As he made his way through the crowd and joined them at the table, she introduced him to the other boy. "Traxx, this is Harvey."

"Henry," he corrected immediately, and shook the boy's offered hand.

Maddie rolled her eyes. "Whatever."

Now that he was up close, Henry thought Traxx actually seemed a few years younger than Maddie.

The boy offered him an easy and generous smile before saying, “Nice to meet you, Henry. How are you getting on?”

“This ship is so huge, I’m afraid I keep getting lost.” Henry held back about his blackouts and waking up not knowing where he was.

Oblivious to his thoughts, Maddie muttered, “Don’t worry; The Dauntless gets smaller every day.”

Under the table, Maddie’s leg shoved out the chair opposite her, so Henry could sit down.

“Thank you,” Henry said, taking it. The velvet tablecloth felt luxurious beneath his fingertips and he didn’t know why, but he dropped the matching cloth napkin into his lap as if it was almost a reflex. This action perplexed him, because the only napkin available to anyone in The Factory was the back of one’s sleeve.

“My, my, aren’t we Mister Manners,” Maddie said, shoveling down a mouthful of dinner roll. While chewing heavily she asked, “So other than a few wrong turns, you’re really doing okay?”

Henry was surprised she cared.

“Well, The Leftenant came by for an inspection this morning.”

"Let me guess..." Traxx cut in. Then holding up a crisp British salute, he said in mock British accent, "A well-made bed creates the appearance of a tidy and pulled-together room."

Henry's eyes went wide and he nodded. "That's right! That's exactly what she said."

Traxx and Maddie burst into laughter and for the first time in a long time, Henry started laughing too.

Henry froze. A Gargoyle had suddenly appeared beside him, and Henry dared not move. It was the same grey demon with sharp teeth and razor-like talons who had sniffed him in The Factory earlier.

"Hi there, can I take your order?"

Henry noted the Gargoyle, in addition to wearing a butler's uniform, was also adorned with a white chef's hat and was presently carrying a notepad and pencil.

Henry continued to hold perfectly still. "Uh, what's that?"

"What? Him?" Traxx asked. "That's Cheeves. He's the chef."

Maddie swallowed another half-chewed roll. "Hey Harry, you okay?"

Henry wasn't sure if Maddie's concern was genuine or not. "I think I may have peed my pants a little," he said embarrassed.

Seeing his apprehension she explained, "Don't worry, he won't hurt you."

This time she did seem genuine.

"But… he's a gargoyle… in a chef's hat."

"Uh-huh. Get over it," Maddie said.

"Would you like to hear about our shpecialthsls?" Cheeves asked.

Henry noted the gargoyle, Cheeves, had a heavy lisp when he talked. He also noted that neither Traxx or Maddie answered him and seemed to go out of their way to ignore him.

Daring to lift his gaze up at the gargoyle in the chef's hat, Henry began to say, "Uh, okay."

"NO, DON'T!" Maddie and Traxx yelled simultaneously.

The gargoyle's eyes went wide as he grinned with pleasure. Both Maddie and Traxx groaned as Cheeves began to recite the day's specials… "Today we have Cat-burgers sah-served fresh with a si-side order of Calico-Fries, and Cat-Sue Flay."

"Ugh, now he'll never leave," Traxx complained.

Undeterred, Cheeves continued. "Or if you prefer, we ssstill may have some Persssian-ssoup ssserved with Burmese biscuitss and to drink, a Ssiamese sshake.

Henry was beginning to see the pattern. "Wait a minute, you people eat cats?"

Traxx had his face down on the table and Maddie laid hers on her arm. The latter of the two grumped, "Just wait, he's not done."

"For dessert, we have Kitty-cakes-sss, Cat-alamode, Calico-pie, Tail-Tea, and my personal favorite, kitten-creampuffs-suss."

Henry held up a forefinger to stop the gargoyle butler, but he prattled on until finally saying… "Oh, and one more th-th-thing, we're out of catss." And with that said, Cheeves began laughing, only it was more like something that was between half-laughter and half-snorting at the same time.

Traxx was the first to speak. "Cheeves, just bring us three specials."

Holding up a pen in salute, Cheeves responded, "Thhhhrrrrree spa-special-thls, you got it, Masth-ter Traxx."

Henry watched as the gargoyle waddled off. Amongst all his other peculiarities, the gargoyle was bowlegged when he walked. The fabric of his butler's uniform was straining against the leg muscles underneath.

Henry shook his head, "I don't know, but there's just something I don't trust about that thing. He really scares me."

Maddie finished her roll and grabbed another. Before forcing it in, she said half-heartedly, "My dad said Cheeves was like his old German shepherd." She changed her voice to a deeper octave. "That dog had a heart-a-gold, but if somebody ever threatened the family, he'd kill 'em."

Henry chuckled. Smiling he asked, "Where's your dad now? Is he on board?"

Traxx immediately dropped his own smile and froze.

Maddie returned the roll to her basket. "Listen kid, The Leftenant said we're heading into a storm front. We should all probably head back to our rooms."

She grabbed her gear and left.

Traxx got up to leave. "Nice meeting you, Henry," he said solemnly, and he too departed.

A shadow fell over Henry from behind.

"Here ya go! Three specialthls…" It was Cheeves holding a giant platter filled with plates of delicious smelling food. "Shhaaaayyy… where'd everybody go?"

Henry could have sworn he had only blinked for a second, but when he opened his eyes, everyone else in the galley had vanished.

Henry wasn't certain what to say. He was about to ask Cheeves what was going on, but even the gargoyle had vanished.

Henry was alone.

Chapter 8

The Leftenant Remembers

As he entered the bridge, Engineer Rick finished off a sandwich he snagged from the galley. The moment he did, he froze; for he had seen a ghost. It was not just any ghost, but the one of his best friend, who had been missing nearly three years.

Under any other circumstances, Rick would've run over to his friend and bear-hugged him right off the floor. But instinctively, he knew something was wrong. Other apparitions were there as well, standing in shadows and all talking in hushed tones. Instead of rushing in head first, he decided to quietly step behind the large chart board and check things out first. Hiding there, he still couldn't believe his eyes.

Standing on the bridge, pretty as you please, conversing with The Leftenant, was none other than his best friend, George Stapleton.

"You're insane," George said grumpily.

In answer, The Leftenant cocked an eyebrow at George and said, "Hmmm… I suppose if I was, there really wouldn't be any point in answering then, now would there? If I wasn't, well, insane people rarely know they are insane. So again, the question is moot. Regardless, I have a message for you."

"A message from who?" George asked.

"I believe you mean, from whom. But in any case, since you must know, the message is from your daughter, Maddie. Would you like to hear it?"

Rick remained hidden. *A message? What message? Maddie's aboard The Dauntless. Why would The Leftenant need to convey a message from Maddie?* This opened a whole new slew of thoughts regarding how he was going to tell Maddie that her dad was still alive.

Conveying his own thoughts, Rick heard George ask The Leftenant, "A message? From Maddie?"

The Leftenant released a quick sigh. "Yes, I believe that is what I said. You aren't the sharpest tool in the tool stores, are you?" She held up a hand toward him. "Before you answer, rest assured, that was a rhetorical question."

George took a hurried step forward. "You've seen Maddie? Is she okay? Where is she?"

"All in good time. But first, as I said, three times total now, I must verify your identity in order to convey the message."

George frowned. "How do you plan on doing that? You know what? I don't care. Just get on with it already."

"I believe that is what I am attempting to do." The Leftenant raised her eyebrow again, as though daring him to interrupt her again.

George didn't.

Finally… she asked. "What is the name of Maddie's cat?"

"What?"

"That is the cipher. I believe the question is self-explanatory. If you wish to receive the message from your daughter, you must answer the question: What is the name of Maddie's cat?"

George shook his head.

"George," The Leftenant prodded. "What is the name of her…"

"I heard you," he said irritably, cutting her off. "I don't know what the name of her smelly cat was."

"Smelly Cat is incorrect."

"I know it's not Smelly Cat," George barked. "I have no idea what the name of her stupid cat was."

"Stupid cat is incorrect."

George seemed to be struggling for the answer, but eventually he opened his eyes and said, “Lucy.”

Rick heard a new voice ask in a Southern drawl, “Lucy? What in tarnation kind-a-name is that?” The voice was familiar, but Rick peeked out a little farther to make certain. The Southern voice went on to say, “I mean I git Tabitha er Mr. Whiskers, but Lucy? That jus don’t make a lick a sense.”

The new voice belonged to one Corporal Dawson.

Rick rapidly pulled his head back behind the chart board. *Corporal Dawson? But he’s dead. I saw it with my own eyes. He was blown up on that dock. Nothing could have survived.*

A fourth voice, deep and baritone, “I dunno, Lucy sounds like a mighty fine name to me.”

Rick knew the voice instantly, but he leaned out one eye just to make sure. Yep. It was Tank.

“Shoot,” Dawson said. “What do you know? Why don’t you go play with your stuffed bunny or sumthin?”

The big, bald man took a step toward the corporal. “It’s a rabbit, and you know it.”

The Leftenant stepped between them. “Now Gentleman, if you would be so kind as to quit talking rubbish, we could go back to talking about yesterday’s proceedings.”

A portly man with a thin mustache stepped out of the shadows. Hiking his belt up over his considerable girth he pleaded, “Tell me again why this is a good plan."

Rick didn't know who this newcomer was, but none of this made any sense. *These people were dead. What were they doing on the bridge? And what is this plan the fat guy with the thin mustache was talking about?* Still feeling as though he was living in a waking dream, he decided the best course of action was to make his presence known and ask them directly. He coughed in to his hand and said, "I'm sorry. If I'm intruding, I can come back."

The moment he said this, George, Corporal Dawson, Tank, and the portly guy with the mustache, all suddenly vanished.

Oh. That explains it. They're holograms, Rick thought. *But why?*

The Leftenant, obviously surprised, (which Rick didn't think was possible), quickly turned toward him, was about to speak, composed herself and then said, "No apology necessary. I was merely reviewing some of our historical records. I'm rather finished."

Dropping his heavy gear bag by the captain's chair Rick said. "Ya know. It's okay that you miss them. We all do."

The Leftenant straightened her coat, brushed some invisible lint off of it. "I am quite certain I have no idea as to what you're going-on about."

The leather seat creaked as Rick eased back into it. He swallowed and said tentatively, "You know, it's the little things that make me miss her the most."

Impatient, and obviously embarrassed, The Leftenant asked, “Excuse me? To whom are you referring?”

“My wife. It’s the little things that sneak up on ya when you’re not looking.” He checked to see if she was still listening. Once he was certain she was, he continued. “I was in the galley the other day and Cheeves served up this clam chowder with a side order of saltines in clear little packets. Without even thinking, I scooped up the packets of saltines and shoved them in my pocket, because I remembered how much my wife loved to find them on road trips.” Rick stared at the palms of his hands. “I remember thinking, Rick, what are you doing? You haven’t seen Chelle-Belle for over six years now, and you probably never will.” He took a deep breath, held it for a moment, and then let it out. “I can tell you right now, I barely got out of there without bawling my eyes out.”

“Although that is truly a very sad-sad story, and I am genuinely sorry for your loss, I fail to see what any of this has to do with me.”

“All I’m saying is... You’re not alone, Leftenant. It’s okay to grieve. There’s no shame in it.”

“I am a hologram, sir. I am incapable of emotion. Your pity is not only unwanted it is unwarranted and misplaced.” Rick noted the tempo in her voice began to increase. “Now if you'll excuse me, I am already overdue to power down and run my regularly scheduled maintenance checks."

Rick held his palms up toward her. "I'm sorry, my mistake. But if you change your mind, I'm always here if you need to talk."

"That is quite..." she began. Stopped. Tilted her head down. Pressed her fist to her lips... and vanished.

As Rick dropped his bag into the captain's chair, he began to wonder if there was even more to The Leftenant than he already thought. Of course, they all knew that there was. For whatever reason, The Leftenant seemed far more self-aware than any other hologram they had encountered. The entire crew knew she was so much more. In fact, anybody who conversed with any other hologram knew that there was something different about The Leftenant. She was their version of Pinocchio, the hologram who wanted to be a *real girl*.

Rick removed his thermos from his gear bag and poured himself a cup of coffee. As he did so, he glimpsed an unpleasant blotch on the radar. "Yuck. That's an ugly storm," he said to no one in particular. He sat down in his creaking leather chair and settled in for the shift.

Perfect.

He picked up the antiquated clipboard, which changed pages on voice command, and examined their food supplies.

We'd better get home quick because with all these hungry mouths on board, the ship's stores won't last much longer.

As he hung the clipboard back on its hook, he gazed over at the magnetic field dampeners' display and noticed something amiss. The variation was minute, which is why no alarms had sounded yet. But the rate of decay seemed continuous, and if they didn't do something soon, the dampeners could potentially evolve into a cascade failure.

Well that's not good.

Rick put down his clipboard and raised his voice to the heavens, "Leftenant... Leftenant... I know you can hear me." When she didn't reappear he added, "Listen, I don't want to talk about you and the holograms, okay?" He thought about this and added more somberly, "I don't want to talk about our friends." When she still didn't appear he said, "Listen, we've got a serious problem here."

The Leftenant immediately appeared directly behind him. This frustrated Rick to no end. She was perfectly capable of reappearing across the room or even giving the appearance of walking into one, but she seemed to prefer to pop up right behind him and scare the living bejesus out of him... every time.

"Mr. Rick. I was gone for exactly ninety-seven seconds. What major malfunction could you have possibly caused in such a finite amount of time? Honestly, it's a new record, even for you. I might as well put the gargoyle in charge."

Rick raised his bushy eyebrows at her. "How long have you been holding back that little gem?" Before she could answer, he pointed to the starboard magnetic field dampener. "I noticed it as soon as I came on shift."

Studying the malfunction, The Leftenant froze, unblinking. "I don't know how I could have missed that."

Seeing how clearly upset she was by her oversight, Rick attempted to offer her some solace by saying, "Hey, it's a mistake, don't worry about it."

The Leftenant's eyes grew wide.

Uh-oh, here it comes, Rick thought, bracing himself for the worst.

"Don't worry about it? If the ship's field dampeners devolve into a cascade failure, the entire ship could li-tra-lly," she dragged out the word literally as far as it could go in her British accent, "...fall out of the sky. Yet, you say, don't worry about it?"

Unflappable as usual, Rick offered. "Hey, it's no big deal. The important thing is we caught it in time. We can't fix it in mid-flight, so all we have to do is find a place to land, repair the damage and recharge the dampening field. Easy-peasy-Japanesey."

The Leftenant harrumphed and responded. “Well then, your racial-colloquialism aside, that does seem like the most prudent plan.”

“See, like I said, It’s no big deal.”

She turned back on him so abruptly, he spilled his coffee. “No. It is a big deal. I don’t make mistakes. I *never* make mistakes.”

Rick brushed the coffee off his uniform shirt as best as he was able. Smiling beneath his mustache at her he said, “Huh, you’re right. The Leftenant made a mistake. Six years I’ve been waiting for that to happen.”

The Leftenant stood up straight, held her nose in the air and said, “I hereby resign, effectively immediately. I am clearly no longer worthy of my post and shall confine myself to my quarters post haste. If that is not to your satisfaction, I shall report to the quartermaster and lock myself in the brig.”

Rick, more amused by the situation than anything else, blew a cooling wind across the remnants of his coffee and said dryly, “Leftenant. We don’t have a brig. Sue turned it into a food pantry.”

The Leftenant promptly stamped her foot, “Well then, perhaps we should.”

“Leftenant, you made a mistake. It’s no big deal.”

“That’s impossible, I don’t make mistakes.”

Rick shrugged, took another sip. "Yeah, everybody thinks that, but the truth is, we all make mistakes and it's okay. Part of being..." he hesitated for he wasn't sure how she was going to take the word, "human. It's what we do *after* we make mistakes that really counts."

The Leftenant tilted her head, narrowed her eyes at him and settled for saying, "Oh, I see."

"So instead of confining yourself to your quarters, or your box, or wherever it is you go when you disappear into never-never land, why don't you help me find a decent place to land The Dauntless before that storm crashes down on top of us?"

She studied the dampener gauge again. "There's no way this could have happened on its own. There are too many redundant systems in place serving as a failsafe."

"My thoughts exactly."

"Of course they were." Realizing that had come out a lot harsher than intended, she added softly, "Sorry. You do realize that if it didn't break on its own, then..."

"Yeah, I know."

"One of us?"

Rick shook his head. "I doubt it. Mainly because if it was one of us, they could have hurt us a lot worse before the rescue mission at The Factory."

"Then, through process of elimination, it must be one of the people we picked up at The Factory."

"That'd be my guess."

Still unconvinced, The Leftenant said, "I find it difficult to believe when one considers our pet gargoyle. Despite Cheeves's annoying and repetitious requests for feline delicacies, he has proven most adept in the past at sniffing out potential enemies. Pun intended as I mean that most literally."

"Regardless, we're going to have to land in unmapped territory..."

The Leftenant stepped up beside him and began surveying the charts. "And, with a saboteur on board no less."

Chapter 9

Leisure-Bot

Can't...breathe...

George climbed out of the moon-pool and crawled across a concrete floor, slick with water. Lying in a puddle on his back, he spat out the depleted rebreather.

I can't believe I made it. I thought for certain that thing was going to devour me.

He lay still, unless you counted him desperately trying to catch his breath. The room was metal and concrete, with lockers and dive gear lining the walls.

Sitting up to breathe, he began to wonder if the others had made it too.

What happened to the Russians? Where's the Italian woman?

It had all happened so fast. He vaguely remembered the leviathan attacking the sub and the bridge filling with water. He was fairly certain that when the kronosaurus thrashed about inside the ruined sub, he and a dozen other crew-members had all bailed out of the sub and swum for the ladder-well.

Am I the only one who made it?

George rose slowly to his feet. He moved over to the circular moon pool at the center of the room. Hesitant at first, he glanced down into the ocean water and saw no one.

I can't be the only one.

He turned in a slow circle. There wasn't much more to the room other than a steel door on a distant wall. Now that he examined the floor more closely, he could see tracks of water where someone, possibly Sven, possibly more, had walked over to the door and exited the room.

He was about to follow, but realized he was wearing only wet skivvies. Remembering the lockers against the far wall, he moved over to them checking for any clothes.

He was about to open nearest locker, when he spied a familiar sight on one of the narrow-steel benches, like the kind you find in a gym locker room.

His clothes!

Moving over to them, he could see a pair of faded blue jeans, a t-shirt, and his favorite overshirt all folded up in a neat little pile. Even the light-brown work boots were his. Lying next to his clothes was a fluffy white towel. Shivering slightly from his swim, he immediately grabbed the towel and began to dry off.

He sighed with pleasure at the towel's fresh clean smell. He brought the towel down away from his face and noticed a note haphazardly taped to one of the lockers.

Was that there before?

He wasn't really sure.

Hi Georgie,

Do try to keep your pants on this time.

Your Pal,

-L.M.

L.M.? he wondered, and then it hit him, Lamppost Man. Oh, how he was really beginning to hate that guy. The last time they had seen each other, he had somehow placed Traxx's multi-tool in his stomach. No, wait. Wasn't he the one flying the bi-plane? An image crossed his mind of the imp tipping his hat at him as he flew past. George was bouncing on a small raft in the middle of nowhere at the time. These memories all ran together, no rhyme or reason. He crumpled up the note and tossed it to the floor.

It took George a little while to get dressed, but he noticed his leg was moving better. It still felt like the shark was latched onto it, but at least he could run if he had too. After dressing, he got about halfway to the door when he stopped. He turned around, went back to the crumpled-up note and pitched it into a nearby trashcan. He felt stupid for being so tidy under the circumstances, but he couldn't change who he was.

George exited the concrete and steel moon-pool room through a heavy door. It was thick metal on one side but a lavish wall on the other. After stepping through it, the door silently closed behind him. If he didn't just pass through it, he wouldn't have even noticed the door was there.

Before him lay a long ornate hallway adorned with lavish carpeting and leafy potted foliage in beautifully-carved ceramic Greek vases. The hallway appeared endless, which always seemed to be the scope of this world.

There has to be an exit eventually.

He didn't see any more tracks in the floor. Instead, about every twenty feet or so, were futuristic looking-doors, like something you might find on a spaceship from a 1990's television show. The only apparent difference between each room was the painting on each door. As George grew closer to them, he could see each painting was a different underwater scene, usually with a diver in the foreground, entering different locales, like a submerged pirate ship, or ancient ruins.

As he walked further down the hallway, George passed another painting; this one was of a diver exploring Atlantean ruins. George was about to take his eyes away from the painting, but the image magically changed to an image of the same diver now entering the ruins. It stayed that way for another few seconds and then changed again to an image of the interior ruins. The point of view was always over and behind the diver as though the camera was documenting the journey. George began to wonder if the diver in each painting was the occupant of each room, so in essence he was watching a little home movie of their personal adventure under the sea.

Pretty neat.

George negotiated the hallway another fifty feet or so, but it still appeared endless. Turning around, he could no longer see where he had entered the corridor in the first place.

Where's the door I came out of? He couldn't locate it anymore.

Fighting panic, he decided to try opening one of the rooms. He knocked lightly, at first, "Hello?" When he didn't receive an answer he knocked with more fervor, "Hello, is anybody in there?"

Instinctively, he reached for the doorknob or lever, but there was none. Scanning the other doors, he saw none of them had handles. But now that he studied the door in front of him a bit more, he could see a small and square, raised press plate; the outlines barely visible.

It's probably dialed into fingerprints or facial recognition or something.

George pressed on it anyway and to his surprise, he heard a bolt unlock and the heavy door creaked open. He suspected the door was so thick because if the corridor flooded, they could seal the occupants safely inside their rooms.

George entered the room. "Hello," he said again, cautiously. The single-bed room was pure luxury: thick shag carpet, king-size bed with extravagant down comforters, and beautiful furniture. Most exquisite of all, the walls and ceiling were made entirely of thick glass, offering amazing views of crystal-clear blue waters, multi-colored corals and vast arrays of dancing fish. The overall effect was that of being in a giant fishbowl; only in this case, the room's occupants were the exhibit.

Under other circumstances, George could certainly see himself enjoying the luxurious underwater resort. Gazing straight up, it seemed shallower here; the surface was maybe only forty feet above.

Too far to swim without gear, but at least I'm not as deep as I thought.

Passing a Greco-ceramic-tiled bathroom, George moved deeper into the room. He was shocked to find a woman sitting on the bed with her back to him. He'd been so overwhelmed by the fantastical room, he hadn't even seen her. Even with her back to him, George could tell right away the woman was stunning: fit, lean athletic build and at least 5'9" in height. She was sitting with her bare feet drawn up and leaning on one arm as she stared into the tropical paradise beyond the glass.

"Um, hello?"

The runway model tilted her head in a way that reminded George of a bird tilting its head when it's studying something.

"Hello, Miss? Are you okay?"

"You speak English." The words were spoken in a very neutral accent, so there wasn't anything indicative of her roots.

"Yes ma'am. I'm an American."

I'm an American, that was dumb, George thought to himself. I'm an American, where do you think you are? Then it occurred to him. Who says we're still in the United States, or even North America for that matter? The crew and submarine that had brought him here were obviously Russian.

The woman tilted her head some more, as though she were contemplating something. George was about to ask her a question when she drew her feet from the bed, placed them firmly on the floor and stood up. Again, all with her back still to him, she said, "I've been waiting for you."

George wasn't sure why, but he took a step backwards and bumped into the wall behind him. Recovering quickly he asked, "Uhmmm... What's your name, ma'am?"

The head tilt again, "My last companion called me, Lotus-Blossom."

George wasn't sure what unnerved him about this woman; she was tall and fit, but certainly not physically threatening. Of course, in this place, this Stranger World, size didn't always mean less dangerous. He checked the door to see if it was still open. He was glad to see that it was, and he had an escape vector if he needed it. "Do you know where we are? Do you know what this place is? Who are you?"

Head-tilt to the left. Head-tilt to the right. "I am your leisure-companion. I am here to serve."

Finally turning toward him, George could see where the flesh of the woman's cheek and jawline had been torn away to reveal tiny gears and extremely-intricate and mechanized components underneath.

"You're a robot?"

Head-tilt to the left. "Leisure-bot, to be more precise."

George gulped, and then stammered, "Uh, sorry, it looks like I got the wrong room." He hiked a thumb over his shoulder toward the door and added, "You know what, I'm sorry to bother you, I'm just gonna leave."

In the amount of time it took him to turn around and take one step toward the open door, she leapt up to the ceiling, crawled across it and over him. Silently, the leisure-bot dropped down between him and his avenue of escape.

"I am your leisure companion. I am here to serve."

George shook off his amazement. "Uh, ma'am. I'm sorry. I don't want to hurt you, but I really need to be going."

As George moved to push past her, a single hand shot out and grabbed him by his shirt. Her grip was incredibly strong. Realizing he could be in mortal danger, he brought up his forearm and slammed it down on her wrist, trying to break her leisure-bot grip.

(Head tilt to the right.)

George saw a quick view of the glass ceiling rushing by as he flew across the room and slammed into the glass wall on the far side. He hit pretty hard and thought he heard glass breaking, or maybe that was his skull crunching.

He got to his feet and immediately became dizzy and nauseous at the same time. He slid back down to the floor. He reached to the back of his head, and his probing fingers found sticky blood.

The door slammed shut on its own accord.

He didn't remember doing it, but he must have stumbled to his feet because he found himself standing. Staring at the door, he wondered drunkenly, Did I do that? He had to put a hand on the glass wall to steady himself and when he did, he noticed the cracked glass beneath his palm. Any harder and the leisure-bot would've killed him instantly, or broken the glass wall and flooded the compartment. Either way, I'd be dead.

Turning back toward the woman, George saw her purposefully walking toward him with fists clenched. Behind her, on the back of the door, he could now see blood-red scratch marks where someone had obviously tried to claw his way out.

She moved in for the kill.

Still stunned, George feebly raised his fists, ready to jab her in the throat, but she stopped just shy of his reach.

"Let me go," he heard himself say.

She answered immediately, "You can never leave."

The leisure-bot, formerly known as "Lotus-Blossom," opened her mouth. There was a slight clicking sound as her jaw unhinged and her mouth opened wider. At the back of her throat was a flickering light, like one of those antique movie projectors.

The flickering light grew in intensity as it flashed him in the eyes, blinding him. He felt a point, like the tip of a spear, penetrating his brain and splitting it in half, so incredibly painful. The world slanted crazily. He must have fallen over because he heard the thump of his own body slapping the floor.

The last thing he heard before he left this world was the sound of her voice, now gentle, soft and whispering in his ear...

"I am here to serve."

Chapter 10

Fishbowl

George was dreaming.

He was standing on the outside decks of The Dauntless. His wife was there, looking radiant, as she always did, pushing strands of hair behind one ear. She was smiling sweetly at him. No. She was smiling, but it was a sad smile. He then noticed she was standing near an edge with no railing.

Get away from there! he screamed in his mind, *You'll fall!*

He tried to go over to her, but something in the dream was holding him back. Or, was it some things.

George fought them. Whatever was holding him didn't budge. *But they would budge*.

Wait, is she falling? Alarm filled every fiber of his being. *The Dauntless traveled at a minimum height of seventy feet. Even if there's water down there, she'd never survive the fall!*

He knew he attacked those holding him, but he couldn't remember how. All he knew was that he was now free, running toward her, his hands outstretched in front of his face.

Tessa fell backwards and away from him.

NO! Did I push her?

'Say, Georgie,' his old pal, Jimmy Stewart, echoed in his head, 'I hate to break this to you, but I think you just killed your wife.'

"Tessa!" He awoke from the nightmare screaming her name.

A soft, female voice called out to him, "George? George, are you okay?"

His eyes were still blurry, but he recognized the voice immediately. It was Tessa.

He was lying on a bed, a really soft comfy one, probably the most comfortable bed he had ever lain upon in his life. His head was on Tessa's lap, and he felt her familiar fingertips running through his hair, just like she used to do back at the beach house in Pensacola. They would sit on the big swing on the front porch that overlooked the ocean and talk about their day.

"Tessa?" he managed.

"There you are George," she said softly.

George opened his eyes. His vision was still blurry, but he could see well enough to see that his beautiful wife was gazing down at him with that soft smile of hers and squinting lightly with her almond-shaped eyes.

"Tessa, is that really you?"

"Who else would it be, silly? You've been out for a long time. You must've really needed it."

The last thing he remembered was the leisure-bot walking toward him with the flickering light at the back of her throat.

Tessa seemed to sense his thoughts and offered, "It's alright now, George. You're safe."

Tessa, and the others, they must have rescued me.

Breathing a sigh of relief, his vision began to clear more. Beyond Tessa's face he saw a school of fish swim overhead.

Well that makes no sense.

Focusing a bit more, he realized the fish were actually on the opposite side of a thick pane of glass ceiling.

Oh no. I'm still in the fishbowl.

The passing fish seemed to stop their ballet and gaze down upon them, watching the show beneath them unfold.

Well that's ironic.

He lurched himself out of Tessa's lap. She tried to grab him, but her moves were slow and sensual, and he escaped, off the bed at least.

"What are you doing?" he asked.

"I'm here to serve," she responded sweetly.

It occurred to him that he could simply give in. His real wife was dead. He was certain of that now. He might have killed her. Perhaps this was what he deserved.

"You're not my wife."

The faux-Tessa gave him that look Tessa always gave him when he would say something incredibly stupid. "Does it really matter? Why, your every wish would be my command."

"Now I definitely know you're not my wife."

He retreated to the door. This time she didn't stop him. She seemed content to sit on the bed. The door didn't budge. The scratch marks on the inside of the door were more apparent than before.

Someone had tried to claw his way out. He doubted it was the leisure-bot. She seemed more than capable of smashing down the door.

"That won't work, George," she said, sounding exactly like Tessa. He briefly wondered, is it like Tessa, or is it the way he remembered Tessa speaking?

"Why don't you come back to bed and I'll run my fingers through your hair some more. I know you like that." He did like that, but now that memory was tainted forever by this...abomination who looked like Tessa, but wasn't her in the slightest.

She moved toward him. It wasn't the same robotic-purposeful movements as before. It was the way Tessa had moved: gentle, casual. Maybe, because she had uploaded his memory of Tessa, she was forced to move only like Tessa, and maybe that, was something he could use to his advantage.

Before she could reach him, he noticed the bathroom door on his right was open. As robot Tessa arrived, he jumped inside. The moment he turned the bolt and locked the door, she calmly tried the handle.

"Let me in, George. I'm here to serve."

"You're not my wife," George yelled back at her, his voice growing angry.

THUMP-THUMP-THUMP! "I SAID... LET ME IN GEORGE!"

He needed a weapon. Scanning the bathroom, he saw only sink, toilet and ceramic tiles.

The Leisure-bot banged violently on the door again.

He backed away from the door and that's when the smell hit him.

That can't be good.

He didn't want to turn around. He knew what he was going to find, and eventually he did. There in the bathtub, submerged in clear water, was the corpse of a short man dressed in a business suit.

Sitting on the toilet seat beside the tub, George reached down into the bath water and searched the corpse. Its flesh was gooey. George didn't find any weapons (even another pocketknife would've been something), but he did find a photo in the man's hand. It pictured a short-statured Asian man, with an elderly Asian woman with a stunning college-aged girl, who couldn't have been more than nineteen.

"What happened to you?" George asked the dead man. He went on to wonder, *In the end, did you kill yourself or did that whack-a-doodle outside do it for you?*

George thought about all the other doors he could've chosen in the endless corridor and cursed his dumb luck that he chose this one.

Laying the picture back down onto the side of the tub, he mumbled in his best Humphry Bogart accent, "Of all the gin joints, in all the towns, she walks into mine..."

As he rose from the tub, his hand grabbed a metallic handicap bar. One end had been pulled free from the wall, and the other end was nearly free.

He gazed down at the corpse in the tub. *Had you tried to pull this bar off the wall? Use it as a weapon?* If he did, the submerged bather had only half succeeded before giving in to exhaustion. George grasped the pipe in both hands, put one foot up on the wall and pulled. The pipe moved, and after several more angry tugs, it came free.

"Come out, Georgie! I want to play with you some more."

George gave one last nod of respect to the man in the tub. "Thanks buddy. This one's for the both of us," and he moved to the door.

"Come out! Come out! Come out!"

George did exit the bathroom and when he did so, he swung mightily.

She caught the pipe easily, held it for a second and then ripped it from his hands. "Oh George. You have so much to learn."

She backhanded him so hard, he flew across the room and crashed into the night table beside the bed.

Ironically, his first thought was, *This has to be at least the fourth thing I have been flung into today.*

The lamp upon it had smashed to pieces, and he could see where the power supply was still sparking.

Maybe I could electrocute her?

He quickly dismissed the idea because, one, she wasn't about to stand there and let him connect the sparking wires to her person. And two, he doubted the wall socket was carrying enough juice to shock her into submission anyway.

To his surprise, she tossed the metal bar back to him.

That's when it hit him. She had done this before. Perhaps dozens, even hundreds of times to anyone unfortunate enough to stumble into her web. Every scenario ran through his mind, but he realized, there was no outcome she couldn't predict or probably hadn't experienced already.

Think George, what is the one thing no one in their right mind would do?

She took a menacing step toward him. "Let's get this over with, George," she said tauntingly. "Get it all out of your system." When he didn't react quick enough she raised her voice and yelled, "I said, try again!"

It was futile. He knew it, and she knew it.

(Tinkling of glass),

George could hear the glass pieces crunching underfoot. He spun around and soon located the source. Pieces of glass littered the floor where he had struck the glass with his head. *Tessa always said I had a thick skull.* Soon, narrow streams of water began pouring in.

The leisure-bot must've seen him studying the fresh hole too, for she said, "Don't you worry about that, George. Room service can have it fixed in no time."

Wrong!

George swung the pipe, only this time, he did the one thing no person in their right mind would ever do. He swung at the broken glass. Water immediately began streaming in with more fervor.

Faux-Tessa's eyes went wide with alarm. "What are you doing?"

The panic in her voice brought a smile to his face. An alarm klaxon sounded and if that weren't enough warning, a spinning, red strobe light dropped down from the ceiling.

"Stop!" she cried, "You'll kill us both!"

The water quickly formed a pool on the floor. Before the water could reach him he hopped up onto the bed. The Leisure-bot did that head tilt thing again, but for the most part she ignored the water rising up over her shoes.

Steel shutters began lowering down over the smashed-out window.

"George," she had to yell now for the water was really gushing in. "All you did was delay the inevitable. The shutters will stop the water, the glass will be repaired and we will start all over again, right where we left off."

The leisure-bot seemed confused when he dropped the pipe... and picked up the broken lamp instead.

"No thanks. You're not my wife," he said, and then threw the sparking lamp into the water that was now rising up to her knees.

Immediately, the leisure-bot jolted from the electric shock. All but the flashing strobe light dimmed for a moment and then the main lights went out completely. A few seconds later, they snapped back on. The leisure-bot fell to her knees and sat there convulsing.

The shutters had completely sealed the windows and a drainage hole had magically appeared in the carpeted floor. Certain that the water no longer carried any juice, George hopped down from the bed and recovered the pipe.

The leisure-bot's head continued to jerk back and forth, and George figured he had only seconds to react. With all his strength, he hit her in the head several times.

The leisure-bot raised her ruined face. It was still Tessa's. Using his wife's voice she begged, "Please..."

George hefted the bar, but couldn't bring himself to strike her. He knew the leisure-bot wasn't Tessa, but he just couldn't bring himself to finish her off.

"Please... George. Please don't hurt me anymore."

In the end, it was the poor deceased man in the bathroom that finally gave him the willpower to deliver that final swing. It was the hardest thing he had ever done in his life, but he knew if he didn't, he would've wound up just like the Asian man in the bathtub.

WHAM!

The Leisure-bot crumpled to the floor and a second later the door to the room unlocked and swung open.

George knew he probably should've taken the handicap bar with him. He had no other weapon, but he wanted nothing to do with it, so he dropped it to the floor.

Chapter 11

Land Ho!

"Hey, Uncle Rick!"

Uh-oh. She called me Uncle Rick, and not just Rick. That means she wants something. Before she could even try, he said loudly, "Nooo."

Maddie had her hands clasped behind her back and half-skipped her way onto the bridge of The Dauntless. Coquettishly, she said, "I haven't even asked for anything yet."

"I know that tone. It's the same tone your mother used whenever she wanted something totally insane. Whatever it is, the answer is no."

Totally ignoring that, Maddie asked, "Seeing how we are grounded until the portside batteries recharge, Traxx and I were wondering if we could take the Hopper out and do a little recon?"

Rick tossed his clipboard onto the console, furrowed his brow and responded with his usual incredulous nature, "Nooooo... you can't take out the Hopper."

"Why not?" Maddie whined, "I'm rated."

Rick put his face in his palms, held them there for a moment, and then drew them down with a heavy sigh. "We're in unexplored territory, that's why. We don't know what's out there. It could be anything."

Undeterred, Maddie shot back, "All the more reason for me to go out and map it." Seeing that her Uncle still wasn't convinced she added, "I'll be armed. And, it's not like I'm going out there all by myself. Traxx is going with me."

"Forget it. What would your da..."

Rick didn't finish the sentence he had so reflexively began. There was an awkward silence between them.

Maddie lifted her eyes to his, and holding back the tears she was first to speak, "What would my dad say? My mom?" Shaking her head, "I don't know. I don't know what they'd say. You know why? Because they're not here. They haven't been here for a long time."

The large engineer averted his eyes, looking anywhere, at the rivets in the hull, out the windows, anywhere but in the eyes of a young girl who lost both parents way too soon.

Maddie sniffed loudly and wiped her tears on the back of her wrist. "Uncle Rick, other than my dad, I've had more rescues under my belt than everyone on the entire ship combined." She moved to where she could meet his gaze. "If you can't trust me to do a little recon with a dumb ole' Hopper, who can you trust?"

She was right. George had trained her well. So well in fact, he often wondered if George somehow knew that one day she'd be leading her own expeditions. *Probably just being his usual self; hope for the best, but plan for the worst.* Grumbling to himself for doing so, Rick moved over to the metal safe mounted on the wall, opened it and removed a set of keys. Before throwing them to her he said, "Four hours, Maddie."

They both knew she'd push that to five.

She went to say as much when Rick sighed and said, "I mean it, Mads, you got four hours at the absolute most. I don't care if you find the Holy Grail out there, after two hours in, you turn your butt around and come right back. You understand?"

Rick could tell by her face that she didn't expect him to be so harsh. She was about to retort with the first thing to come flying out of her mouth when he added, "Maddie, before you lay into me, please keep in mind you're getting what you wanted."

Maddie let that one go, and he tossed her the keys.

"Sure, Uncle Rick. Um, thanks."

He didn't respond. He was too angry. Instead he turned back around and slammed the door to the safe shut.

Maddie retreated to the exit where Traxx was waiting for her in the shadows. He kept his voice low, but Rick could still hear the boy when he said, "That was pretty mean the way you talked to him. He's done nothing but watch out for you."

Rick knew deep down that Maddie appreciated the way he had tried to fill in for her missing parents, but it still hurt him just the same when she said, "Just mind your own business, Traxx," and stomped out the door.

"Sorry," Traxx responded, but Maddie was already gone.

Rick watched the two of them go, and thought, *They're just kids.*

Tessa appeared next to Rick on the bridge. She was resting one elbow on a console and sipping a mug of chai tea. This wasn't an illusion or even a clever hologram like before. Rick knew that much.

Tessa's ghost took a sip from her mug, smiled sweetly, and finally said, "You know, Rick. You can't keep an eagle in a canary cage forever. At some point, you're going to have to let her spread her wings."

Of course, she was right. Tessa and George were the two most adventuresome people he had known in his life. So, it shouldn't surprise him that their daughter would share the same recklessness.

Tessa was always the parent who was a little more free with Maddie and her escapades. On the other hand, George would've been perfectly content if Maddie were wrapped up in a plastic bubble made of titanium. Sure, he trained her, but that was because he was always hovering protectively over her or nearby.

Rick knew he should go over the repair list one more time, but he couldn't shake the feeling of melancholy. *How did it all go so wrong?* When was he going to tell Maddie the truth as to what really happened to her parents. *I mean, how do you tell a kid something like that?* How could he ever possibly hope to tell Maddie that her father, the man she loved most, was the man who murdered her mom?

Chapter 12

The Launch Bay

"You still haven't told me where we're going."

Maddie led him down several flights of stairs into the belly of the ship. "Yes, I did, I'm taking you to the launch bay. It's located near the aft of the ship."

Henry trailed down the stairwell behind her. She certainly did not tell him that. Or had she? *Maybe I blacked out again?* Henry didn't feel comfortable walking past signs that read: Authorized Personnel Only. But, he dutifully followed her nonetheless.

Arriving at a massive hanger bay, Henry stared up at an enormous box-shaped vehicle parked within. The craft before him was drab yellow in color and about the size of the heavy cargo truck he had seen in The Factory. But despite this craft's great size, it seemed more like a Land Rover with large-paned windows; like the kind Henry had seen in those National Geographic magazines on African Safaris; only this gargantuan rover didn't have any wheels. Instead, it was floating on air, as if by magic.

"Whoa," was all he could manage. *Whoa. My, aren't you articulate Henry.*

Henry wasn't sure who this new voice in his head was, but he continued to follow Maddie around the back of the massive vehicle even so. More than once he saw her caress the hull with a gloved hand. They passed the nomenclature, H-04, stenciled on the side in blue lettering.

Abruptly Maddie said, "Oh, that's right; I forgot. You haven't seen a Hopper before."

As they finished circling the craft, Henry could now see the front of what Maddie called, *the Hopper*. The front was more akin to a helicopter's cockpit and looked as though it had been slapped on as an afterthought.

"See that?" Maddie asked, pointing to an accordion-looking passageway that connected to the payload area. When Henry nodded, Maddie explained proudly, "That allows for the cockpit to swivel back and forth, like a hound dog sniffin' out prey".

Henry noted that Maddie was just full of delightful colloquialisms, and she often switched to a southern drawl when she said them.

"So, where's the pilot?" Henry asked.

Maddie didn't answer. Instead she grabbed a vertical bar and slid open a side door that reminded Henry of the heavy doors on old freight train cars. The moment the door finished sliding all the way open, metal, corrugated stairs unfolded from beneath the hovering vehicle. When the unfolding stairs got stuck, Henry could hear whirring motors groaning in protest. This continued until Maddie gave the stairs a swift kick with her boot. "She's an old girl, but she's still plenty reliable."

Henry thought he detected the tone of a much more seasoned man behind her words, *her dad maybe?*

Despite the craft's obvious modern design, it had seen better days. The drab yellow hull was pitted and heavily dented in several places. Henry could see where two of the large window panes had splintered cracks.

Maddie climbed up the short stairwell and into the payload area. Henry cursed himself under his breath for following.

Inside the payload area, Henry saw Traxx and the gargoyle pulling on thick overalls similar to the ones on the rack behind them.

Traxx slipped into his easily, whereas Cheeves was having a bit more difficulty pulling his suit over his large paws.

"Cheeves," Traxx complained, "We've been over this, buddy. You don't need a survival suit." He yanked the suit from the gargoyle, causing the gargoyle's ears to lower like a sad puppy.

A sad puppy with fangs and razor-sharp claws, Henry thought. Despite how welcoming Cheeves had been, Henry still couldn't explain his strong apprehension around the friendly butler.

Seeing how crestfallen Cheeves had become, Traxx explained, "Cheeves, your skin is tougher than the hull of *The Dauntless*. You'll be fine."

Cheeves, quickly recovering from his pouting session, perked up at some new thought, "What about goggles? Do I get to wear goggles thhhiiisssph time?"

"No, Cheeves," Traxx said. "I could shove a screwdriver in your eye and it wouldn't hurt you. Besides, you broke the last pair. Remember?"

Maddie tossed her head over to Henry. "If you haven't figured it out yet, Cheeves is practically indestructible."

Spotting Henry, Traxx asked Maddie, "Why's he here? Henry can't go. He's not checked out to do map surveys. We barely are."

Hearing an opportunity for escape, Henry piped up with, "Maybe he's right, Maddie, maybe I shouldn't go. After all, I wouldn't want to get anyone in trouble."

Maddie smiled at him. "Don't worry about it. Back in the galley, you said so yourself, you wanted to get off this ship and explore."

Henry shook his head. "No," he began slowly. "No. I don't believe I ever said that. In fact, I'm fairly certain I said the exact opposite of that. I distinctly remember telling you how big the ship is and how I keep getting lost."

Maddie tilted her head and lifted an eyebrow. "You sure? I'm pretty sure I remember you telling me how you were looking for an excuse to get off the ship and get out to explore."

Henry stammered, "I literally have never said that, not even once. I know, because I don't think it now."

Maddie shrugged. "Well, look at it this way, this is a much smaller vessel. No way you'll get lost in here."

Henry gave a dour smile, "Hardly comforting."

"Oh, c'mon!" Traxx complained, snatching a newly-broken pair of goggles from Cheeves.

Finally realizing Traxx wasn't going to let him wear any expedition gear and spotting her, Cheeves exclaimed, "Oh, hi Maddie! So nicethhhh to see you. Do you have any..."

Maddie cut him off with a curt wave and asked him, "Cheeves, did you remember to bring your cat?"

Cheeves eyes went wide and his ears perked up at this. "Muh Cathe?"

Maddie switched her focus from the gargoyle to Traxx, "You didn't tell him?"

Traxx shuffled his feet and stared at the floor. "Maddie, I don't think we should leave him behind. Maybe we should take him with us like Rick told us to."

Maddie's brow furrowed and through gritted teeth she growled, "Traxx..."

The younger boy sighed and spoke directly to the gargoyle. "Yes, Cheeves, that's right," he began, giving a less than stellar performance, "I almost forgot to tell you. We found a kitten in The Factory, and I brought it back to your quarters and hid it there." Now that he was committed to the ruse, his acting was beginning to improve. "It was supposed to be a surprise for you. Did you get it?"

Henry doubted the gargoyle would believe this. Nothing was ever wasted in The Factory. Any animal unfortunate enough to stray out onto a work floor of starving workers rarely lasted long. Despite knowing this, he kept silent for fear of incurring the wrath of Mad Maddie.

To Henry's surprise the gargoyle asked, "You have a Cath?" His head shook from side-to-side with excitement, "And it's a kitt-ton?" Cheeves lips pursed closed as he spoke in baby talk, "A cute, little, adorable, kitt-ton?"

"That's right," Maddie sang, "and he's all yours."

Cheeves face suddenly looked skeptical. "Wait a second. You guys are puttin' me on. There's no kitt-ton in my quarter-thsss."

"O-kaay..." Maddie responded, stretching out the word to a full measure. "I guess Sue Sablan will probably just adopt him, and we'll never see him after that."

"WHU-UH-TTT?" Cheeves asked, and then complained, "Not Sue. She's the quarter..." he struggled with the word, "...quarter-quartermasth-ter. I'll never get to play with it then."

Traxx jumped in with an enthusiastic, "Or eat it!"

Bouncing on his taloned-toes Cheeves gasped and quickly said, "I'll be right back. Don't go anywhere withhhppp-out me."

Maddie assured him, "We're not going anywhere until you get back."

"You promise-thhpp?"

Traxx crossed his heart. "Promise and hope to die."

Henry thought that sounded a bit ominous.

Cheeves nodded vigorously. "Kay, I'll be right back."

Cheeves nimbly bounded out of the Hopper and down to the launch play floor. After a moment of preparation, that involved some butt-waggling, he leapt mightily into the air and cleared the railing of the upper catwalk, a good twenty feet above the main floor. The gargoyle stopped for a second to make sure they were still there and hadn't left yet, and then vanished into the hatch.

"Okay, we haven't much time before he gets back." Turning toward Henry, Maddie held up one of the uniforms to his frame and then another. Deciding on one pair, she roughly tossed him a pair of overalls. "Here, this is about your size, put it on."

"Uh, alright."

As Henry climbed into the thick leather trousers, she explained, "Once we get where we're going, we'll give you a quick crash course on your survival suit."

Alarmed Henry's raised his eyebrows at this. "Perhaps I should wait until a full class becomes available."

Ignoring this, Maddie removed some gloves and a soft, leather helmet from a shelf and tossed them to him. "Aw quit your griping, Snowflake."

Henry was so busy shouldering the rest of the way into the (one piece) uniform that he missed the catch as it sailed past his head.

Maddie chuckled slightly and waited for him to finish and recover his helmet.

Henry placed the soft leather helmet on his head, but couldn't see anything. After a moment he heard Maddie giggle and Traxx say, "Uh, Henry, you've got it on backwards."

Henry removed the helmet and began to say, "I really don't think this is such a good idea,..." But, Maddie cut him off by saying, "We don't have time for this. We've got to get out of here before Cheeves comes back."

Hearing this, Henry asked, "Wait a minute, aren't we *waiting* for Cheeves?"

"Uhmmm..." Maddie began. "Yeah, about that. Cheeves isn't coming."

Henry was confused. Cheeves was their protector, their bodyguard. Leaving such a formidable bodyguard behind absolutely made no sense. "What do you mean he isn't coming?"

Before she could answer, not that she looked as though she were about to, Traxx asked her, "Do you think we'll need the spare generator this trip?"

"No," Maddie replied. "Get rid of it. We only need the one charge. We're not going that far, and I'd like to lighten the load as much as possible in case we find something really worth bringing back."

"Copy," Traxx said coolly. He reached up and opened a bulkhead overhead and removed two discs with handles on them. He magnetically attached the discs to the generator, one on each side, hit a button on each of them and the massive generator suddenly floated six inches off the floor. The younger boy walked around the heavy generator, placed himself between it and the wall, raised up his legs and kicked it. The generator shot out of the Hopper, as if floating on Aladdin's magic carpet.

These people. Their technology was far beyond anything he had ever seen in The Factory, or had ever read about. Yet, these two teenagers seemed to have no problem with operating it.

Henry jumped slightly as things began CLANGING to the floor. Maddie was roughly tossing things out of the Hopper she didn't deem mission-worthy.

Henry held up his hand, and immediately felt foolish. "Uhmmm... why are we doing this again exactly?"

Maddie answered him as she worked. "We're in unexplored territory. We're on a mapping expedition." Maddie made a face and added, "Duh."

Traxx, now standing on the launch bay floor, reached up into the Hopper's payload area and began removing Maddie's discards, too heavy for her to fling to the floor. Traxx explained, "Not only that, but we could be sitting on top of a huge pile of foodstuffs, medical supplies or ammo and not even know it. All we're going to do is take a quick poke around, see what we can scrounge up, load it into the Hopper and bring it back."

"And you're sure it's safe?"

"No, it's not safe," Maddie shot back, but she must've seen something in his face because she quickly added. "Stop worrying, Snowflake. Ninety-nine times out of a hundred we never see anyone or anything out here in the Madlands."

"And the other one time?"

Traxx took the last of Maddie's castoffs. "Don't worry, Henry. The Hopper's fully equipped with automated defenses. As long as we don't stray too far from it, we'll be perfectly fine."

As he worked, he explained to Henry, "It's a good thing we're making room. One time we left behind so many crates of canned chocolate pudding. You wouldn't believe it."

Henry was confused. "I thought your machines on board The Dauntless could replicate any food?"

"Oh, they can, but there's nothing like the real thing; especially when you know what the food really is."

Henry was more confused. "What's the food?"

Maddie interjected, "Don't tell him that, he'll never eat again."

"What's the food?" Henry asked, now wanting to know more than ever. *What could it possibly be?*

Traxx patted him on the back. "Henry, you seem like a nice kid. Trust me when I tell you that you don't want to know."

Henry nodded that he did indeed want... to... know.

Traxx stuck his tongue out and made a flagellant noise.

Henry finally figured it out. "Oh, gross, really?"

"Traxx, I told you not to tell him."

Traxx shrugged in response.

Immediately Maddie announced, "Okay guys, let's go."

Maddie led him and Traxx from the payload compartment, through the accordion causeway and into the cockpit. They had to go down a short set of stairs because the cockpit sat a bit lower than the payload compartment. Henry saw four captain's chairs, two in the front, and one in back. A fourth seat was situated near a wall of monitors. Traxx and Maddie immediately dropped into the two seats in front, donned headsets and commenced flipping necessary switches Henry couldn't even hope to understand. Below their feet, he could see that they had a clear view of the ground through the clear re-enforced Plexiglass floor plating.

Concern bubbling up inside him, Henry asked again, "Wait a minute, where's the pilot?" he spotted Maddie and Traxx as they shared a look between them. Henry raised his eyebrows toward her and asked, "You're telling me you're the pilot? You're just a kid."

Traxx adjusted his headset on his head and sighed. "Oh boy, here we go."

Seeing Traxx do this, Maddie offered, "No, no. It's okay. He's new around here and doesn't know any better. He's just a stupid kid."

Henry took offense to this. "Hey, I'm at least one year older than you are." In truth he figured he was at least two or three years older, but he figured he would be polite.

One of the switches must've activated the payload compartment door, because Henry could hear the stairs tucking underneath, and the door sliding shut with a hiss. This was followed by a pneumatic THUMP sound as the door sealed closed, and the cabin became pressurized.

Seeing how Traxx was obviously the one with some semblance of reason, Henry asked him, "Don't you think Cheeves will get mad when he finds out we left him behind?"

With practiced hands, Traxx flipped several switches in rapid sequence. As he did, numerous things came on: The front lights, spinning yellow strobes announcing their departure and various hissing sounds. The boy had obviously driven this *Hopper* many times before. Without slowing down in the slightest Traxx answered, "Nah. Cheeves is easily distracted. The first thing that's going to happen is he is going to get to his quarters and tear apart his room trying to find a cat that isn't there."

Henry swallowed. "He's going to tear apart his quarters?"

"Yep," Traxx answered, "He'll literally shred pillows, tear stuff off the wall, rip up everything trying to find a stupid cat that doesn't exist."

Wait, what? Henry thought. As of last night, Sue had reassigned him to another berth to give the refugee family their own quarters. "But *I* share a room with Cheeves."

Traxx let out a hearty laugh. "Oh yeah, I forgot about that."

While checking things off her pre-flight checklist, Maddie asked him, "How do you put up with his snoring?"

Henry's face fell. "I don't. He keeps me up all night."

Traxx offered, "Try hitting him with your boot."

"What?"

Maddie grinned. "Yeah, bean him in the head with your shoe. Usually he'll turn over on his side, and he'll stop snoring."

Traxx chuckled again, "Or he'll tear your arms off in his sleep."

Henry recalled the way Cheeves had leapt up onto the balcony twenty feet in the air.

"Yeah, I don't think I'm doing that."

Maddie laughed. "He's just kidding… sort of." Switching to a very serious voice, much more serious than Henry would have thought her capable of, she spoke into the microphone of her headset, "Dauntless bridge… Dauntless bridge… This is

Charlie-Zero-Four, all systems are in the green and we are requesting a go for launch."

Henry knew this was a lie. All systems were certainly not in the green, because even as she said it one of the buttons overhead was a fire engine red. Maddie kept flicking it until the bulb popped and was now dead.

The comm system crackled and a man's voice came back over it. "Copy that, Charlie-Zero-Four, you are cleared for immediate launch."

"Copy that Michael, and tell Sue thanks for fixing my suit."

"We'll do kiddo. You kids be careful out there."

Henry leaned forward and searched for an exit. "So how do we get out?" he began, when without warning the platform dropped out from beneath them. Henry could hear loud motors working as the platform began lowering them down out of the belly of the ship.

Traxx laughed. "You should've seen your face just now."

Another, deeper, more disgruntled voice came over the intercom speaker. "Maddie, you and Traxx read me?"

"Yes Uncle Rick," both she and Traxx chimed back together. Henry was unsure as to whom this Uncle Rick might be, but it was very apparent that Maddie and Traxx were not brother and sister.

"I want you to let Traxx drive."

Maddie shot out her hands and splayed her fingers like a nervous cat, "What?" she questioned. "Traxx drives like a grandma. He drives slower than a grandma. In fact, he drives slower than a great-grandma who is dead."

Rick radioed back, "That's the point."

Traxx nod his head back at him and said, "It's true, compared to Maddie I do drive pretty slow."

"Four hours, Maddie. No more. I mean it."

"Yes, Uncle Rick."

"And Cheeves... You keep a close eye on them."

Maddie and Traxx stared at each other wondering what to do. Maddie gestured for Traxx to do something, but he shook his head. Maddie punched him in the shoulder, hard.

Traxx rolled his eyes, lifted his headset microphone to his lips, and in a pretty good facsimile of Cheeves's voice said, "Do you have any cathhssppp?"

With the Dauntless landed, Henry could see that the airship's large metal struts did not match the color or design of the rest of the ship. *I wonder if those were added later?*

The Hopper shuddered as the platform reached the ground.

Maddie switched to her command voice again, "Dauntless Bridge... Dauntless Bridge... we are go for disembark."

"Copy that, Charlie-Zero-Four. Good hunting."

Chapter 13

Kelpi's Moon Pool

George passed through another door and gently closed it behind him. He wasn't sure how long he had been walking around the underwater complex, or base, or resort; he really had no idea what to call it.

The first area, where he had met the leisure-bot (he shivered involuntarily from the memory) had seemed as though it was more like a lavish hotel. After searching for hours, he finally found a stairwell marked EXIT and left the hotel section.

He then traveled through a tubular causeway that connected to other underwater complexes. Guests didn't even have to walk. They rode on conveyor belts while listening to soothing music and whale songs. Despite this, the tube-way made George extremely nervous. At any moment he expected the leviathan to swim out of the shadowy depths and crash through the glass.

The causeway had given him time to think. He hadn't encountered anyone else since escaping the leisure-bot. Nor did he come across the crew of the submarine that had brought him here.

He recalled how one day, he and Tessa became separated from each other in one of those brand new super stores. They were young back then and these were the days long before everyone had a cell phone. He had been on one side of the store in camping equipment, while she was on the grocery side. Then, when they went to find one another, they had swapped sides. At one point, they had even taken turns waiting out at the truck in the parking lot, only to miss each other again. It had been maddening. George found it ironic as he was a search-and-rescue pilot. So, it was no surprise to him that he had not stumbled across the submarine crew in a place that was easily fifty times bigger than any super-store.

George also noted that he hadn't seen any more dead bodies, at least not since the one in the bathtub. Not that he wanted to, he just expected to. Oh, there was that one body floating outside one of the causeway windows. The water-logged corpse was wearing a cheap blue suit, like something a shady accountant might wear. He sported a thin mustache and a floating comb over. Fish had been picking at the poor man for some time, rendering his flesh all kinds of gooey. Despite being a gross mess, George almost felt as though he recognized the man. In the end, George tore his gaze away from the watery cadaver and pressed onwards.

What George didn't know, was the moment he turned away, the leviathan scooped up the dead accountant in his jaws and swam off.

George exited the causeway and entered a new complex. The inside was wide open, with ceilings at least four stories high. Representations of giant sea creatures hung from every ceiling and large window panes afforded generous views of sea life outside.

Along the walls and scattered about the main floor were several interactive displays depicting underwater life. One life-sized diorama was of a diver in one of those antiquated diving suits with the large round helmet. Other life-sized suits were also on display. It appeared to be a timeline on the history of diving equipment. The first being the antique diver, his knife drawn, and doing battle with a giant squid, that had its tentacles wrapped around his waist and arms.

George began to wonder, *Was this merely a history of diving suits or was this an adventure you could sign up for?* In Stranger World, you never knew what to expect. Were it not for the dire circumstances, he certainly would have been impressed by the notion.

He continued to explore more of the massive open area. Whereas the lavish resort complex had seemed unscathed, this new area was a torrent of a mess, like there had been some sort of battle. Several ceiling tiles were hanging down from water damage, and in many places the beige carpeting was sopping wet. He noticed several sets of tracks recently made in the moist carpet.

The submarine crew must have come this way.

His footsteps made squishing sounds as he walked through the puddles and past a nearby gourmet seafood restaurant. He made a note to check it out later for some food.

Because many of the overhead lights were burned out in so many places, shadows lay everywhere. It wasn't until George reached the center of the gigantic room that he saw her. A mermaid. At first, he thought his imagination was running amok, which was saying a lot considering where he was.

Under normal circumstances, seeing a mermaid was enough reason to give any sane person pause. But here in Stranger World, George had seen mermaids before. Well, technically, those weren't mermaids. Those darlings with sharp teeth had been shape-changing river-nymphs on the Fantasy River. But, the thing that bothered George the most was this mermaid wasn't swimming outside the windows in the ocean, where any self-respecting mermaid would be. No, this mermaid was inside, swimming through the air.

He had first spotted her at a distance, but now she was aware of him too. Slowly, but with purpose, she propelled herself toward him.

He took a few steps back, unsure of where to go. He could see she was smiling the entire time, so that was at least something positive. She had long purple hair, tied back with a seashell and a bikini top comprised of two yellow starfish. When she caught his eye, she offered him a friendly-little wave as if to say, 'Hi there.'

George found himself waving back. He didn't know what else to do. Out of the corner of his eye, he spied one of the divers on display. The early scuba diver (battling a shark) was holding a knife the size of a machete. Even if the blade was real (and sharp), George doubted he could get over to it in time. He took another few steps backward.

When she arrived, she blurted out, "Hi there, my name's Kelpi the Helpful Mermaid. I'm here to assist you." George couldn't help but notice that when she spoke her words were dripping with enthusiasm and her speech even had an annoying happy rhythm to it.

"But you're a mermaid."

As she levitated up and over the gift corner walls, Kelpi nodded enthusiastically, "Yes, yes, that's right, Kelpi *the Helpful* Mermaid. How may I assist you today?"

How may I assist you? This is new, he thought. *What to ask her first? Where am I? No, she'll just say something coy like, 'You're right where you're supposed to be.'* No, instead he decided to ask her, "Have you seen anybody else come through here recently?"

Kelpi the Helpful Mermaid hesitated before answering then said, "No. I... have... not... seen... anyone... come... through here."

Wow, that was an award winning performance, he thought, and said, "You're lying."

The Helpful Mermaid blinked a few times and surprised him when she asked, "Whatever do you mean?"

George responded reflexively by saying, "You hesitated way too long before answering. Plus, most people, when they access information from their memory, look up and left. You looked straight up. So, either your either lying, or you're a psychopath."

"Huh, you figured that out a lot faster than the others."

The others, George thought. *Does she mean the submarine crew?* "What do you mean the others?"

"Oh, you'll see. When you get down there."

George was confused. *Others? Down... there? Down where?*

Kelpi flicked her tail and she swam around him.

"Can I assume you already know about the prison?"

"Prison?" George asked, "What Prison?"

Kelpi turned her head to the side. "Nobody told you about the prison?" When George shook his head to indicate that *they* didn't, she put her hands on her hips. "Now Mr. Stapleton, what is it you've been doing with yourself all this time."

George thought about this before answering. "The only people I've met were those crewman on the sub," he was growing impatient now, "We were a little busy trying to not get eaten by an aquatic dinosaur."

Kelpi made a pouty face and spoke in baby talk, "Did that bad ole dinosaur, Mister Croney, try and eat you again?" She swam to a nearby window. "I really do need to have a talk with management about him. It isn't as if you didn't have enough problems already."

George couldn't believe what he was hearing. He blurted out, "Ya think?"

He was about to ask her another question when she turned from the window and said, "Well, "I'm afraid the rest of you took all of the other good equipment. There's not much left for you to use."

George shook his head, "Kelpi, what the devil are you talking about?"

"Oh right. They were supposed to brief you on the submarine." What she said next came out half-serious. "I swear, I have to do everything myself. I'm going to have to have a talk with management about those bumbling land dwellers when this all over."

"When what's over?"

Kelpi put a finger to her chin and thought it over before answering. "Okay, here goes. There's a whole presentation. A slide show and everything. They actually did a very good job putting it all together..."

"Kelpi!"

Her shoulders jolted from being startled. Composing herself, she said, "Right." She drew in the air with her finger and lines magically appeared out of thin air. As she spoke, a stick version of a man in a diving suit pantomimed her words.

"It's really quite simple. I don't know why so many of you have failed before. All you have to do is dive down to the prison, navigate the gauntlet and free the prisoner."

George didn't like the sound of that. The last thing he wanted to do was go diving with *Mister Croney* swimming around out there. But he was curious, so he asked. "What prison, is it here?"

"No silly," she gestured over toward what appeared to be an indoor swimming pool, and added, "Down there. You'll need to swim out through the moon pool."

They crossed over to what appeared to be a modest-sized swimming pool, but once next to it, George could see an opening in the floor of the swimming pool with a gentle-grade ramp allowing easy access to the ocean outside. As an Air Force Rescue Ranger, George was familiar with moon pools and their uses. Normally moon pools were used for marine drilling platforms or underwater research facilities. Here, he suspected this moon pool was used by tourists to gear up and go on scuba diving expeditions, like the ones he saw on the moving paintings outside the hotel rooms.

George recalled how the young, blond submariner had gotten gobbled up in one bite.

"Yeah, I'm not going anywhere, especially not down there." He hiked a thumb toward his chest. "I have to get topside and reunite with my daughter and friends. I don't have time for some suicide rescue mission. I'm sorry."

Kelpi blinked a few times before answering. "Do we really have to do this every time?" She straightened her posture. "Okay, skipping to the end, it's like this. There is no way back up to the surface. Not without the help of the..." she hesitated and searched for the right word, "...the prisoner. If you don't rescue him, you'll never get topside."

George shook his head, and then shook it some more. "Even if I did agree to this suicide mission, I don't have any gear, or air. Besides, I wouldn't get two feet with that thing swimming around out there."

"Mr. Croney?" she asked.

George nodded, "Yuh-huh."

Kelpi waved him away with her hand. "Oh, he won't bother you down there. He prefers to stay closer to the surface." She then took in her surroundings.

"My, my, this place certainly has been picked over, hasn't it?"

George was fairly certain she was being rhetorical and allowed her to continue.

"I'm afraid you're right. There isn't much left in the way of diving equipment." Staring back at him and smiling. "You just might be stuck here... with me... forever." She brightened up at this new train of thought and spoke rapidly, "Ooohhh... we could talk for hours. I know where they keep all sorts of board games. We could visit the library. We could go on diving expeditions together."

"Uh..." Spending the last of his days with Kelpi, the Annoying Mermaid, had about as much appeal as being eating by the kronosaurus. Staring at the diving suit displays and moving over to them, George asked, "What about this stuff?"

Kelpi's happy grin dropped. "Aww..." Pouting, she swam over to him. "I'm sorry, but those are museum pieces and you couldn't possibly... and he's stepping over the velvet rope."

As George inspected the dive gear, he said over his shoulder, "Let's call this *an emergency*." He removed the spear gun from the diver's hands. He was thankful the diver didn't come to life and start making him balloon animals or something.

Empty. No spears. He tossed it to the side, where it clanged on the floor.

The other dive suit had a sheathed knife strapped to its chest. George removed the leather binding holding the blade upside down in its sheath. Because it was a museum piece, he didn't expect it to be sharp. But in inspecting it, he found the blade would have cut paper floating in midair.

His bolstered confidence was quickly shattered at the thought of the leviathan attacking the sub. Although formidable, using the knife would be like trying to fight a tiger with a toothpick. Still, it was better than nothing. He sheathed the knife back in the harness and began removing it from the mannequin.

After about an hour of both of them searching the open area, nearby locker rooms, and gear shops they found nothing. Out of options, George returned to the first display with the antiquated diver. A dive suit like this would normally have hoses that ran up to a compressor that fed down air, but this one had none.

"I don't see any air hoses or support system. What am I supposed to use for oxygen?"

Kelpi shrugged. "It's like I told you. There's not much left around here."

George spied some cylindrical yellow tanks on the wall. "What about those?"

Kelpi shrugged, "Those are oxygen tanks for the window cleaners, but they're just air tanks. I don't see a suit." George used a knuckle to knock on the old-fashioned helmet.

"Oh... right." She laughed. It wasn't entirely annoying.

It had taken him nearly three hours and a bit of spot-welding, but by the end, he had a pretty good suit. It was a hodge-podge/hybrid suit that was a combination of the old diving suit and the futuristic modern tanks.

About an hour ago, Kelpi had brought him some deli sandwiches and raspberry iced tea. He found it odd that she knew his tastes so precisely. Furthermore, she seemed to converse with him as though they had known each other for weeks and not just the past few hours.

As George began pulling on the dive suit, Kelpi swam over to him and dropped a pile of gear. "Here. You'll need some flares." She tsk-tsk-tsk'd several times and added to herself, "We're running out of those too." Studying him again she added, "You're gonna need a flashlight. You forgot that last time."

She's insane. That's the only logical conclusion.

George picked up a roll of duct tape out of the pile. "What do you want me to do with this?"

"Attach the flashlight to your wrist. You came up with that a few times ago. I thought it was pretty good idea."He decided to play along with her insanity. The last thing he needed was another leisure-bot situation.

He nodded. "Alright, thanks Kelpi."

Kelpi beamed. She scrunched up her shoulders and said, "You're welcome, George."

Knife, flares and flashlight in place, he took his absconded helmet from Kelpi.

"Alright, here we go." She helped him don the helmet and as soon as it snapped into place, he became very aware of his own, very loud breathing.

Alright, George. Slow and steady. You've got to conserve your oxygen.

His feet were heavily weighted down with blocks, and it was difficult to move in the suit, but he managed to lower himself down into the moon pool.

At the top of the ramp, the water was only about waist deep. In addition to his breathing he could hear the thick boots clunking as they hit the deck.

"Wait a second. How do I get back up?"

Smiling, Kelpi seemed confused by his query. "With the aqua sled, silly."

"And where do I get that?"

Kelpi pointed to the far side of the pool. George turned in the direction and said, "I don't see anything."

"Look where I'm pointing." It was the first time she had a tone with him.

Turning all the way around in the pool, George saw something about the size and shape of a moped hanging on hooks. He lifted the sled off its hooks. It splashed as it hit the water. He didn't see any signs of propulsion, little blades connected to motors or even an engine. It was only a frame. "Where's the engine?"

Kelpi blinked those ridiculously oversized-eyes at him. "What do you mean? The throttle? It's on the handlebars."

George shook his head. "No. I mean the engine, the propulsion unit. What makes the thing go?"

She swam around him and examined the device again.

"Oh. I see. You really do have to stop thinking in twenty-second terms. There is no propulsion system. It's a fusion-based magnetic frame that operates off the magnetic pull of the earth's core."

"Sure, okay. I must have missed that in my future-planet physics class."

Standing in the moon pool, he slowly slid onto the sled.

She swam over his shoulder and hovered there. Kelpi definitely had no concept of what personal space meant. Extending her finger, she punched a button and a holographic display appeared over the handlebars. He could see five bars that grew in ascending order. Only half of the bars were light green. "You only have about a half charge, but that should be more than enough to get you down there and back."

"Down where?" He still had no idea where he was going.

Kelpi tapped the holograph display once more. A large green arrow pointed the way. It seemed overly-simplistic, but then he remembered it was probably originally designed for tourists and not Air Force Rescue Rangers.

She sighed. "Well, that's it. You've used up every last bit of our resources. I'm afraid you're the last one, George." Seeing that he was staring up at her, she raised a fist and gave a half-hearted, "Carpe Diem."

"Seize the day," George said automatically.

"Ah, a man who knows his Latin." She tilted her head to the side, "Then again, all of you did."

"All of you? There's that phrase again."

"No time for that now. You really need to get going. But, I have a good feeling about you, George. I think you just might be the one."

"Um, thanks?"

"Of course, I also thought that about the last one too. The one before that, and the one before that."

"I get the idea."

CRASH!

George and Kelpi both turned toward the sound of a door being smashed off its hinges. He could barely see it through the circular faceplate in his helmet, but he glimpsed the heavy door as it finished skimming across the floor.

The leisure-bot, now fully revealed as the *cyborg* she was, scanned the room until she found him. "George!" she screamed, then held her hands to her ruined face. "Look at what you've done to me, George. Look at what you've done!" She began limping on her ruined leg toward him. "I'm coming for you, George! We'll never be apart again."

He and Kelpi exchanged a glance. "Awwww, you've made a friend."

"Buy me a few minutes?" George asked in a tone a lot meeker than he intended. Kelpi smiled down at him and nodded.

"I'll try, but once the leisure-bots latch on to someone, they can be pretty tough to shake."

"I've noticed."

"Get going. I'll buy you as much time as I can." Switching to her happy smile again she added, "And George... have a super-duper-funtastic day!"

"Thanks, Kelpi," George said as he pulled back on the throttle and drove the sled down the ramp and into the watery depths.

"Hi there. I'm Kelpi the Helpful Mermaid. How can I assist you today."

George could hear the leisure-bot screaming behind him, "George, I'll never stop chasing you! Do you hear me? I'll never stop chasing you. Never!"

Chapter 14

The Last Dive

No sooner had he cleared the underwater base's moon pool ramp, George heard a splash above him. His first thought was Mister Croney had instantly found him. But then he saw the leisure-bot falling toward him like an underwater skydiver. Fortunately, she swam like a rock. With a gentle twist of the sled's throttle, he easily avoided her outstretched grasp.

This still didn't stop the leisure-bot from screaming at him underwater. He wasn't sure, but it sounded like, "Guhrorge, come back to me, Guh-rorge!" as she sunk past him and vanished down into the murky depths. "Guhrogeeeee..."

George hit the throttle lightly again and continued his descent. To distract his mind from the notion of becoming a light snack for a colossal dinosaur, he checked the holographic navigational display over the handlebars. He steered the sled in the direction of the green arrow. George fully expected the sled to make noise, sort of like those futuristic flying cars on the Jetsons, but it didn't. *Probably just as well, bubbles or vibrations in the water might attract you know who.*

The waiting was the worst part. Any second now, he was certain the leviathan was going to return and devour him as he had that poor submariner. His heart was hammering so hard that he thought it was going to beat right out of his chest. *You gotta stop,* he told himself. *You gotta slow it down or you're going to consume all of your oxygen before you get there.*

Get where though? he wondered. He still had no idea where he was going or what he was doing down here. He was so busy re-checking the holographic display that he nearly ran into an algae-covered dome structure. The dome went on for miles in every direction. At first, he was thinking it was about the size of a football stadium, but now he was thinking it was at least four times the size of that.

He thought about stopping and getting off. But, even though the dome was a gentle slope, he was afraid if he got off, the sled would slide off without him. Then he definitely would have no way of getting back up. Instead, he simply puttered along sans George Jetson space-car noises.

There was no sign of a hatch or an entrance of any kind, just a smooth dome covered in algae and coral.

He checked the navigation console again. Four red arrows indicated he was on the right spot. He went to brush some of the algae that had collected on the monitor. When he did, the picture in the display suddenly zoomed in further, and he realized there was a zoom function. He wished that Kelpi had told him that. He might have saved a considerable amount of fuel and oxygen.

He saw the light blinking, with four red arrows. Now that he was zoomed in, he could see that he was close to the target area. Turning the sled in the direction of the new arrows, George traveled another ten minutes.

The power gauge was dropping to nearly one-fourth. He was approaching the point of no return. Once he passed that, there was no going back up. His dive suit didn't come with any buoyancy control devices that he could inflate with his oxygen to ascend to the surface. This suit was much too heavy for him to swim back up. It only went one way and that was straight down.

Zooming along, George realized the arrows were pointing one way, and then suddenly changed directions. Whatever coordinates he was supposed to go to, he had missed them.

Steering the sled in a tight arc, he turned around. Now that he knew where to look this time, he saw it. A shadowy opening, about the width of a man's shoulders, lay hidden amongst the pink coral crusting the dome. The dark abyss had to be a runner-up to what a black hole in space must look like.

To conserve power, he hopped off the sled and parked it next to a coral outcropping so his ride wouldn't drift off or slide down the dome without him.

The suit was difficult to maneuver in but he was getting the hang of it. He lay down on his chest so he could peer into the hole.

George looked down. *Can't see, too dark.* He reached down to the pouch on right thigh and removed a flare. He snapped it open and was rewarded with a painfully-bright, red phosphorous glow. George dropped the flare down into the abyss, and it descended into darkness.

If he dropped down there, it was most likely he wouldn't be able to get back up in time. He checked his air gauge. Not much left, one hour tops, and he need most of that for his ascent.

This is looking more and more like a one-way trip.

The flare continued dropping without landing, then it dropped some more; and still nothing. *I can't see anything.* He looked back at the sled propped up like a kid's bicycle without a kickstand. *It would be a tight fit, but I suppose I could squeeze the sled through the hole, and then jump on the sled on the other side of the dome's ceiling. But, what if I can't get the sled back up through the hole?*

As he was thinking about this, movement beyond the sled caught his eye. He picked up the sled like an adolescent boy picked up his bike.

The Leviathan was back.

It had spotted him.

The sea monster knew he had nowhere to go, so it circled him, seemingly relishing the notion that he was helpless.

George remembered seeing a dinosaur movie back in the nineties. The paleontologist hero had discovered something about how a dinosaur's sight was based on movement. He stared at the sled. Whether this was true or not, he wasn't sure, but what other options did he really have? His toothpick of a knife?

He took a flare, popped it, and stuck it in-between the handlebars and throttle, so it was jammed. He had to brace his feet against the rocks to keep the sled from motoring off too soon.

Wait... wait for it.

The leviathan seemed to sense he was up to something now and was shooting through the water toward him with the speed of a torpedo. George held onto the sled for as long as he dared and then let it go. The sled sped off without him.

The Leviathan had a choice: either go after the moving, glowing sled or the motionless diver.

It was closing in on him. *Gosh that thing is fast.* Twenty yards, ten yards... George squeezed his eyes shut and waited for the inevitable.

CRUNCH!

The plan worked; sort of. The monster chomped the sled up in one bite and veered off, but it had swum so close to George, that he had been swept up in its wake and blasted off his feet.

He survived, for the moment, but for how long? Even if the kronosaurus swam off, there was no getting back home now.

George got to his feet. He could see the leviathan turning around in a large swooping arc like a fighter jet.

They both seemed to spot the hole between them at the same time.

George ran for his life, but the water slowed him down; he could only lumber toward it like a man walking on the moon.

Stopping only for a moment at the edge of the hole and staring at the black abyss, he realized the choice had already been made.

He spotted the creature hurtling toward him. Not daring to hesitate a second longer, he stepped off the edge and entered into oblivion.

Chapter 15

The Malt Shop

As he dropped down into the hole of the dome, George didn't see the jaws of the leviathan CHOMP overhead, but he sure felt the ripple of the wave caused by them.

That had been a lot closer than I had planned.

Splayed out like a starfish, George floated downward, feet first. With the dome blocking out the sun overhead, he was soon completely immersed in darkness. The light from the hole above him was getting farther and farther away.

Checking his depleted oxygen gauge, he was now well aware this was a one-way trip. Maybe that was Kelpi the Annoying Mermaid's purpose all along. *But why not just kill me on the surface? Maybe she couldn't kill people.*

Still sinking.

How fast? Is it too fast? He really had no idea. The suit was heavy. That much he knew. If and when he did land on the sea floor, he didn't want to strike it so hard he'd break his legs.

Still descending, but to where? George tapped the flashlight but it did little to penetrate the inky blackness. His training kicked in and he began reporting what he saw, "Visibility--only about ten feet." He was well aware that this was ridiculous since no one could hear him. He was on his own, but reporting the details aloud somehow gave him something else to think about.

George reached down to the pouch on his thigh. *Only three flares left.*

He decided to risk it. He popped one and dropped it down below him.

Before the flare winked out completely, he thought he glimpsed something far below, in the darkness.

It almost looked like...rooftops. Like those belonging to a middle-sized town. *Yeah, those are rooftops. Am I saved?*

As though sensing his presence, lights in various buildings began winking on. First the ones in the gas station on the outskirts of town, and then other lights were coming on too.

It wasn't an undersea city, or some futuristic sea port. It literally looked like a submerged small town, with a white-steeple church at one end of the street, and a main street running through a modest downtown.

As he slowly descended overlooking the town, he felt a bit like Mary Poppins, holding her umbrella and coming in for landing.

He popped another flare.

Unless he found more oxygen soon, this recovery mission was over before it began.

He finally touched down in the middle of the street. It was weird. It was like he was transported back in time to a small town in rural America, only back in the late fifties or early sixties.

The only thing separating it from Middletown, USA in the sixties was the entire town was completely submerged underwater.

More lights in buildings were coming on, streetlamps were coming on. Even the single traffic light at the main crossroads began working. He was glad he didn't hit any powerlines or buildings when he flew in and touched down onto the middle of the street--like Superman swooping in for a landing. *Which is it, George? Mary Poppins or Superman?* He thought*, you need to pick one.* He grinned, *Superman.* Maddie and Tessa would've said Poppins.

George noted that several starfish had made their home on many of the walls of the buildings and streetlamps.

As more lights continued to flicker on, he leaned back and tried to stare up at the hole in the roof of the dome. He could almost make out a pinprick of white light. If he hadn't known where to look, he would've never known that it was there.

What is this place?

It occurred to him he might be hallucinating from the effects of nitrogen, but before he could contemplate this possibility any further, a nurse shark swam lazily down Main Street, meandering back and forth. Other than putting his hand on the hilt of his knife, he remained perfectly still. Fortunately, the shark wasn't interested and continued to swim on past him like a parade float in the Thanksgiving Day Parade.

His feet still heavy from the weights, he walked slowly to the nearest building.

It was a malt shop.

He was surprised he could hear the bell above the door jingle when he went inside. The interior would have been perfectly at home in any Norman Rockwell painting. The one with the two kids sitting at the counter, checkered tile floor, came to mind.

He half expected some smiling young man (*what'd they call 'em? Oh yeah, soda jerk)* to pop up from behind the counter and ask him, "What'll it be?" He chuckled to himself. Since when do you use words like soda jerk?

Even with the lights coming on, most of the joint was bathed in shadow.

The oxygen alarm in his suit began going off.

Movement caught the corner of his eye. He turned his head to the right and only saw the inside of his helmet. He shuffled around and stared out from the large glass-paned window with the words, Jack's Malt Shop on it. He thought he saw a man outside the front window wearing a business suit and a fedora.

As soon as he turned away, he could've sworn he saw another person. Actually, this time, it was persons. Two young women wearing skirts, walking arm and arm started giggling as they walked past the window.

I must be hallucinating. Breathing in my own carbon dioxide. That's the only answer.

This seemed likely, especially since the people weren't moving through the water like he was, slow and cumbersome. No, they were walking at normal speed, like the entire town wasn't submerged in water.

Were they ghosts?

It was getting more difficult to breath, and soon he began gasping for each breath.

Gosh, I would've loved to have seen this place without all the water in it. It's beautiful. The architecture is amazing.

He sat on the nearest bar stool, rested his elbows on the edge of the counter and placed an order, "Soda jerk. I'll have a malt for me and my little buddy." No soda jerk popped up behind the counter to reply with a cheery, "Right away, Sir!" Instead, all he got was more flotsam floating by his face plate.

He became dizzy and the world tilted crazily, but he managed to hang on a little longer. He concentrated and was able to ride it out until it passed.

His suit alarm increased in tempo and was a harsh reminder that he didn't have much time left on this world. Forcing himself to sit up straight once more, George noticed a sign hanging on the wall at the end of the counter.

He stumbled over to the little sign and found it draped over a giant lever. *That's weird.* The sign and lever were the only things out of place in the entire Malt Shop.

The sign read: PULL LEVER

He dropped the sign and watched it float lazily float to the floor.

Pull lever, he thought drunkenly. *What else do I have to lose? I'm going to die anyway.*

George raised his right hand, grasped the strange lever firmly and pulled.

It didn't budge.

He raised both hands to it, grasped the handle even tighter and pulled. Still it did not move. George hung from the handle with the combined weight of his body and the diving suit.

The lever dropped and he heard a giant KER-CHUNK. Then a CLANK-CLANK-CLANKING noise, but as far as he could tell, nothing was really happening. He had expected a secret door to open or a sliding panel, but nothing happened.

Must be broken.

He backed up to the counter, his legs growing weak from a lack of oxygen. He lowered himself to the ground. He was really sucking air now as black spots began appearing before his eyes.

He wondered what Kelpi had meant by 'the others.' There were no *others* here. It was a 50's town, under a broken dome, completely flooded with sea water. There was nothing here. No prison. No answers (no escape, no rescue). Nothing.

It was a dead end. A decoy. A stinkin' red herring. He tried to think of more synonyms, but his oxygen deprived brain couldn't come up with any.

He wheezed a few more breaths and wondered how many more he had left to him.

This is it. He wondered what explorers of the future would say if they ever found his corpse a hundred years from now, in diving suit, in a malt shop, in a flooded 50's town.

I'm sorry Maddie. Daddy's not coming home.

"Tessa, I'm on my way."

George closed his eyes for the very last time.

Chapter 16

Hopper 04

"See that?"

Maddie pointed to a flashing blip on a display screen mounted on the dash between the two front seats. Henry leaned forward and saw the blip just before it vanished. Seeing this too, Maddie thumped the console with her gloved fist, and it soon returned.

"So," Henry started. Judging by his tone he was obviously unhappy. "What is it?"

"It's our heading," Maddie responded and hit the accelerator so hard that Henry fell back into his seat. As the Hopper circumnavigated several obstacles, Maddie studied the landscape as much as she was able. Judging by the dilapidated buildings, broken city streets and jagged hulks sticking out of the frozen tundra like marooned ships, they were obviously entering the ruins of some mid-sized city of days long gone by.

After a few seconds of zipping around the obstacles at high speeds, Maddie eased back on the throttle to avoid hitting anything that might be hidden under the thick layer of snow. The Hopper was tough, but there was no point pushing its structural limits.

Traxx began to explain to Henry how the sensors were calibrated to pick up possible weapon caches, medicines, or foodstuffs. Maddie stopped listening to him, as she often did, when he would happily launch into a tirade of technical jargon.

As Traxx's voice droned on, Maddie recalled how her dad used to take her on salvage and mapping expeditions. At the time, she was more interested in learning how to drive the Hopper, fight and shoot weapons. As they explored, he would tell her how the world used to be, how cities were filled with millions of people living ordinary lives.

Growing up in Pensacola, Florida, Maddie remembered tourists walking on the beach and all the traffic her mom would complain about whenever they drove into town. As years passed, it was getting harder and harder to recall her youth. It was harder still, because Traxx couldn't remember anything about his life before Stranger World. Like Henry, he was a boy without a past. Maybe that's why the two of them were getting along so well.

Maddie turned the Hopper down another street filled with rusted cars, bent-over street signs and flooded fissures, until finally pulling up to what appeared to be a dilapidated mall.

Traxx double-checked his readings and stated what she already knew. "I think we're here."

Outside the forward window, snow weighed down the thick branches of a nearby evergreen, and ice crystals hung everywhere the eye could see. Even with the ruined buildings and city bus half-submerged in snow, for Maddie, this was real beauty. Not like that fake garbage they were peddling in the parks that most people seemed to prefer.

She breathed the words, "It's beautiful."

"What did ya say?" Henry asked, still in his seat behind her.

She set the Hopper in Watchdog mode and got up from her seat. Squeezing past Henry, she replied, "I said, c'mon snowflake. It's time to gear up."

Henry Gears Up

Henry dutifully followed Maddie and Traxx through the accordion-like causeway back into the payload compartment.

Once there, Maddie began opening up lockers and removing gear. First, she pulled on a thick wrist gauntlet made of worn leather over her forearm. Like the rest of their gear, the homemade gauntlet was purposeful, yet piecemealed together. Also haphazardly sewn into her gauntlet was a flashlight, compass and a sleeve for some sort of multi-tool.

Maddie must have seen him staring because she was now staring right back at him with raised eyebrows. Before he could explain, she pointed at him and asked, “See that thing on your chest?”

He lowered his eyes to the chest plate of his harness and saw a round, red knob fastened to his left pocket. It almost looked like an e-stop button from back in The Factory. When he raised up his hand toward it, Maddie quickly stepped forward and slapped it back down.

“No! Don’t touch it, *now*.”

While rubbing the sting out of his hand, he asked, “Why, what does it do?”

This time, Traxx, who was donning his own gear, was the one to explain.

“If you get into trouble, you smack that button with the palm of your hand as hard as you can.”

“And then?” Traxx spun him around and patted his back.

“You feel that thing attached to your back?” Henry flexed his shoulders like someone feeling for back pain and felt a metal disc about the size of a Frisbee sewn into the inside of his jumpsuit. When he acknowledged that he did feel it, Traxx continued.

"You hit that rubber button on your chest plate and a disc will come shooting out of its launcher and go straight up into the air."

Maddie finished clipping more gear to her belt. Without even looking at him she added, "It comes out pretty fast so make sure you keep your head tilted forward slightly."

Unsure he wanted to know the answer, he asked, "Why, what if I don't lean my head forward, *slightly*?"

Maddie punched in a few buttons on her gauntlet. When she didn't get the information she wanted from her wrist computer, she slapped it a few times with the palm of her hand.

"Most likely the buoy will shave off the back of your skull."

Henry swallowed, "And I want to carry around something that will take off my head off, why?"

Maddie blew some errant strands of hair out of her face. "It doesn't take your head off, just the back of your head. Gosh, you are such a baby."

Traxx, who had nearly finished getting dressed, offered, "It's an E.L.T." when he saw Henry still didn't understand he added, "An Emergency-Locator-Transponder."

Maddie sighed. "He doesn't know what that is, you're just confusing him."

Henry's pride wanted to disagree, but Maddie was right, he was totally lost. He should have stayed on The Dauntless. He didn't belong out here in the...*The Madlands?*

Maddie stepped up in front of him and began checking over his uniform and harness. When her hair brushed his face, he smelled an aroma of fresh raspberries that wasn't entirely unpleasant. She tightened his gear straps in some places and loosened it in others. As she did this she explained, "Look, all you need to know is, after you hit the red button, a disc shoots up into to the air and hovers high over your head. It serves as a distress beacon to let rescuers know where you are."

Maddie held up some leather gloves. When he didn't grab them quick enough, she lifted his hands and smacked them into his palms. "Okay, now these are you gloves. Don't take them off, ever. There are a lot of bugs, contagions, and broken glass out there that you don't want to get inside you." She paused for a moment and then asked, "That reminds me, did Dr. Bob give you your inoculations?" Before he could answer her, she said, "No, wait, of course he didn't. You haven't been to the Sanctuary yet."

The Sanctuary, Henry wondered. *Is that where the Dauntless was headed?* Up until now, nobody had told him anything other than that he was safe and they were taking him to a safe place.

Mistaking his silence for panic, Maddie offered in a tone that would almost pass for concern, “Don’t worry, Henry. The gloves will protect you. Just don’t take them off.” She studied his uniform once more and began rattling off each item as she inspected it.

“Survival suit... check. E.L.T. ...check. Gloves... check.” Catching his eyes staring at the Skull-Shaving-Death Button she added, “Remember, don’t hit the red button until I tell you to or you get separated from us. And, whatever you do, don’t get separated from us.”

“Oh, and in each pocket, you’ll find some form of survival gear: warm packs for your hands and feet, matches, a needle-and-thread, a knife, and a nice warm hat. In the cargo pocket of your,” she had to think about this for a moment, “Uh, left leg I think, there’s some energy bars if you get hungry. These suits were designed by my dad. George was a survival expert. There’s even a compass sewn into the cuff.” She flipped his wrist over to show him where a compass spun loosely.

Henry began tapping the glass of the spinning compass with his finger and heard himself say, “Hey, that’s pretty neat.”

Maddie smacked his tapping finger away from the compass with another painful slap.

"Stop that." She pointed to the goggles mounted on his soft leather helmet. "Those are your goggles. Once we step outside, keep them down over your eyes at all times. I don't want to be plucking micro-bots out of your eyeballs."

Henry wasn't sure what a micro-bot was, but the thought of Maddie, *with her spectacular bedside manner*, plucking them out of his eyeballs sounded about as unpleasant as having the back of his skull shaved off. He reached up to pull the goggles down over his eyes and...

SLAP!

Henry began rubbing the sting out of his hand for the third time.

"Not now. I said when we step out of the Hopper to go outside. If you're going to survive you really need to pay more attention."

He nodded, feeling as though he had just been told he was demoted back at The Factory.

"Any questions?"

He had several, but when he meekly raised his hand, Maddie had already turned away and slammed a gloved fist onto a dull-yellow button next to the door.

A sharp decompressing sound made him jump slightly, and he was glad Maddie had already turned around. This time, it was the back door that opened. Instead of sliding open like the side door did, this one lowered down all the way to the ground to form a ramp.

Maddie and Traxx exited out the rear payload door; their boots clanged on the metal incline.

As Henry tentatively walked down the ramp to join them, Maddie warned, "Watch your step on the ice. You don't want to slip and fall out here." Seeing Henry had forgotten to don his gloves she barked, "Henry, put on your gloves. You cut yourself outside the *parks* and a tetanus shot will be the least of your worries."

He wasn't entirely sure what a tetanus shot was, but it didn't sound like something he would enjoy. He reached the bottom of the ramp unscathed, and his eyes filled with wonder.

"Henry, gloves."

Mouth agape, he only nodded in response. The lower parts of the mall were submerged in debris and ice, but he'd never seen buildings so tall, or so numerous!

When he didn't don the gloves fast enough, she barked once more, "Henry, gloves!"

The Leftenant

Henry finished donning his gloves... and nearly jumped out of his survival suit when The Leftenant suddenly appeared beside him.

The Leftenant, hands clasped behind her back, opened with a cheery, "Hello children, where are we off to today?" Not waiting for answer she began to take in their surroundings.

Traxx gave her a friendly wave. "Oh hi, Leftenant."

The Leftenant nodded to him and responded with a curt, "Mr. Traxx."

Maddie on the other hand, was obviously not pleased to see The Leftenant. She sighed and said, "First of all, we are not children. And second, no one invited you. We were cleared to do this expedition all by ourselves."

"No. You were cleared to take out an expedition provisionally."

Henry found himself backing up toward the lowered ramp of the Hopper. *She's onto us.* He was pretty sure he saw Traxx gulp too.

The Leftenant continued. "That provision was conditional upon the fact that you were escorted by Mr. Cheeves." The

Leftenant feigned looking around for the pesky gargoyle. “I don’t see him anywhere, do you?” She lifted a palm to her mouth and called out half-heartedly, “Mister Cheeves, I say, Mr. Cheeves, are you there?”

The Leftenant turned back toward Maddie and fixed an icy gaze upon her. “Hmmm... not here. Perhaps that’s because he’s still back in his quarters, hunting for a non-existent feline.”

Traxx lifted a quaking finger toward Maddie, “It was her idea.”

Maddie growled, “Shut it, Traxx.”

Traxx’s eyes went wide. “Sorry Maddie, but we’re in unexplored territory, the Madlands no less.

The Leftenant piped in, “Proper jammy, Mr. Traxx. I always did think you were a good bloke.”

Traxx continued, “Maybe it’s not a bad idea to have The Leftenant along.”

Maddie shook her head and grumped to Traxx, “Don’t say that. Don’t encourage her.” Then to The Leftenant, Maddie explained, “Leftenant, you’re not coming with us, and that’s final.”

The hologram woman fizzled out for a second and then raised her eyebrows at Maddie and replied, “Oh my being here suggests that in point-of-fact, I most certainly am.”

"Leftenant, we don't need a babysitter, okay? This expedition was sanctioned by Uncle Rick," she stammered, "Er... I mean, Chief Engineer Rick."

"Oh, how nice," she cooed softly. "Chief Engineer Rick sanctioned this expedition." Her tone changed, and she said more harshly, "When I need a *Chief Engineer's* permission, which I don't as it is a lower rank to myself, I'll ask for it. Good to know though. Thank you." She practically sang the words thank you.

To Henry, The Leftenant didn't sound the least bit thankful.

Maddie squinted her eyes, scrunched up her nose and asked, "How'd you even get here anyway? I shut down your hologram emitter on the Hopper the moment we left The Dauntless."

The Leftenant continued to scan the immediate area like a sentry whilst answering, "For me to know and you to never know."

Maddie checked her clothes and appeared to be searching for something. "Guys, check your clothes. She must've planted a hologram emitter on one of us."

Henry was barely aware of what a hologram emitter's purpose was; let alone what one looked like. Nevertheless, he reluctantly began patting down his clothes to comply with *Her Madness*.

Maddie first scanned his clothes and then focused on Traxx's. Judging by her harsh stare, she seemed to have found something on the youngest of them. When Henry turned toward Traxx too, he saw the briefest flickering of light coming from the corner of Traxx's goggles.

Maddie confirmed this by saying, "Darn it, Traxx. She's on your goggles." She stomped over to him in her big clunky boots and pinched the emitter off his spectacles.

The emitter couldn't compensate fast enough, and this caused The Leftenant to appear first sideways and then upside down.

By the time The Leftenant righted herself, Maddie held the emitter out to her and spat, "You're not coming with us. Not today!" She dropped the emitter onto the ground and crunched it beneath her boot.

Henry was aghast. "You killed her," he heard himself say. "Why would you do that? Is she okay?"

Traxx, looking about as happy about as he felt, explained, "The Leftenant's fine. The remotes are just an extension of the true Leftenant."

Henry didn't have the foggiest idea of what Traxx was talking about, and he doubted he ever would. Not in a million years.

While Maddie twisted the ball of her foot for good measure she added, "It's just another way for her to spy on us."

"Hello," The Leftenant's voice sang when she reappeared unharmed. "Yes indeed, I am quite alright Mr. Henry. Although, I certainly do appreciate your obvious and heartfelt concern."

Maddie shook her head. "Everyone check your clothes. She must've put an emitter on each one of us."

As the three of them began patting down their clothes, Henry with the least amount of fervor, The Leftenant said, "You can check as much as you like, but I have placed no less than 126 holograms emitters on your personage."

"You didn't," Maddie spat venomously. Composing herself, Maddie said, "Leftenant, Traxx and I are both well-armed. We don't need you always watching over us."

"Ohhhh... I'm certain your parents would disagree."

"But my parents aren't here anymore, are they?" Maddie then stuck her finger in The Leftenant's face. It was another mannerism that seemed far beyond her age. "My dad might've thought of you as a daughter, but that doesn't make us sisters, okay?"

The Leftenant's face softened dramatically. "Your father said that?"

Maddie Harrumphed. "Yeah, like you didn't know."

To Henry, it was very apparent she didn't know. This was the first time Henry had ever seen The Leftenant display any kind of emotion other than righteous indignation. He was kinda feeling sorry for her.

Great, now I'm feeling sorry for a hologram.

Maddie placed her gloved hands on her hips. "I didn't want to have to do this but," she called out over her shoulder, "Traxx. Do it."

Standing on a pile of debris behind her, Traxx appeared sheepish. "I don't know Maddie, maybe it's a good idea to have her along. Another pair of eyes can't hurt anything."

Maddie cut him off. "Traxx, nobody is ever going to trust us do missions by ourselves if we can't even do a simple mapping expedition."

Reluctantly, Traxx opened a panel on the computer he wore on his thigh. He punched in several keys on the keypad within.

The Leftenant took a keen interest in this. "Mr. Traxx, whatever are you doing?"

Traxx finished punching in a sequence of numbers and hesitated before pressing the last button. "Sorry about this Leftenant," he said, and punched in the final key.

The Leftenant fizzled for a moment, "Oh, bother," and then was gone.

Each one listened, but all they heard now was the sound of the escalating wind.

Henry was the first to speak. "I know I'm the new guy here and all, but I'm not sure that was such a good idea."

Maddie stomped past him and headed toward the mall. "Aw, suck it up, Buttercup."

Chapter 17

The Mall

"Door won't budge."

Traxx released his grip on the bottom of a rollup, galvanized door. The three of them had wasted nearly thirty minutes walking around the outside of the mall searching for an entry point. Every other entrance was either locked or blocked by debris.

Finally, just as they were about to give up and head back to the Hopper, they discovered a loading dock on the back side of the mall. It was marked by a heavily stained sign that read, *DELIVERY ENTRANCE ONLY.* They found the rollup door only slightly ajar. Traxx had been the first to grab the bottom and started tugging, but thus far, no effect.

Maddie checked their six before taunting him. "C'mon, Traxx. Ya gotta pull on it like a man."

Traxx grunted as he tried again. "Nothing. I'm telling you, it's stuck fast."

Maddie stepped forward and shoved Traxx out of the way. She clutched the bottom of the door with both hands and began yanking. When it still didn't budge, with a single look, she urged for Traxx to help pull at the same time.

The first two attempts were a no go and Traxx said, "See, I told you, it's jammed or something."

Maddie caught her breath and then over her shoulder she called, "C'mon, Henry, you get in here too. Let's all try, one more time, together."

Henry joined them and they pulled as one. Just as they were about to give up, they heard the sound of metal snapping and the rollup door rumbled upwards on its tracks.

All three fell inwards.

Henry immediately noticed the floor was checkered tile, and heavily stained with time.

Maddie was the first to her feet, she dusted herself off, smiled and said, "Alright boys, let's see what treasures await." She cracked a flare, its red glow illuminating the darkened interior with a red haze.

Henry wasn't sure leaving the daylight behind was a good idea. After all, he had been nervous enough outside the mall with the rustling of garbage blowing in the wind and rocks sliding down the piles of debris surrounding them. But the

inside of the mall seemed worse; it was as though the air had the silence and the stillness of an ancient tomb.

Before following, he glanced back at the angry sky outside. It was still shrouded in an ominous gray. For the first time since he was rescued, he wondered, *Maybe I should have stayed in The Factory, at least there I knew where the dangers lie.*

Both Maddie and Traxx had their weapons drawn. Henry became even more aware that he didn't have a gun and followed them as quietly as possible. To guide himself, he slid his gloved hand against the wall.

Maddie, still carrying the red phosphorous flare out in front of her like a torch, barked at him in a tense whisper, "Hey Henry, check those lockers for anything useful."

Henry hoped she hadn't seen him jump slightly. He stared over at where she was pointing and saw a large bank of lockers against a cream-colored wall. Totally unhappy with the present situation, as he was fairly certain he would be dead within the hour, he asked grumpily, "Search them for what?"

Maddie immediately answered, "Medicines, food, ammo. Survivors like to hide stuff. You have to think like them."

Traxx walked past him shining his own flashlight. "Watch out for booby-traps."

Henry felt himself blanch at this, but he summoned his courage anyway and opened the first locker with the trepidation of a member of the bomb squad. Nothing was inside. Opening several more, each one about as tall as he was, he also found nothing, that is, unless you count all the vermin that skittered away the moment the light from his flashlight was upon them. "We're never going to find anything."

Hearing this, Maddie's voice said from the darkness, "Not with that attitude we're not. Keep looking."

Henry was mockingly miming Maddie's words under his breath when he opened the next locker and a not-so-fresh corpse tumbled out at him.

Henry shrieked as he jumped back and immediately regretted doing so. To his surprise, neither Traxx nor Maddie laughed at him. The body, now lying at his feet, was dressed in coveralls, with most of his flesh eaten away by rats and insects. Henry found himself wondering what had happened to the man. *Was he stuffed in the locker or was he hiding from something? If the latter, what would be so bad that he'd never want to come out?*

Stepping up beside him, Maddie asked, with a smirk, almost as if judging him, "What's the matter, kid, you've never seen a dead body before?"

Henry *had* seen dead bodies before. He wanted to tell her he had seen lots of them. After all, body disposal had been his job, and he was darn good at it. But, he had never seen a corpse like this. In The Factory nothing was ever wasted.

Bodies were stripped down of all belongings, and even their flesh was used as fuel for the furnace. This body had been dead for a long time and barely resembled a human being.

He felt a comforting hand squeeze his shoulder. “You gonna be okay, buddy?” The hand belonged to Traxx. “You kinda look like you’re gonna puke.”

Henry shook his head. “No. I’m fine. I’ve seen dead bodies before. Just not like this.” With his next breath, the smell hit him. Henry felt himself shudder involuntarily, and may have thrown up in his mouth a little. He quickly swallowed the bile back down so Maddie wouldn’t see.

As they moved farther away from the rollup door, and daylight, Henry felt the air growing colder and could now see his own breath. He grabbed his shoulders and rubbed them for warmth. To no one in particular he muttered, “Whew, it’s a bit cold in here.”

Hearing this, Maddie turned back toward him. He hadn’t meant it as a complaint. After all, in The Factory he had been cold many times before. He fully expected her to fire off some insult regarding his masculinity, but she surprised him.

Instead, she handed her flare to Traxx for safekeeping, and then grabbed him by his wrist. She examined the gauge sewn onto the outside of his forearm and said, “No wonder you’re cold. Your thermostat’s turned off.” She brushed off some of the light crystallized air that had gathered there and thumbed a button. "There, I set it to 69 degrees Fahrenheit. You should be feeling better shortly."

She gave him a reassuring nod, reclaimed her flare from Traxx, and led them out of the receiving area through swinging doors.

The outer rooms were void of anything useful, so they moved deeper into the mall. The walls were thicker now and the outside storm became muffled. As the light grew dimmer, Maddie and Traxx had to click on their flashlights. Using their gun barrels to clear away the cobwebs, they managed to navigate another abandoned and ransacked department store unscathed.

Exiting the store into the main mall, they stepped into a wide-open area. Daylight was streaming in through broken skylights overhead. Henry, thankful for the additional light, joined Maddie and Traxx who were standing at the railing and overlooking two sub floors. Maddie discarded her dying flare and took in their surroundings.

They were standing in a main causeway with numerous stores and shops lining both sides of the main thoroughfare. Dust, dirt and debris had settled over everything, along with the ripe stench of decay. If you removed all the dilapidation, the mall was similar to the ones Henry remembered from his youth.

Wait, since when were you in a mall? he wondered. An image of holding someone's hand, much taller than himself, flashed across his memory. *Parents perhaps?*

Glass crunched beneath Maddie's boot as she abandoned the railing and headed for a nearby escalator. As they descended the broken stairs, Henry became very aware of the ripe odor of dead animals, rotting wood and disuse. He purposely chose not to guess the origin of the yellow and brown stains smeared on the walls between storefronts.

Maddie was first to reach the floor below ground. As she moved deeper into the mall, Henry sidled up next to Traxx and asked in a harsh whisper, "How much deeper into the mall does she plan on taking us?"

Traxx studied Henry's face for a moment. It was as though the younger boy had forgotten he was with them. He checked in with the data pad he wore on his thigh. "We're nearly at the turnaround point now. If we don't find something in the next ten minutes or so, we'll start heading back."

Traxx didn't sound very convincing, not even to himself.

As they moved deeper within, Henry felt a growing sense of unease, mostly because they were moving farther and farther away from the Hopper, and the delivery entrance. Periodically, Traxx would pause, open his computer strapped to his thigh, enter coordinates into it, and move onward again. The only reassuring thing Henry could cling to was the way Maddie and Traxx moved with relaxed precision, seldom checking with one another and speaking only when necessary. They had obviously done this sort of thing before.

The bottom floor appeared as though it had been picked over for the last two hundred years and little remained. Staring at all the dereliction, Henry tried to suppress all the new questions he had. In as calm a voice as he could muster, he asked Traxx, whom was walking only slightly ahead of him, "Where is everyone? What happened to all the people?"

Traxx kept his voice low when he answered. "Depends on who you ask. The Leftenant says war wiped everyone out. But, Maddie's dad was beginning to believe it was something else."

"Like what?"

Before Traxx could answer, Maddie stopped suddenly and held up her fist indicating for them to stop. Without saying a word, Traxx immediately stopped in front of him. The younger boy had stopped so abruptly, Henry nearly crashed right into him.

Maddie's fist changed into a forefinger gesturing that something lay ahead. Henry leaned over to peer around Traxx and saw another wide open area lit by candles. As they moved closer, Maddie and Traxx kept scanning the upper floor and their immediate surroundings. If they had seen anything hiding in the shadows or behind the piles-and-piles of debris to either side of them, they didn't say it.

I hate this place... I really-really hate it... Henry thought.

"Look there, up ahead," Maddie said, training her light down the causeway. He and Traxx hurried up next to her and added the illumination from their own flashlights.

Henry watched them forge ahead without him. Refusing to take another step, he stared past them at what appeared to be a modest encampment made up of crates and supplies, all neatly arranged in a nice semi-circle. Seeing that he wasn't following, Maddie called back over her shoulder to him, "C'mon Henry, hurry up," and immediately began rifling through the open crates. "Looks like we hit the jackpot boys."

Henry moved closer. She was right, they had indeed hit the jackpot: A dozen or so First Aid kits, hundreds of canned foods, and tons of miscellaneous tools, weapon parts and mechanical devices.

"We can't take this stuff," Henry said aloud. "It doesn't belong to us."

Maddie flashed him a look of incredulousness, as if he had just spewed-up something completely insane. "Do you see anybody else here? Cuz I sure don't."

Traxx must've been okay with the stealing too, because he was also searching the ragtag grouping of supplies.

Henry stared at the candles burning down. “Somebody must’ve been here because somebody must’ve lit those candles.”

Hearing this, Traxx explained, “Henry, those candles are holograms.” Dropping his found treasures back into the crate, he walked over to the nearest one and said, “Here, watch.” Henry watched as the younger boy passed his hand through the candle as though it were a ghost. “See?” Traxx said. “Don’t worry, Henry. You’ll get the hang of spotting what’s real and what’s an illusion before you know it.”

Henry doubted he ever would.

Maddie Harrumphed. “Yeah, especially after you hang around The Leftenant long enough.” She grabbed a duffel bag from one of the crates and began loading supplies into it.

That was when Henry first saw it… the giant, not-so-white rabbit.

Chapter 18

Pack of Mechanized Misfits

"Uh, guys..."

There were a lot of things that Henry noticed about the giant not-so-white rabbit, the moment it had emerged from the shadows, madly chittering away only a scant few yards from where they stood.

The rabbit wasn't a *giant* per say. Standing on his hind legs like a man, he was only about five feet tall. Also, he wasn't exactly white. Maybe he once was, but now his fur was filthy and caked with dirt and mud. Still further, Henry could see mechanical gears protruding grotesquely out of various places of the creature's molted skin.

As the not-so-white rabbit took him in, and then Maddie and then Traxx, its head moved with jerking movements, accompanied by distinctive clicking sounds (like gears grinding against one another). The broken rabbit's head click-click-clicked back in his direction and now Henry could see a tiny, pink tongue lick its blood-stained mouth in eager anticipation.

Despite knowing beyond a shadow of a doubt that thing was some sort of mechanized monstrosity, Henry couldn't shake the feeling that the rabbit was alive. Staring at him, its features contorted, as if dealing with an extreme amount of inner torment.

Henry shuddered involuntarily.

"Oh look," Maddie cooed, "Henry made a friend."

Falling rocks were first heard, then seen tumbling down into a huge pile of debris closest to Maddie. Lifting their eyes to the rockslide's source, Henry saw a medieval Knight standing atop the mountain of garbage. The knight had only one arm, but the heavily-worn mace he wielded with it, still seemed dangerous enough.

Almost simultaneously, a metal grating at Traxx's feet suddenly lifted up on its own accord, scraping the pavement as it slid off to one side. To Henry's horror, reptilian claws slowly began pulling a slimy inhuman monster out of the sewer's murky depths.

Traxx unslung his rifle as he backed away from the scaly monstrosity and was soon standing even with Henry. Without taking his eyes off the subterranean monster he said, "Don't worry, Henry, these are only first gens."

"First gens?"

"Yeah, think of them as extras in a movie."

Hearing this, Maddie said in a harsh whisper, "I don't think Henry has ever seen a movie."

Henry picked his head up at this. Despite the worrisome circumstances, he managed, "Yes I have." But, at the moment, he couldn't exactly recall a specific one. *At least I think I have,* he thought inwardly.

Traxx must've seen how scared he was because he offered, "Seriously, you've got nothing to worry about. They probably just wandered off from their respective lands, found their way here, and formed a pack. They almost never attack."

His words sank in slowly, "Almost... never attack?"

Calmly, Maddie also began to retreat from the one-armed knight. "Alright boys, nice and slow, let's make our way back to the Hopper. Smooth and easy, no sudden movements."

As though hearing this, the one-armed knight shouted down to her, "You there, knave. Prepare to be bested!" He raised his mace high above his head and charged down the hill of garbage toward Maddie with a loud battle cry.

At the same time, the lagoon monster lunged for Traxx's feet.

By all sense of logic, the one-armed knight or the lagoon monster should have scared Henry the most. However; for some reason, that honor belonged to the Not-So-White Rabbit creeping toward him. The moment the rabbit got about halfway to him, everything erupted in total chaos. Maddie was shouting at the knight, "Stay back, I don't want to have to shoot you!" and the knight was yelling back, "Have at me knave! Have at me!"

Maddie did have at him.

"Boring." In a move far beyond her age, she calmly drew her pistol and shot him in the head.

The knight's helmet (presumably with his head still in it) went bouncing past Traxx, whom was already taking aim at the subterranean creature.

Maddie then shouted at him, "Henry, the rabbit, watch out!"

Henry was horrified to learn that the Not-So-White Rabbit was no longer where he had last seen him. It had vanished. An eerie shadow rose up on the stack of crates in front of him. The shadow behind his had tall rabbit ears. Henry spun all the way around just in time. He jerked his face backward as the rabbit's yellow-stained teeth CHOMPED down on the air space his nose had occupied only a few seconds before.

CHOMP-CHOMP-CHOMP!

The chittering rabbit continued to snap its jaws with each step closer to him. Henry backpedaled. Seeing this, the gnarly creature hunkered down, leapt into the air and dove on top of him, pinning him to the ground.

Henry gripped the motley rabbit by its disgusting narrow shoulders with both hands, while barely managing to keep its chomping teeth out of his face. In one last bite, the rabbit's eyeball fell out of its socket and dangled by a silvery cord over Henry's face.

As the rabbit's remaining good eye examined him, Henry shouted aloud, "Maddie, help!"

Henry risked a glance to the side, but Maddie was busy thundering off shots at more attackers prowling in the darkness beyond the candle's light. If he was going to survive, Henry realized he was going to have to save himself.

He dodged his head to the left and right to keep his face from getting chewed off. Still on his back, and pinned by the rabbit, he drew up his knees and planted his feet squarely on the rabbit's abdomen. He then shoved with every last ounce of muscle he had earned in The Factory. The rabbit flew off and landed on its back.

Fearful the rabid bunny would pin him again, Henry scrambled quickly to his feet. He could see the rabbit violently kicking its legs in an attempt to turn over, all the while screaming a sound that was a cross between metal grinding and an animal shrieking in rage. Henry knew it wouldn't be long before it got back up again.

There was a loud explosion as Traxx began shooting at the creature climbing out of the sewer. Maddie was also busy fending off even more assailants. Henry thought he glimpsed one dressed like a spaceman, another like a zombie, and still another like an oversized lawn gnome.

The rabbit regained its feet; twitched its one good eye at him and crouched down like it did before. Any second now, it would dive on top of him again, only this time, Henry knew it was unlikely he'd escape.

If only I had a weapon. The only thing that was even close to being a weapon was the metal disc he carried on his back that could shave off the back of his skull.

The rabbit leapt.

Henry dropped to all fours, remembered to tilt his head slightly forward, and slammed the palm of his hand on the button on his chest.

WHOOSH!

Henry felt the air on the back of his neck and head as the disc shot out of his harness and whisked past him. He didn't see the not-so-white rabbit catapult backwards into the darkness. When Henry finally did lift his head, he saw the remainder of mechanized Misfits (the ones that hadn't been cut down by Traxx and Maddie) were scampering away as best as they were able.

Certain they were gone, Maddie holstered her pistol. Her astonished eyes did little to reassure him. "Henry, are you alright?"

His ears still ringing from the gunshots, Henry could only stand there in dumbfounded shock.

Maddie, raising her voice, asked again, "Henry, I asked you if you are alright. Did he bite you? Are you hurt?"

Now that the ringing was beginning to die down in his ears, he could hear the concern in her voice. He shook his head, surprised he was in fact unharmed. He saw the medieval knight's helmet now lying at his feet. He didn't dare look inside it. "You killed them." He hadn't meant to sound so accusatory, it had just sort of come out that way.

Maddie made a derogatory sound akin to a deflating balloon. Henry noticed she liked to do that a lot.

"Please," she said. "These guys are barely first gens." Picking up the helmet, she tossed it to him so he could peer inside it. When he finally managed to, he could see that there was nothing inside. She explained, "These guys aren't people, they're merely background scenery that wandered off from their lands."

Henry, not knowing what to do with the empty helmet, solemnly placed it on a nearby pile of cinder blocks. A second later, it tumbled off. He went to pick it up, but ended up kicking it away with his foot by accident.

"Just leave it," Maddie said.

Dusting his palms off on his jumpsuit, Henry asked, "So they're not...people?"

"No," Maddie shot back. Clearly, she didn't appreciate being called a murderer.

Traxx intoned, "Sides, if they were, they would've killed us and torn apart our Hopper." He slung his rifle, and both he and Maddie immediately began loading up supplies into absconded duffel bags, only this time with much more fervor.

Without slowing down, Maddie called back to them. "Let's grab what we can before they come back with reinforcements."

Chapter 19

This is Not My House

A severed robot head.

This was the first thing George Stapleton saw when he awoke. It was propped up on a chair across the room and was just staring at him.

As his vision began to clear, he realized the severed robot head wasn't a robot head after all; in fact it was one of those old diving helmets.

Why does that seem familiar?

The room wasn't like any he'd woken up in before. It wasn't an underground hospital room, or a commercial air-liner surrounded by giant sunflowers with human faces, nor was it a Russian Cold War submarine. No. This room was nothing like any of those rooms. It was totally normal. That in itself made it entirely abnormal.

A set of clothes were neatly folded on a nearby dresser.

Lying on top of the covers, he realized he was wearing old boxers and a white t-shirt that reminded him of the G.I.'s in the 50's. Not that he was old enough to remember them, but he had seen the undergarments in the movies. To add to the illusion, his dog tags jangled about his neck when he moved. Examining them, he saw that they were in fact his dog tags and not part of some historical costume.

He groaned as he threw his stiff leg over the side of the bed. Tentatively, he put some weight on it. Testing it, he found it was painful, but manageable.

As far as bedrooms went, this one wasn't bad. It was kind of like the one he'd grown up in as a kid. A bird chirping drew his gaze outside the window. He didn't see the tweeting bird, but he did see the leaves of the trees dripping with water as though from a recent downpour.

Wait, this isn't right. I was on a deep dive...underwater. More images began coming back to him. *I remember something about a malt shop. And...I was running out of air.*

As though confirming this, the dented, beaten helmet continued to stare silently back at him. A modified diving suit was draped over the back of the helmet's chair. It would've been far too heavy for the thin metal-wire hangers that hung in the closet like skeletons.

Metal wire hangers...I forgot about those. I haven't seen those since I was kid. Modern hangers were plastic junk.

The modest room was sparse when it came to furniture. Aside from the single bed he woke up in and the chair holding his helmet and dive suit, there was only a night table and a midsize dresser. George noted his clothes were neatly folded on top of the latter.

He stood up and a sharp pain shot through his leg. Wincing from it, he decided to move a bit more slowly, at least until he got the blood flowing into his limbs once more. He stared at himself in the dresser mirror and saw his normal visage, wearing boxers and a t-shirt, staring back at him.

He waited for someone to come in. When they didn't, he put a hand on the door knob of the six-panel door. Expecting it to be locked, he was surprised when he turned the knob and it opened right up.

He took one step into the hallway laden with hardwood floors. Gazing down the off-white hallway, he saw other bedrooms with their doors open and stairs at the end of the hall. He remembered spotting the leaves outside the window and realized he was on the second floor of a house.

I can't go running around in my skivvies, he thought, and went back into the room to dress.

The clothes on the dresser were a pair of khaki pants and a short-sleeved polyester shirt. They weren't his, but they fit perfectly. Feeling a chill in the air, he picked up the heavy fisherman's sweater and slipped it on as well. More than the rest of the garments, this seemed the most familiar.

He seemed to recall his dive suit had a knife. A real big one too, about the size of a machete, but staring around the room, and checking under the bed, he couldn't find it.

Not wasting anymore time, George went downstairs and entered the kitchen. What he had first assumed to be a farmhouse, was actually more similar to the houses in the late 1950's or early 60's suburbia. There was an old style fridge, the kind with the big honking chrome handle. The rest of the house could have passed for a television set on *Lassie* or *Leave it to Beaver*. Spotting the refrigerator again, his stomach groaned for attention. *If only there was some*...the heavy refrigerator door opened with a loud cracking sound, and he was surprised to find the interior stocked with apples, a jar of pickles, a pitcher of lemonade, and plenty of sandwich meat.

I'm not sure what's going on here, but I'm starving.

It occurred to him that the food might be poison. Every time he had woken up in this world, there was always that chance. *But why bring me back to life only to kill me again?*

'Why, for their amusement.'

Oh, haven't heard from that guy in a while, George thought.

George's inner voice (his Jiminy Cricket, if you will) had always been the voice of Jimmy Stewart. Or, to be more precise, the character Jimmy Stewart played in the Christmas movie, "It's a Wonderful Life." The character's name was George Bailey.

This sparked a new memory. It was more than a coincidence that he and George Bailey shared the same name. He was actually named after that character. Something about how his parents had been watching it about a month before he was born and they both said at the same time, "What about George?" and that was it. That would be his name for the rest of his life.

He stuffed an apple in his mouth and loaded his arms up with as much food as he could carry. As he dropped it all on the modest kitchen table, a hot, fresh baked loaf of bread caught his attention. *Was that there a second ago?* He was pretty sure he would have noticed the delicious smell. Regardless, he grabbed the bread. Even though he was in a survival situation, he took the time to grab some butter out of the fridge.

One of these drawers has got to have a butter knife in it. Grabbing the first drawer closest to him, he slid it open. It was a junk drawer filled with scissors, and scotch tape, even a big brown ball of rubber bands. *Huh, I guess junk drawers are universal.* He scanned the junk drawer a second time and realized when he moved the drawer back and forth, nothing inside the drawer moved. *It's a fake. I couldn't take any of this stuff out, even if I wanted to. So, there are limitations to this place.* He tugged on another drawer and as soon as he heard the jangle of silverware he declared, "Jackpot."

George buttered the fresh baked bread. *Wow, it even smells good,* he thought, but as he enjoyed the first bite, he was forced to wonder who had baked it for him.

Jimmy Stewart's voice popped in his head again. 'Stop asking so many questions there, Georgie, and just enjoy your food. Just this once. Whadya say?'

George gulped down two thick slices of buttered bread. On his third, he spotted a white hat through the window of the front door.

"Uh, hey!" George said reflexively, getting up from the dining room table. He had gotten up a bit too fast and slammed his pelvic bone painfully against the corner of the table. He dashed out of the kitchen and into the living room. He couldn't help but notice the massive, wood-framed television set on the floor with rabbit ears on top. Its wood frame matched the coffee table perfectly.

Reaching the door, George clasped the handle half-expecting nobody to be there, just like the ghosts had vanished in the malt shop. That's why he was surprised when he flung the door open and saw a thin short-statured man walking down the concrete pathway out to the sidewalk. The man was carrying a metal, wire-framed carrier of a half-dozen, empty milk bottles.

George exited the house and began yelling, "Hey, buddy, excuse me," but the milkman, who was whistling a happy tune to himself, either didn't hear him or chose to ignore him.

George was about to pursue the milkman when he tripped over bottles of milk left behind in a little wire-framed crate left on the stoop. Lifting his eyes from the broken bottles of milk to the curb, George watched as the milkman marched into the open sliding door of his truck, sat down promptly, turned the ignition, put the vehicle in gear, and drove off.

George stumbled all the way down the driveway. Reaching the curb, he watched the milkman drive off and turn down a distant corner.

Looking in the other direction, George could see now that he was on a typical suburban street in the 1950's.

How did I get here?

'Maybe you traveled back in time, Georgie. After all, I did. Why not you, too?'

“Stow it, Jimmy,” he said aloud. Tessa had long ago broken him of his habit of talking to *Jiminy* Stewart, but it seemed the bad habit had resurfaced.

His memory was all a jumble. It hurt his head every time he tried to remember.

He scanned the neighborhood a bit more. All the houses were the same size, and roughly the same architecture. But each of them had their own color schemes and landscaping; the same, but different enough to express individuality. In its entirety, it was an attractive street, pleasantly wide, with ample sidewalks and numerous streetlamps. He didn’t remember neighborhood streets ever being this wide, even in his youth.

Instinctively, he thought, *Tessa and I should look into moving here.*

‘Sounds fine to me, Georgie. Just fine.’

George took a few more steps down the street. Further memories were coming to light. The Leisure-bot, the moonpool, and the world’s most annoying mermaid.

But how did I get from the Welcome Center to a 1950’s neighborhood?

A dive suit. The same suit that was in the upstairs bedroom. It was coming back faster now. A gaping hole, in the roof a dome, over a town. A town that looked a lot like this one.

George lifted his eyes and expected to see a dome overhead. But he didn't see anything of the sort. All he saw was a blue sky, with a yellow sun. It was a nice day. A flock of Canadian geese were flying south for the winter in a V-formation. He could only assume it was south because the sun was directly overhead and he didn't have a compass. He was about to tear his eyes away from the cloudless sky, when he saw a flock of birds flying in V-formation.

Wait a minute? Is that the same flock of birds?

He scanned the rest of the sky, but saw only the one flock.

Either that was deja vu or the image of those birds just repeated itself.

He watched the sky a little longer, but the birds only continued to fly off. *Was that some kind of mistake? A glitch? Am I looking at the inside of the dome but it's a holographic projection of the sky? If that's the case, where'd all the water go?*

As though in answer, a memory assaulted him. He was in a malt shop, submerged underwater. His oversized gloves were reaching out to a ridiculously gargantuan lever; and he was pulling it down.

Did that seal the hole in the dome and drain the water?

Armed with this theory, George studied the houses a bit more. Even though there wasn't a cloud in the sky, the gutters were still overflowing with water and every leaf and surface was dripping with moisture. Everything was soaking wet, the pavement, the street and sidewalk.

Across the street, George saw a brightly-colored star fish stuck fast to the windshield of an old station wagon. The more he looked, the more he saw other starfish stuck to other windows. Still further, he saw many of the houses were covered in algae, but even now seemed to be evaporating with the meeting of air.

In the sewer at the end of the street, George was pretty sure he glimpsed an octopus, one about the size of large dog, clinging to the sewer opening before being pulled into the drainage system below by torrents of water.

So, this was the town I floated into. I still don't know where all the water could have gone.

He was about to take another step into the street and nearly stepped onto the louvered slits cut into the street.

Whoa.

The louvers were so well disguised that he didn't even see them before. Now that he was standing over them, he could see in-between the cracks. Watching the water rush down into them, he was reminded of the torrential Florida downpours as a kid. He and his little brother would make sailboats out of old newspapers and watch them voyage down into the gutters. Several fish swam by and when one got left behind by the departing water, George bent down and helped it along until it went down the drain.

As the last of the water flowed into the louvers, they mechanically snapped closed and became a street once more.

So why let it flood in the first place? he wondered.

Ring-Ring!

George dodged nimbly out of the way when a young boy wearing a striped shirt and baseball cap rode by him on a bicycle with balloon tires, large fenders and a hulking frame.

"Hey mister," he said. It had come out 'Hey, Misth-tir' because the freckle-faced boy was missing his two front teeth.

"Wait, can I talk to you?" George called out after the boy.

But the boy kept peddling merrily along.

George turned to check the direction the kid had come from to see if anybody else was coming. There wasn't. He turned back around in the direction of the boy on the bicycle, but he was gone, despite the fact that the street went on for several blocks.

Another ghost? Was the milkman a ghost too?

He seemed real enough.

George looked to where the milkman had dropped off the small crate of glass milk bottles. Milk continued to drip off the front stoop where he had tripped over glass bottles and broken them earlier.

No. Whatever the milkman was, he wasn't a ghost. Not like the kid on the bicycle.

He scanned both ends of the street. The suburbia seemed endless. Glancing back at his house (Well, it wasn't his house, merely the one he had woken up in), he decided he needed a higher vantage point.

He walked back up to the concrete path, stopped at the stoop and took the time to pick up the only remaining milk bottle.

"Meow!"

A black cat had come out of the bushes and immediately began lapping up the spilt milk. He thought about petting it, but George had never really been much of a cat person. He was more of a dog guy. It was Maddie who really loved cats. He decided to let the cat be.

Taking the milk inside the house, he opened it up. *Smells fresh, just like the bread,* he thought, and immediately drank half of it down. He was about to leave the nearly empty bottle on the dining room table but for whatever reason, he decided to play along, and took the time to walk back into the kitchen and put it in the fridge.

He could feel the cold air within.

The frigid air made him realize it had been freezing outside. Even though the boy had been in shorts and a striped t-shirt and the milkman only his uniform, George remembered seeing his breath in the air. It's still cold. They might've removed the water from the town, but as of yet, they still hadn't had time to remove the cold from the air.

He jogged back upstairs to his room. Again, it wasn't his room, but he had come to think of it as much. Moving to the window, he saw the reflection of sunlight on all the moisture of the leaves.

Putting both hands on the windowsill, he leaned out. From the higher vantage point he could see other houses. Lots of them. They all had antennas on them. Thick, heavy gruesome things, of different sizes and shapes; all designed to carry TV airwaves into houses for free TV. *Gosh, I forgot about those too.*

Beyond the rooftops, George could just make out the center of a town. So, he was in suburbia but nearby was a downtown area. A large water tower loomed over the houses like one of those giant robots from Orson Wells, *War of the Worlds*. George read the lettering upon it: SAFE HAVEN.

Safe Haven? When I was being held captive by the Zombie-Pirate-King, didn't the Lamppost Man say something about not bringing Tessa to the Sanctuary? That's what they want. George still didn't know who *they* were, but it seemed pretty important that Tessa never reach the Sanctuary. *Did he mean this place?*

Tessa... why can't I remember what happened to Tessa? A flash of his wife standing at the railing of The Dauntless, tucking her hair behind her ear, whooshed across his mind. *What happened?* For the life of him, he couldn't remember. It made him sick to his stomach not knowing, or was there another reason?

He left the windowsill behind and went back downstairs. He was about to go back outside, but saw a door that most likely led to the garage.

'Say, Georgie. Now there's an idea. Why walk when you can ride?'

Opening the door to the garage he saw an old light-blue pickup truck, a real antique too, maybe 1950's, but in mint condition.

Out of the corner of his eye, he spotted truck keys on a hook mounted near the door. *That's convenient.* Instinctively, he twirled the ring of keys around his finger as he walked around the hood of the truck, opened the driver's side door and hopped in behind the wheel.

The truck fired right up.

BUH-BUH-BUH-BUH...

George checked the truck cab's visor for a garage door opener and realized, *Duh, this is 1950's. They didn't have remote control openers back then.*

He got back out of the truck, but left the motor running. Gas wasn't an issue, it had three-quarters of a tank. While he opened the garage door he wondered, *Why three-fourths of a tank? Why not a full tank, or even a quarter of a tank?*

The garage door was locked but it was a simple fix, and he slid the inside bolt restraining it. Hopping back behind the wheel, he saw the truck had a clutch. Fortunately for him, his first pickup had a clutch just like this one. So, it was easy for him to put it in drive.

George drove the truck down to the end of the driveway and stopped. He checked for traffic, checked for the kid on the bicycle, and even checked for the milkman and his truck. He didn't see any of those things. So, he hit his turn indicator that went PLUNK-PLUNK, PLUNK-PLUNK until he completed the turn. Using the old-style hand crank, he rolled down the window, placed his elbow on the frame and headed into town in the same direction the milkman had gone.

As George left *his* house behind, he didn't see the bloated corpse sticking out of the bushes across the street.

If he had, he would have recognized the man immediately.

It was him.

Chapter 20

Downtown

George drove past a water tower, an elementary school, and an old movie theater playing, Alice in Wonderland.

'Well, we certainly tumbled down the rabbit hole this time, didn't we, Georgie-boy?'

Ignoring Jimmy, he continued on past the post office where Old Glory was already dried out and flapping briskly in the wind. That is, if it was a flag. It occurred to George that the flag might be another hologram, like the sky and the birds. It certainly made the most sense since everything else was still soaking wet, and yet the flag was flapping briskly in the summer breeze that was non-existent.

Whatever Safe Haven used to be, it was now broken. Despite these minor nuisances, it was the perfect town with its white picket fences and well-manicured lawns.

Coming into town, George saw it was little more than a crossroads with buildings to either side. There was a saloon and barber shop on one side of the street, with the court house, bank and antique shop on the other. A tiny park broke up the buildings and came equipped with a white bandstand and a modest playground. This was no eco-friendly plastic playground either; the slides were made of steel and the swings rubber and chain. Despite the bizarre circumstances, the town was beginning to grow on him.

He slowed the truck's speed to about 5 mph when he passed the Malt Shop he had visited earlier. Directly across the street from the Malt Shop was City Hall. Thus far, he hadn't seen a single other person; only parked cars of the same era.

He decided to go to City Hall first. Leaving his stolen truck curbside, he jogged up the steps and pulled on the door. Locked. All the pounding in the world did nothing to alleviate his growing frustration.

The sheriff's office was next door and beyond that was the barber shop, complete with the candy-striped carousel for a sign.

A honking sound caused him to jump and turn back toward the street. He was surprised to find the street suddenly filled with passing motorists going up and down the street. Even the stoplight was now working. Nearby, kids were laughing, and playing a game of stickball in the park. Women went in and out of the beauty salon across the street. Just as he was beginning to wonder if they could see him too, for maybe he was the ghost, a man wearing a fedora tipped his hat at him.

In fact, all the men were wearing hats. He needn't have worried about whether or not they could see him, for now he was attracting attention. The passing pedestrians seemed to take notice of the fact that he wasn't exactly dressed the way they were in these here parts, but thus far, they were too polite to say anything about it.

George spotted the milkman's truck parked by the curb. After a few seconds, the same milkman he'd seen earlier climbed out of the truck. Now that he saw him up close, George could see he was a scarecrow-thin of a man and had this creepy smile that reminded him of a Halloween Jack-O'-Lantern.

"Hi George."

George felt his eyebrows knit together. How did he know my name? he wondered. The scarecrow man's nametag read, SIMON. "Do I know you?"

Without dropping his creepy smile, or intense gaze for that matter, the milkman said, "No friend, but I know you. I believe what you're looking for is the Stranger residence."

George nodded. His Spidey-sense was definitely tingling. This guy was just plain creepy.

"The Stranger residence," George repeated. The milkman nodded briskly.

"That's right. You'll find it at the edge of town." The milkman began to turn away, but then, as though deciding something, he added, "You'll want to speak with the boy."

Without warning, George felt something crash into him. Turning toward the aggressor he saw a young woman pushing a baby carriage. She seemed aghast over running into him.

"Oh, I'm terribly sorry. I really should have been watching where I was going. Are you alright? That is to say, I hope I didn't hurt you in any way. Did I say I was sorry?"

George nodded. "You did ma'am." He turned back toward the milkman only to see him driving off.

The woman spoke up again, "I really am sorry."

"That's quite alright, ma'am. It really just startled me more than anything else."

"You must be new in town."

"Yeah, in fact, I just got here." Not knowing what else to say he asked, "You?"

The baby in the carriage began crying, and she removed his blanket and took him out. "Looks like little-baby Barnaby is waking up from his nap."

Barnaby, why does that name sound familiar?

The woman removed a very chubby and very ugly baby from the carriage and held it up for him to see. She then hugged it fiercely. George was glad she didn't ask him for his opinion of her baby. He hated lying and was never very good at it. Smiling sweetly, she finally answered his query, "Fourth generation Safe Haven. I lived here my whole life."

"Really, no kidding?"

She nodded. "Are you going to be attending the barbecue this Saturday in the park? I hear the band is putting on a real hum-dinger."

"I wouldn't miss it," George answered, trying to sound as cheerful as possible. In truth, it was easy being nice to the young woman. With the exception of the creepy milkman, what wasn't there to like?

She studied him a bit longer and seemed to take in his appearance a bit more. "I'm sorry for saying so, but you appear a bit lost. Do you need any help, or assistance?"

George smiled. Had folks in the 1950's really been so cordial? If so, he'd time travel back there in an instant. He was about to tell her that he was fine, but then realized she could help him with something. "I'm looking for the uh, Stranger residence."

The young woman put a finger to her lips and thought about it for a second. Then, "Oh sure. You must mean John and Belle Stranger. My goodness, you are lost aren't you. You see that stop sign at the end of the street?" When George nodded that he did she continued, "You simply go down there and make a left. Then you go on for, I don't know, five or six miles. Don't go left, don't go right, you just go straight ahead. You keep going until you see a little farmhouse right there at the edge of town. You can't miss it."

"Well thank you for your time, Ma'am." He made a hand motion to tip his non-existent hat, but when he realized he wasn't wearing one, this made her stifle a giggle with her white-gloved hand.

He turned to walk back to his truck, but what he saw there caused him to freeze in his tracks.

An overweight man in a business suit was standing next to the blue pickup with two policemen. When the truck's owner spied him, George overheard the man say, "That's him officer. That's the man who stole my truck."

The two police officers, one young and the other a bit older with a gray mustache, locked eyes with him. The older one yelled out, "You sir, I'd like a word with you."

George didn't like the sound of that, especially since the older policeman was removing his wooden billy club from his belt.

"I can explain," George began.

Following the senior officer's lead, the younger man also removed his heavy, wooden billy club and both began walking briskly toward him.

The people on the sidewalks, the cars passing in the street, even people on the other side of the big glass pane window in the malt shop had all frozen, and then slowly turned toward him. The police officers however did not freeze and were already racing across the street.

George figured himself trapped until he saw an alley made of brick next to city hall. He took a few cautious steps toward it. When he did, the younger officer let out a quick shrill from his whistle, while the older man cried, "I said halt right there!"

George ran.

Chapter 21

The Death of Maddie, Traxx and Henry

"Henry, will you stop worrying? Once we get back to the Hopper we have nothing to worry about."

As he exited the abandoned shopping center, Henry adjusted the heavy sack filled with their *stolen* supplies so it carried better on his shoulder. He glared back at Traxx and grumped, "That's what you said inside the mall!"

Maddie dropped her own sack of loot onto the edge of the loading platform, hopped down, turned around, and snatched it back up again.

"C'mon, Henry, there's no way we could've seen that coming." When he didn't respond she added, "I'm sorry, okay?"

Henry dropped down beside her. "You're sorry? Sorry for what? Nearly getting me eaten by a giant rabbit?"

Traxx hopped down next to him. Trying to lighten the mood, he responded, "If you ask me, I think it was more like a giant Easter bunny."

Henry pursed his lips and gave the younger boy his most venomous stare yet.

Seeing this Traxx said, "But... that's probably not helping."

"Just leave me alone." Henry hefted his own sack on his shoulder and stomped off.

Constantly checking over their shoulders for pursuers, they began their long trek around the mall back to the Hopper. As they walked, Henry noticed Maddie had lost a bit of her swagger. At first, he thought it might be good for her to lose a step or two. But now, he was beginning to wonder if she was beginning to doubt herself. He soon realized he had found a measure of faith in her confident leadership style, and now that it was gone, he was already beginning to miss it. He hefted the heavy sack up onto his shoulder again and thought, *I think I liked it better when she was more sure of herself.*

They turned one corner of the mall, and then another, and after walking down the street for a few blocks, the Hopper was soon in sight. He thought he could never possibly be as glad to see the dingy-yellow hovercraft as he was now. No matter how hard he tried, he just couldn't shake the image of the Not-So-White Rabbit from his mind. For him, the last few hundred yards were going to be the worst. At least Maddie and Traxx walked with their guns drawn, and down by their sides. *For all the good it will do us if the Misfits attacked again in force.*

As though reading his thoughts, Maddie turned her chin over her shoulder and said back to him, "We're almost there. Just keep moving."

Henry was so angry, he refused to respond. But when his eyes met hers, he immediately saw the alarm on her face. She wasn't looking at him, but rather behind him.

Henry turned and saw a trio of hideous orcs, casually appearing in their wake. They were short, with upturned canines and dressed in medieval leather armor. Soon others were peeking out over the tops of various mounds of rubble and joining them.

Maddie must've seen the pack of Misfits too for she tightened her grip on her sack, put her chin down and increased her speed. "C'mon guys, pick up the pace."

The sound of glass breaking was heard above, and Henry saw a man in a superhero costume lean out of a two-story window and make ready to drop something large and made of concrete.

"Traxx, look out!" Henry screamed. When he realized Traxx didn't see the cinderblock about to drop down onto him, Henry dropped his sack and barreled into him.

Both of them went sprawling. Henry felt a tremendous amount of pain in his shoulder.

Maddie soon appeared above them. Her weapon was drawn, and she was taking aim at their pursuers, which even now were gaining in number. Without looking at them she asked, "Henry, Traxx, you guys okay?" Before they could answer, she raised her pistol and fired a few rounds at the three trailing orcs.

Henry grabbed his left shoulder with his right hand and massaged it profusely. It hurt badly, but it didn't feel broken. His suit was torn and his shoulder was scraped badly underneath, but he figured it must've been a glancing blow or it would've been a whole lot worse.

Traxx, wide-eyed saw the broken cinderblock only a few inches from where he lay. "Thanks Henry," he breathed. "If that had been any closer, it would've killed me for certain."

Maddie fired off another round and yelled down to them, "C'mon you two, get up. You can braid each other's hair later."

The bravado was false, but Henry was grateful for it just the same. When Maddie saw him go back for the sack she barked, "Leave it. The only thing that matters now is getting you both back to the Hopper."

"Agreed," Traxx said, leaving behind his own sack.

They quickened their pace and Henry saw at least twenty more Misfits trailing behind them. They were of every variety too: Army men from various countries, space men wearing bulbous helmets, a bunch of firemen who also happened to be vampires, and an athletic woman wearing high-heels and a cape.

"C'mon, the Hopper's just around this pile," Maddie said leading them onward, but even before she finished navigating it, she slid to a sudden stop.

Henry finished rounding the pile and his worst fears were confirmed. As many Misfits that were behind them, there were at least twice that number blocking their path to the Hopper. The Misfits were everywhere, in the windows overhead, and strewn all over the mountains of debris around them.

Henry struggled for breath. They were surrounded. He figured the Misfits would pull them apart, and then what, eat them? Regardless, it was hopeless. Maddie and Traxx couldn't possibly hope to shoot them all.

Traxx swallowed and said to no one in particular, "All that noise we made inside the mall must've attracted them. We might as well have rung the dinner bell."

To his surprise, Maddie didn't seem very flustered. If anything, she seemed to have regained a bit of her confidence back. She called over her shoulder, "Traxx, you got this?"

"I got it," he answered. He immediately flipped open the hatch on his data pad strapped to his thigh and began punching in code.

"Sorry about this guys," Maddie said apologetically, and hit the dirt.

Henry wasn't sure why she dove to the ground but after seeing Traxx dive down too, he figured he probably should as well.

Henry watched as a large panel unfolded on the Hopper. Twin cylinders mounted on a platform slid out from within. The noise they produced was deafening, but their effect was even more devastating.

Henry lifted his head to the Misfits surrounding them.

Maddie shouted, "Henry! You trying to get your head blown off? Stay down!" When he didn't comply fast enough she dove on top of him and shoved his face down in the dirt.

Overwhelmed, Henry couldn't help but peek, at the mayhem exploding around him. The chain gun rapidly spent hundreds of shells in mere seconds, its automatic-targeting system cutting down ninjas, robot-tigers and a pack of raptor dinosaurs in mere seconds. The shadows in the upper ramparts that didn't retreat fast enough, were either blown backwards into the shadows from whence they came or were blasted from their perches.

The chain gun ceased firing, but continued searching for more targets.

Several more minutes passed before Maddie eased her grip on him and allowed him to get back up. His ears were ringing something fierce, but as he surveyed the carnage, he was pretty sure he heard Maddie say, “Alright Traxx, I think you got them all.”

Henry saw Traxx punch a few buttons on the keypad on his leg and the chain guns folded neatly back into the Hopper.

Henry held his shoulder where the cinder block had hit him as he continued to survey the carnage around them.

Closing the hatch to his leg computer, Traxx asked, “I've never seen a pack that large before, have you?”

Maddie shook her head, “Nuh-uh. I've never even heard of anyone encountering so many. They were like a small army, and so organized.”

Henry saw a face pop out from the top of a pile of debris, and then another. A few seconds later a pack of lions casually strolled out of the nearby parking garage and narrowed their eyes at them.

Seeing this, Henry tapped Maddie repeatedly on her elbow, “Uh, Maddie.”

Maddie saw them too. Before she could say anything, Traxx bellowed, "Already on it." He began punching in codes in his thigh computer, lifting his head at the Hopper, but nothing was happening.

Now Maddie seemed nervous too when she said, "Anytime Traxx."

Traxx kept repeatedly punching in the same code. "I'm trying, I'm trying. Something's wrong."

Maddie moved over to him, "Traxx, now would be an excellent time!"

Traxx shook his head. Eyes wide with fear, he gazed up at her, "It's not working, Maddie!" Now they could all see where progressively more Misfits began closing in. Where there had been fifty before, there were now a hundred Misfits, if not more.

Maddie shook her head. Clearly, she did not know what to do. Henry picked up a pipe and yelled at the nearest of them, a jester-looking fellow, and told him to stay back.

In the end, Maddie and Traxx would shoot every last round they carried on their person. Henry would swing his pipe until his very last breath. They were finished, and they knew it. The Misfits knew it.

It was time for their little adventure to be over; it was time to die.

The first explosion propelled five Misfits twenty feet into the air. The second missile strike had propelled dozens. Strike-after-strike, each missile had exploded with deadly accuracy, blowing apart nearly every last attacker. The few who survived the onslaught quickly retreated from whence they came.

Maddie was the first to speak, “Traxx, did you... ?”

Traxx shook his head indicating he did no such thing.

Maddie looked over at him and scrunched up her face, “Henry, you didn’t have anything to do with this? Did you?”

Henry held up his hands in supplication. “Are you crazy? How would I... I don’t even know...” Words were hard to come up with so, he settled for just shaking his head.

“Hello children.”

The words echoing on the wind had practically been sung.

All three of them turned to see The Leftenant standing behind them, her hands clasped firmly behind her back.

“I do hope you enjoyed your little excursion, but it’s time to put away your toys, collect your things and come home.”

Stupefied, Maddie asked, “Leftenant, you did this?”

The Leftenant purposefully waggled her eyebrows at her, (something she’d been practicing, but still hadn’t quite got the hang of), and replied, “Yes. Fortunately for you, an orbiting defense satellite was within range. Were it not, I’m afraid that pack of miscreants might have carried you off... in teensy-tiny little pieces."

Traxx flashed her a look of confusion. "I don't understand. I disabled you."

"Please," The Leftenant replied, kicking a decapitated ninja head with the toe of her boot. "As if I could be outsmarted by a child, even one as clever as yourself." She straightened out her jacket, marched past him.

"Now, if you are all quite finished mucking about in the rubbish, the defense satellite has now moved out of range, so I suggest you recover your absconded properties and we return to the Hopper at once, post haste."

Henry felt himself nodding profusely. "Sounds good to me."

Chapter 22

Henry Stranger Residence

George had given the cops the slip.

'I bet there's something you never thought you would say.'

Jimmy Stewart's voice in his head was right. George had been a law-abiding citizen his entire life, he never thought he'd find himself running from the law. After spending years working alongside The Leftenant, he had no doubt those holographic cops would easily cave his skull in with the billy clubs they so menacingly clutched in their outstretched hands. Whatever game Stranger World was playing, he knew he couldn't do anybody any good if he got locked up in jail.

'The slammer; I think that's what they call it Georgie-boy.'

Shut up, Jimmy; let me think.

For such a tiny town, they certainly had a large police force. He must've counted at least six squad cars out searching for him. Despite worrying about his pursuers, it was hard not to notice how each unit was the old kind with those single dome light on top of the roof.

After ducking down the alley, he had made several more turns. He ducked inside the back door of a public library, passed through it, and hid out in a shed behind a church. After a few hours, the artificial daylight had given way to dusk. Under the cover of darkness, it was a short hike out of town down a narrow, dusty road. Before long, George came upon a mailbox at the edge of town that had the letters *J. Stranger*, stenciled on the side of it.

He thought about the sky dome overhead and the tons of water above it. *What did Kelpi the Annoying Mermaid call this place? A prison? A prison for whom, or what?* For someone so important as to build all of this, the place before him didn't look like all that much; just a quaint little farmhouse. As he walked up to the front door, he passed a red barn that had seen better days and heard chickens clucking in a nearby coop.

Mounting the porch, he pressed the doorbell. When nothing happened, he knocked lightly on the door.

Abruptly, he heard singing coming from within. It had just started up, mid song, or maybe it was more like a pleasant humming. Also, there was a faint smell of fresh baked cookies in the air.

Was that there before? He doubted it.

He heard sirens in the distance crank up again. *They must've figured out where I went. Maybe they even talked to the woman with the ugly baby.* George knew if that was the case, the town wasn't very big and they would arrive in minutes.

A kind voice beckoned him inside the antiquated farmhouse, "Come on in, door is open." The screen door creaked loudly as he opened it. The voice that called him inside sounded like it had belonged to a woman. But the only person inside the modest living room was a balding man sitting in a faded lime-green chair, with his face hidden behind an oversized newspaper.

"Um... hello sir. My name's George Stapleton. I'm looking for," he began, but fumbled for the words. Who was he searching for? The creepy man had something about a boy. *Well I am certainly not going to say that.* Realizing too much time had gone by without him saying anything he opened his mouth to speak, but the man in the chair merely shuffled his paper and turned the page. When he did, George could clearly see the man's face. He didn't have one.

George took a few steps back toward the door without even realizing it.

This wasn't his first faceless person. Even in his nightmares, he recalled the faceless Nazi's on Lady Wellington's pleasure barge. He was about to leave when he heard the sound of pots and pans clanging together. Turning toward them, he saw the noise was radiating from an adjoining kitchen. He couldn't explain it, but there was something comforting about that sound.

"In here," a woman's voice sang.

Too afraid to take his eyes off the man without a face, George backed out of the living room and into the white-tiled kitchen.

The woman at the sink had her back to him and continued with the task of washing dishes. He fully expected her not to have a face as well, and could only wait in trepidation as she finished washing every last dish. When she was done, she shook the excess moisture from her hands and dried them on her apron. She then removed the apron and hung it up to dry.

Finally, she turned toward him. Thankfully, she did have a face. She was middle-aged and actually kind of pretty, with big, bright-blue eyes.

"Hello there, darling," she said with a voice that was as lovely as it was disarming. "I'm Mrs. Belle."

There was something familiar about her. "Do I know you? Er... what I mean to say is, have we met before?"

Mrs. Belle studied him for a moment with those big bright blue eyes of hers and smiled. It was the kind of smile that had a way of disarming you the moment you saw it. At last, she asked, "Don't you remember?"

"I'm sorry..." George struggled to find the words. He had to admit, it was difficult in her presence. He seemed to remember something about the interior of a commercial airliner. In his memory he saw several empty seats, but the moment he came up to a pair of seats with two women in them, a piercing white light struck his mind's eye like a bolt of lightning.

It was so painful, George shot out a hand for the kitchen table to keep himself from collapsing to the floor. He held his other hand to his temple to help keep the pain at bay. The instant he gave up on trying to remember, the pain faded away.

The ominous sound of police sirens in the distance was a harsh reminder, *I'm running out of time.*

Opening his eyes, he saw Mrs. Belle was now sitting at the opposite side of the table with a steaming cup of coffee in her hands. A second cup was also on the table directly in front of him. Smiling up at him she said, "Don't worry hon,

I'm sure it will all come back to you in due time. Why don't you sit a spell?"

George, eager to sit down before he fell down, motioned a thumb back toward the living room, and asked, "Is he... your husband? Is he alright?"

"Oh, don't mind Mr. Stranger. He's fine. My son had a lot of trouble remembering John's facial features, that's all. I don't blame him. His father rarely spent time with the boy."

None of this makes sense.

"Do you know why I'm here?"

Mrs. Belle regarded him patiently again, then moved over to him. Her perfume smelled like orange blossoms, and when she placed a hand gently on his shoulder, it was light as a feather. He was surprised to find he was no longer sitting at the table but standing again. Guiding him toward the back door she said, "Of course I do, hon. You are here to see my boy, Henry. Just like all of those who came before you."

Suddenly George noticed the white curtains in the living room were bathed in red flashing lights. The cops had found him. Outside, a senior officer yelled, "Open up in there. This is the police. We've got the place surrounded."

Mrs. Belle's words suddenly registered with him. "What people? Who came here before me?"

There was a loud knocking at the door and the cop barked, "I said open up in there. There's no use running anymore."

"Why you did," she said, opening the creaky screen door to the backyard.

George shook his head. Exasperated, he cried, "Why do people keep telling me that? I've never been here before."

George was confused, but he allowed her to practically shove him over the door's threshold. Ignoring the sirens, barking cops and flashing red lights, Mrs. Belle stated calmly, "Now, Henry's outside in the backyard, probably building one of his *stories* again." She was about to close the door, but stopped, looked him square in the eye and said, "You know what? You're a bit different from the others somehow. I can't explain it, but I really hope you make it this time. I really do."

"I'm sorry, I don't understand."

The door banged closed. She smiled sweetly through the greenish-mesh of the screen door. "You were never meant to." Lightly shooing him away, she said, "Go on now. Henry won't wait around for you forever."

Chapter 23

Henry's Backyard

The backyard was surprisingly large.

It was about 5 acres of un-mowed grass, with a dirt track running around just inside the border. The track's edges were bordered with two-by-fours, railroad ties and any other miscellaneous planks of wood the builder could get his hands on. George took a few steps closer and could now see where the improvised road passed dozens of improvised structures. Each was different from the other, but from this distance, it was too hard to make out any real detail.

Turning back toward the house, George saw only Mrs. Belle staring at him through the green mesh with her big, bright-blue eyes. Occasionally, she would raise her coffee mug to her smiling lips and take a tentative sip. The cops could have easily charged through the house, or around it, but surprisingly, they had not. In fact, the moment George turned away from the screen door he no longer heard their blaring sirens, shrill whistles or snarling commands. It was as though the entire police force had been swallowed up by some unseen sinkhole.

"Hi there!"

George jumped slightly.

Wearing a worn and tattered ringmaster's tailcoat and top hat (with a sewn-on patch), the thin ten-year-old gazed up at him and smiled. "Welcome to Stranger World my good man!" He tucked his walking cane under his armpit and produced a white-gloved hand in the form of a handshake.

As he shook the boy's hand, George noted the boy's gloves also had been ravaged by time. "Are you Henry? Henry Stranger?"

The boy released his hand, snapped his fingers and smartly said, "Right you are, sir." He placed a hand at the small of George's back and ushered him forward. "Now if you'll be so kind as to step this way. *You,* are next in line."

George noticed the boy walked with a limp and leaned heavily on his cane. Whether this was a well-performed act or not, he did not know.

Seemingly from nowhere, two pig-faced, redheaded boys strode up, pulling a big, heavy, makeshift cart behind them. They each had a bit in their mouth and were strung up like oxen. Both boys, wearing signs around their necks, had pinched, angry-red faces with a classic bully *look* carved all over them. The sign on the left read, *I'M DUMB*, and the one on the left confessed, *I DUMMER*.

The boy in the ratty ringmaster outfit, leaned his head back to look up at him, held out a white-gloved palm, and said, "That'll be 25 cents, sir."

Startled, George was almost as panicked as the moment the leviathan was coming for him. Patting his pockets, he said, "I'm sorry, but I don't have any change."

The slender boy put a hand to the side of his mouth and whispered, "Check your pocket."

"Uh, okay." He checked his pocket and sure enough, there was a quarter in there, well sort of. It was actually a piece of cardboard in the shape of a quarter, only oversized, like it might appear to a child, and had 25¢ written on it. "Here you go," George said loud enough for the bullies to hear.

"Thank you, kind sir." Before pocketing the quarter into the breast pocket of his frayed costume, young Henry bit into it, so as to ascertain its genuineness. He held up an improvised megaphone fashioned from a tin can, cardboard and tape, and exclaimed far louder than was necessary, "Right this way, sir! Right this way!"

The makeshift carriage was a mishmash of four red wagons and a thick sheet of plywood topped off with two unmatched and discarded couches.

"All aboard!"

Feeling as though he were moving in a dream, George boarded the makeshift chariot. As he did so, he felt guilty about adding his weight to the chariot for the two young bullies to pull. Henry seemed to have no such reservation and climbed up into the raised dais positioned for the driver. George noted he did this with slight difficulty due to his leg.

Satisfied George was in place; the young ringmaster removed the whip from its hook and cracked it high above the bullies heads. "Hee-yaw! Onwards noble steeds!"

George felt his head snap back as the buggy jolted forward.

In an announcer voice, Henry shouted, "Ladies and Gentleman, please stay in your seats at all times while the ride is moving."

The wagon passed beneath a white banner strung up between two stripped tree trunks serving as poles.

In full announcer voice, Henry read the sign aloud:

Welcome to Stranger World!

The first "attraction" the buggy passed was a *tea party* made up of a plastic table and chairs. The venue was enshrouded by potted plants, and attendees included three stuffed Teddy bears, a pink elephant, and at the head of the table, a creepy porcelain doll.

Standing off to one side, as though they had just arrived at the party, was an original G.I. Joe doll, "with life-like hair," holding hands with a little girl doll wearing a blue dress.

George remembered Lady Wellington's mask falling off and the fight that ensued. He spied another doll behind the porcelain doll holding a giant feather. A sense of loss filled up inside of him at the thought of his friend, Barnaby who had given his life for Maddie.

With a crack of Henry's whip, the ride continued onward through the un-mowed grass. Still using his announcer voice, the boy heralded, "Your attentions please, your attention. Next stop is Dino-Land USA. Remember to please keep all hands, limbs and other appendages inside the carriage at all times. Our dinosaurs do bite and would appreciate any bite-sized snacks." At this, Henry giggled at his own joke. When he saw George wasn't laughing too, he cleared his throat, sat up straight, cracked the whip and they were off once more.

The carriage passed makeshift paddocks made of wooden poles and chicken wire. A haphazard sign attached to the cage read: *Beware the Raptors*. When George gazed within the cage, he could see where Henry had attached dinosaur masks to the chicken heads inside.

After the paddock, the track suddenly dipped down into a trench about four feet deep. Embedded in the walls, were steak bones and other animal bones you might find on a farm, each neatly arranged to form the outline of dinosaur fossils. As soon as the carriage exited the trench, Henry wiped the imaginary sweat from his brow and exclaimed, "Whew! That was a close one."

Up next, they passed a Victorian village on a raised dirt pile. The village pieces looked as though they had been pilfered from a standard Christmas train set. Standing outside the doors of a large manor, and a bit out of scale, was a stone gargoyle dressed as a butler and holding a bright yellow balloon in one clawed hand.

After the Victorian village, they passed a sand box with a toy airplane in the dirt. The tiny commercial airliner was surrounded by potted sunflowers. Each sunflower had the face of a doll embedded in them. One of them had round-rimmed glasses and a bowler hat.

George scanned ahead to see how much longer the ride was when he saw a wooden fort, like something a child might build. It was in the shape of a pirate ship complete with a skull-and-crossbones flag. As the carriage grew near,

George could hear pirate-themed music crackling over a tiny speaker wired up on a pole.

Henry announced, "Coming up next are the Swamplands of the Zombie-Pirate-King!" As the carriage sauntered by, George could see various stick figures comprised of broom sticks and tree branches. Each of them was dressed as pirates with zombie faces drawn on paper plates.

Henry pulled on the reins and brought the carriage up to a stop next to a wooden post. "Uh-oh, keep your heads down," he said ominously. "It appears as though the zombie pirates are out in full force today and they're looking to shanghai themselves more crewmembers."

Standing up in his seat, Henry pulled on a brass ring attached to some twine. The twine led all the way back to a pulley-system over and above the makeshift pirate ship. The moment Henry pulled on the ring, several of the pirates lifted their wooden swords in salute. George tried not to giggle when one of the pirate's arms fell off. Henry, now wearing a worn-out pirate hat, turned back to him slightly, changed his voice to a more ominous tone and added, "Perhaps, it will be you... Arrrgghhhh."

Henry released the ring mechanism causing the pirates arms to drop back down by their sides. He dropped the pirate act by switching back to his top hat and in an efficient manner, flicked out his coattails and sat back down in his seat. With a crack of his whip, the ride was off once more.

As they departed, George noted one figure in particular. He was standing in the makeshift bow with one black boot up on the railing. This pirate was a bit more fleshed out than the rest. Upon closer inspection, George could see where white rocks, painted to look like skulls, were woven into his thick, charcoal beard. Further, two Christmas lightbulbs had been installed in the Pirate Captain's eye sockets, giving off a green phosphorous glow. George couldn't swear to it, but the moment he began to look away, he thought the Zombie-Pirate-King turned his head toward him slightly.

The track curved left at the end of a dilapidated wooden fence and continued onward along the back wall. The bullies grunted in complaint as they made the turn.

George leaned forward to talk with the driver. "Henry, can I talk to you for a moment?"

Henry, obviously uncomfortable responding to a request made in mid-ride, chose to ignore him.

"Henry," George repeated.

In his usual announcer voice the ringmaster answered, "Out of courtesy for the other passengers, any and all questions will be answered at the end of your ride." Then added, "No extra charge, of course."

George decided to play along for a bit longer.

Leaving the zombie pirates behind, the carriage approached a scene George wasn't familiar with. A modest wooden sign read: Welcome to the Himalayas. Mounted on the back fence were cardboard mountains, cleverly arranged to give one the impression of a vast mountain range. Some of the higher mountains were even capped with aluminum foil to represent snow and ice.

Turning to his left George saw a fenced-in paddock with two shaggy dogs dressed up like wooly mammoths. When one of the younger dogs tried to remove the vacuum cleaner hose attached to its snout, Henry shouted at him under his breath, "Barnaby, stop that!"

Henry leaned back and put his chin over one shoulder, "Coming soon is the Wooly-Mammoth train, over 70 feet tall and featuring a world famous dining car!"

George could see the track weaved in and out of makeshift scenes all over the property. He was about to ask how much longer when he spotted a plastic swimming pool. Peering inside, he saw a wind-up leviathan swimming around a half-submerged city. "If you need to relax, our underwater hotels are the most luxurious and relaxing on the planet."

His patience wearing thin, George leaned forward again and said, "Henry, we gotta talk."

"Sorry sir, no time for questions now, coming up next is the Sands of Insanity. But don't worry, if you get thirsty, there will be plenty of lemonade available for purchase at the end of your ride."

"Henry..."

Both of them jumped at the sound of a loud CRASH.

Locating its source, George saw the screen door on the back of the house had been smashed open so hard it was now half-hanging on its hinges. Standing just outside the house was Henry's faceless father. He was wearing a sleeveless t-shirt and holding his belt in his hands. Behind him was a cadre of police officers, now also faceless, with batons clenched in their fists.

A brisk wind blew up in the scant two acres between them.

Spotting the faceless men too, Henry's proud shoulders slumped forward and he turned back around to him to say, "It seems time has run out for both of us." The boy shook his head sadly, "And, I had so much more to show you too."

After a moment of staring at them, the faceless John Stranger led the charge toward them, knocking over Henry's set pieces as they went.

A woman's voice shrieked, "Run, Henry, run." George was fairly certain it had been Mrs. Belle.

"C'mon!" Henry shouted and leapt from the moving carriage. George quickly dove after the boy.

Glancing back at their pursuers, George saw several cops tripping over set pieces, but the majority were closing in. When they reached the track, they had to stop and wait for the carriage to slowly saunter past them.

"Through here," Henry exclaimed and stepped through a row of hedges. George hadn't seen the exit even though he was standing right next to it. They dashed over a lunar landscape cleverly made out of old sponges. Impressive spaceships were linked together by causeways and while studying all the astronauts and moon vehicles, George collided into one of the spaceship towers and knocked it over. "Sorry, Henry," he said immediately and tried to pick it back up. The top piece broke off in his hand. "Sorry, sorry."

"That's okay," and staring at the spaceship in his hands the boy added, "That one was yours anyway." Then tugging on his arm, he said, "C'mon, hurry up. It won't be long before they figure out how to get through the hedges."

Leaving the lunar landscape behind, they soon entered a jungle scene surrounded by transplanted bushes. There was a grouping of toy-sized African pavilions with a dirt runway strip next to it. Like the other scenes, the attention to detail was amazing, right down to the propeller of a doll-sized biplane spinning wildly and the sock flag blowing in the wind and at the end of the runway.

"Keep going," Henry urged, disappearing into the folds of the jungle.

George followed him through the thick underbrush until he came upon a dirt clearing. At its center was a large, wide dirt mound with a cave dug into its center. The cave's walls and ceiling were supported by thick wooden beams.

Henry pointed to it and exclaimed, "You need to hide in there!"

George didn't see how much good it would do to hide in a cave only as high as his waist and about six-feet deep.

They heard John Stranger and the faceless cops crashing through the jungle behind them. George scanned the jungle for a weapon and found nothing. "Henry, stay behind me."

Instead of doing as he was told, Henry gripped him by his shirt and pulled him down next to him. The boy was impossibly strong and George fell to his knees. Gripping George's face in his hands, Henry said evenly, "Remember this George. You have to find the knife in the cave."

Over the boy's shoulder, George could see the bushes rustling as the first of their pursuers was about to come through.

Henry gripped his face tighter, "Say it! Say, I have to find the cave with the knife in it, just like this one."

George began, "Henry, we have to..." but the boy slapped him.

"Say it!"

George couldn't believe what was happening. The absurdity of it all. This was a whole new level.

The boy whacked him again.

Through squished up lips, for Henry was still holding him by his face, George said, "I have to find the knife in the cave."

Henry nodded. "Good." He took one last look at his father stepping through the bushes. As John stood there with the belt in his hand the faceless cops poured around him in an endless parade. "Now go."

With impossible strength, Henry flung George into the mouth of the cave. "Go!" the boy yelled after him. George crawled toward the back of the cave. In fact, he was surprised he hadn't reached it already. From the outside the cave couldn't have been more than six feet long and yet he felt as though he had already crawled twice that much.

Police whistles shrilled after him and George heard the crack of leather against bare skin. "Keep going, George!" the boy cried in anguish. George stopped crawling forward, looked over his shoulder and saw faceless cops filling the mouth of the cave. Within seconds, some were already beginning to crawl after him in a most unnatural manner.

As he was trying to figure out how he could turn around, with the intention of beating the snot out of every last one of those faceless jerks beating Henry, his hands slipped down off of a dirt ledge. George tried to catch himself with his other hand, but the dirt edge collapsed beneath his weight, and he fell.

George could only scream as he toppled down into a pitch-black bottomless pit.

Chapter 24

Okay, Let me have It

"Wait, let me get this straight. You want *me* to drive?"

Maddie wasn't in the mood to offer Traxx an explanation, but she gave him one anyway. "Yes, Traxx. The chain guns jammed. They shouldn't have, but they did. And yes, I cleaned them both out, and ran a full diagnostic before we left. I want to find out why." She grabbed Traxx's diagnostic kit off his thigh and strode to the back of the Hopper.

Traxx buckled his safety harness and replied enthusiastically, "Copy that. The Dauntless here we come." Immediately delighted to take the wheel, he cracked his knuckles like a pianist about to begin a command performance. "Alright Henry, you might as well come sit up front and I'll show you how it's done."

Before doing so, Henry watched Maddie as she left the cockpit. It seemed as though he wanted to say something to her, but she didn't give him the chance to work up enough courage to do it as she hastily brushed past him.

Maddie navigated the accordion causeway and strode to the rear of the craft. In the payload compartment, she opened a panel and began connecting leads from Traxx's portable diagnostic kit.

"Hello," The Leftenant said, appearing beside her.

Maddie slightly shook her head, grimaced a little and managed, "Come to gloat, Leftenant? Well, go ahead. Today's your lucky day. I got nothing left."

The Leftenant tilted her head to the side, "Really, I can't imagine why."

Maddie wasn't entirely sure what The Leftenant was working up to, so she settled for asking, "Weren't you watching?"

"Yes," The Leftenant readily confessed, "I was watching. I was watching the entire time."

Maddie blew some errant bangs out of her face and finished hooking up the diagnostic to the hopper's pc. "Then you know... we got jumped by a pack of Misfits in the mall." Tears formed at the corner of her eyes, but she refused to let them fall. Despite her efforts, one slipped out like a dirty thief. "I nearly got Traxx and Henry killed." She wiped the stupid-stupid runaway tear from her cheek onto the back of her glove. More to herself she said, "What was I thinking, taking out an expedition all by myself?"

For a moment, The Leftenant didn't say anything. She simply stood there studying her. *Why would she? She's just a stupid hologram. She's not programmed to deal with a crying baby like me.*

The Leftenant surprised her, as she often did, when she said, "You know what? I believe if your father had been here to see you today, I think he would have been very proud of his daughter."

Maddie furrowed her brow. "Now you're hitting below the belt."

"No, no. I mean it. The way you dispatched those baddies in the mall, and then later outside.." The Leftenant pumped her fist for emphasis.

"Jolly good showing young lady, jolly good."

The Leftenant rolled her eyes a little and said, "You did make some mistakes, such as leaving Cheeves and me behind, most certainly. But the fact of the matter is Traxx and Mister Henry both trust you completely, as they should. You, like your father, are a good leader."

"I'm not so sure about that. I was a blazing idiot to think..." Maddie began, but The Leftenant cut her off.

"No. No, no, no. Quit talking rubbish. I was the one who was wrong." She held up her forefinger toward herself and said playfully, "If you tell anyone I said that, I will personally box your ears off young lady." Brushing off some non-existent lint from her shoulder she continued, "The truth is I should've trusted you more. Like or not, for better or worse, you and Mister Traxx are the next generation. Heaven help us." She flicked her eyes skyward for a moment, and added, "Our lives will one day be in your hands. We have to let you make your own mistakes and hope you emerge on the other side all the better for having made them. So I'll state it again, I am certain if your father had seen your achievements to-day, he would have been most proud; very proud indeed."

Maddie heard herself gulp, and then let loose. She gave The Leftenant a fierce hug and let the tears flow. She had never truly mourned the loss of her mom or her dad. Maybe that was part of what this was all about. In the end, she wasn't sure how long she stood there like that, blubbering like a baby into The Leftenant's jacket, but it felt good.

"There, there," The Leftenant said, patting her gently on the head. "You stay here as long as you have too."

Maddie sniffed loudly, wiped her nose on the back of her sleeve (much to the chagrin of The Leftenant), and said, "Thank you for that."

The Leftenant gave her a crisp nod. “Fortunately for me, I drip-dry easily.” By the time she finished her sentence, the tear-soaked coat was completely dry.

“I’m sorry for what I said back there, ya know, that whole thing about my dad thinking of you as one of his daughters.”

The Leftenant’s smile seemed strained for a moment, but she fought through it and responded by saying, “Think nothing of it. I am only a hologram, after all.”

Before Maddie could tell her otherwise, The Leftenant vanished.

Chapter 25

Raggedy Man

"Maddie, get up here!"

Traxx brought the Hopper to an abrupt stop. Rain was falling steadily now and even though the front windshield was thick with frost, Henry could see a man standing in the middle of the street with his hands held high above his head. The man was dressed in tattered clothing and wore a thick bandage wrapped around the top of his head, concealing one eye.

Henry wasn't sure what all the controls did in the cockpit, but he knew enough to know that Traxx was already keying up the Hopper's defenses just in case. Seeing the younger boy do this he blurted out, "No wait!"

Traxx flashed a look over at him as though he had just grown two heads.

Maddie entered the cockpit, and as she put her hand on the back of his seat, she asked him, "Would you relax? He's not going to shoot him unless it gives us a reason."

Traxx seemed hurt by Henry's accusation. "Hey, it's not like Misfits are people. Heck, they're barely biologicals, they're practically background scenery."

Maddie chimed in, "Besides, you saw what those Misfits are capable of? They nearly tore us to pieces." Then she told Traxx, "If that thing out there does anything funny, save your ammo and just run him over."

"Really?" Traxx complained. "Run him over? I was going to make sure the targeting system was functioning properly."

Maddie thought this over. "Hmmm... that's a good point. Plus, if we run it over, its body might damage the undercarriage." Henry couldn't believe what he was hearing.

"You're not serious are you?" He raised a hand toward the man in the street. "How do you know he's one of those," he struggled with the word, "Misfits back there. What if he's a person who's injured? What if he's human?"

Henry watched Maddie and Traxx exchange a look. Traxx was the first of them to speak, "If you talked to a misfit you'd know they're not all that intelligent. They just have a set of pre-programed responses."

Maddie finished for him, "And if this guy was human, what would he be doing traveling with a band of Misfits?"

As though hearing this, the man in the street cupped his mouth and shouted, "Hello! Can you hear me in there? If you can, I mean you no harm."

Fearful they were about to make a mistake, Henry exclaimed, "Wait! I get it. We've all had an extremely bad day, and yes, the Misfits back there had tried to kill us, but that doesn't give us the right to become murderers."

Traxx's finger hovered over the firing mechanism and Maddie bit her lower lip. Henry could see he was getting through to them.

Which was why he was caught by surprise when Maddie said, "Traxx, fire off a warning shot. If he doesn't scamper away, let him have it."

Traxx began keying up the targeting laser again.

The raggedy man cupped his hands to his mouth again and shouted, "I know where your father is."

Hearing this, Maddie lunged forward and grabbed Traxx's hand to keep him from firing. Tentatively, Maddie picked up the microphone and brought it to her lips. She thought about what she was going to say for a few seconds before flicking on a switch marked intercom. Henry could hear her voice echo over the exterior loudspeakers.

"You don't know me, and you certainly don't know who my dad is."

In the rain, the crippled raggedy man squinted his one good eye as he listened and then responded by nodding with exaggerated movements. “I do. I do know your father, George. Your father’s name is George Stapleton. You’re Maddie,” turning to Traxx he added, “and you’re Traxx.” He studied Henry for a moment through the windshield. “I’m sorry, but I don’t know who you are.” He seemed troubled by this. “In fact, I’ve never seen you before in my life.”

Maddie slammed her palm down on the console. At first Henry thought she had shot the man outside, as did Traxx, but both were relieved when the side hatch opened instead.

Greeting him at the stairs with her rifle and leaving him to stand out in the swelling rain, Maddie asked, “Alright, talk. Who are you?”

The raggedy man kept his palms up and well within view. “Please don’t shoot. I don’t know my name, but I do remember my last job. I used to watch everything. I’m a sort of watcher. I can view any and every form of surveillance in all the lands. I’ve been watching you and your family for years. As have others. I know where your dad is and I can lead you to him.”

“You’re lying. My dad is dead,” Maddie shot back, her voice cracking. “If he were alive he would’ve come back for me already.”

Slightly delirious, the raggedy man held two fingers up higher than the rest, "Not true... not true..."

Maddie raised her rifle toward him for emphasis and ordered, "Tell me where he is. Tell me right now or I swear, mister, I *will* blow your head off."

Henry noted that even Traxx seemed a bit shocked by Maddie's swiftness to kill another human being. When Traxx saw Henry staring at him, he smirked, "You can see why we call her Mad-Maddie."

Henry whispered back, "I never wondered that. It's always been quite apparent." Leaning closer he whispered, "But I never thought she'd kill another human being."

When the raggedy man didn't answer fast enough Maddie shrieked, "Tell me right now or I'll cut you in half just like we did to all of your friends."

Hearing this, the raggedy man made a sour face, "Those things were *not* my friends. Those are scavengers. I was their prisoner. They only kept me alive because I could lead them to more parts and supplies."

Traxx frowned. "If you were their prisoner, how is it you were able to spy on us, on Maddie, and on her father?"

The raggedy man hesitated, and just when Henry thought he might actually be guilty of some sort of deception, he said, "How do you think I found the supply caches? The Misfits would allow me to access surveillance stations located around the parks. We would move from one supply cache to the next, while the Misfits replenished themselves," the raggedy man convulsed involuntarily from the memory, "I would watch you, and other members of the Dauntless, on your expeditions. " Smiling to Henry and Traxx he added, "It was better than television."

This seemed to placate Traxx for he leaned over to Maddie and whispered, "Maybe he's telling the truth."

Without taking her eyes, or her aim, from his head, Maddie whispered back, "He could have been spying on us; maybe heard us talking in the mall."

Surprisingly, Traxx didn't back down from Mad-Maddie this time. "We can't stay like this forever. We're running out of time, we've got to get back to The Dauntless."

Hearing this too, the raggedy man spoke up, "I can prove it. All I need is a monitor and an open line of communication."

"Oh goodie. You've picked up a stray." The Leftenant stepped out from behind Henry.

Maddie explained to her, "He says he's a watcher, and he says he can find my father."

The Leftenant regarding the raggedy man for a moment, seemed to be accessing some distant memory before saying, "If it's true, that he is in fact a watcher, he may not be the prevaricator he seems. He just might be capable of locating your father."

Maddie scoffed. "Since when do you trust anybody from Corporate?"

The Leftenant regarded the raggedy man with a raised eyebrow. "This man is clearly a low level worker. He's probably as much a victim as anyone."

Traxx thought this over. "The Hopper isn't equipped with that kind of communications array."

Maddie lowered her rifle. "No, but The Dauntless is."

The raggedy man nodded profusely. "It's true, I can. I can. Just get me to a monitor and I'll show you. But, we have to hurry."

"Why?" Maddie asked, suspicion still intertwined in her voice.

"Because when I saw him last, your father," again with the twitching fingers over his head, "he was entering the gauntlet, and the gauntlet is the one place from which no one has ever returned."

Little Alice fell

D

O

W

N

The hole, bumped her head and bruised her soul.

-Lewis Carroll

Alice in Wonderland

Chapter 26

Down the Rabbit Hole

Flailing his legs and arms, George screamed the entire way down.

After dropping for so long through the impenetrable darkness, it was almost a welcome relief when he finally hit water, even if it did feel like getting hit by a Mack truck.

After the impact, his body sank like a stone and carried him deep.

Instinctively, he clawed and kicked for the surface, popped out and gasped for air. Treading water, he coughed and spit in an attempt to clear his lungs of water.

As his eyes adjusted to the dim lighting, he found he had surfaced in a massive cavern. Behind him, a roaring twenty-foot waterfall cascaded down from a hole in the ceiling overhead and dumped into the pool George now occupied.

In a lot of ways, the subterranean grotto was quite beautiful. Gentle rays of sunlight sprinkled in from above and lit up the glowing, aquamarine pool like a distant lighthouse, gently illuminating a foggy mist. Opposite the raging waterfall laid a sandy beach cut out of a rocky outcropping. He swam for it. Once he got there, he crawled upon the shore.

Turning over onto his back, his clothes wet and heavy, he studied the ceiling over the grotto's pool once more. He tried to find the hole *he* dropped out of, but if it was there, he couldn't see it now. Like most entrances in Stranger World, it was cleverly concealed.

As usual, there was only one option to try. This time his only choice was to go deeper into the cave down a tubular tunnel nearby. Staring at its mouth and darkened interior, Jimmy Stewart's voice warned ominously, *'Oh, I wouldn't do that, Georgie-porgie.'*

"Shut up, Jimmy," he grumped, and left the sandy beach behind.

As he entered the narrow tunnel, crudely-made wooden torches mounted on the walls flickered to life upon approach. George tried removing one of the torches, but they were bolted into the rock and stuck fast.

The tunnel narrowed down to a point. Staring at it, George recalled this was what most folks in the military and law enforcement liked to call a *bottleneck* or a *chokepoint*, the perfect place for an ambush. George felt wary just looking at it, let alone walking through it.

The moment he did, he was assaulted by thunderous and violent winds. He automatically covered his head and face with his hands as the torrents of air emanating from narrow crevices battered him mercilessly. Eventually, he realized the forced air wasn't hurting him, so, he lowered his arms.

He stepped forward a few feet and the winds died down, his hair and clothes were completely dry. He thought he even detected a slight fragrance that reminded him of a fresh meadow.

Wow, talk about full service, he mused, humor always was his coping mechanism.

Exploring along the rocky tube-tunnel, he could see light up ahead and slowed his approach. Hugging his back to the wall, he slid along it until he could peer into the next chamber. It looked massive.

It was a subterranean tropical paradise with a primitive stone path weaving its way through beautifully colored trees. He gazed up at the ceiling. It had to be seventy feet high. *At least it appears that way,* George mused. *For all I know, it's just another hologram, and the ceiling is actually only about twelve feet high*. He resisted the urge to pick a rock up and hurl it skywards. For the time being, it didn't really matter.

Staring at the pathway of stones through the jungle, and remembering past encounters, he hopped from one stone to another to avoid potential booby-traps. This didn't last long however, for he missed one and overstepped another. Before long, he decided the pathway wasn't booby-trapped; for all he knew, the stones themselves were the actual trigger.

Much of the trail was overgrown and the thick underbrush to either side often brushed his shoulders. He soon came upon an opening on his left. It held a modest clearing surrounded by the same thick underbrush with a sheer rock face at its back.

Staring at the rock face at the back, he thought, *I wonder if I'm at the edge of the dome*.

Moving into the clearing, he spotted words, sloppily written on the back wall. The letters were in black paint over a circular hole that was about twice the width of a man's head. The words read:

Go No Further, Have No Fear
If you Must, Look in Here.

At the base of the wall, underneath the circular hole, was a crude, makeshift step stool. The idea was to step onto the stool and peer inside. George was about to do just that when he spotted something else in the clearing.

Off to one side was a man lying on the ground. He was wearing lightweight chainmail armor, leather gauntlets, and a thick garment with a hood (which would have been perfectly at home in the Fantasy Realm with the river running through it).

The man was also missing his head.

It had been taken clean off.

Studying the body, George could see the man was approximately six feet tall (assuming he had a normal-sized head, because thus far, one had not presented itself), and guessed him to be about 180 pounds. He knew this, because that was almost his height and weight exactly. Judging by the gruesome remains, this was obviously a real person and not some construct created here in Stranger World.

After checking for tripwires, he carefully moved over to the headless corpse and began searching him for weapons. Immediately apparent was the crossbow strapped to the dead man's back. George thought about going through the trouble of recovering it, but didn't see any bolts for the bow, so he opted to leave it behind. Most likely, the poor guy had lost his crossbow bolts back in the grotto when he fell in the pool. No other weapons were forthcoming.

You'd think he'd at least have a sword or something; maybe a dagger.

As he stood up, George had the most peculiar feeling that he was not the first person to stumble upon the clearing and search the knight for weapons. The more he scanned his surroundings, the more he got the sense that others had come before him. Taking in the clearing as a whole, George deduced the headless knight must have walked up to the rock face, followed the instructions written on the wall and peered inside. Once inside, something removed his head, *some sort of guillotine device perhaps?* The headless corpse then stumbled backwards to where he now lay.

George pitied the man and was reminded of *his* first day in Stranger World. He and Maddie had stumbled upon a sign, much like this one, in Lady Wellington's Fairy maze. They'd followed the sign's instructions only to find another, much deeper in the maze that read: *Ha! Fooled you!*

That about summed up what must have happened here, only this 'fooled you,' had cost this poor hapless knight his head. *But it still doesn't quite add up. If it had been a guillotine device in the hole, his body would have simply dropped right to the ground.* George studied the jungle floor more carefully. It was mostly grass, but he didn't see any drag marks. *It's almost as though something had tossed him here, something really-really strong.*

Keeping his distance, he slowly approached the circular hole and peered inside. A few feet within, glowing silvery eyes, imbedded in a slime-green colored snout, stared back at him. George's first thought was a *giant snake*, but as the creature slowly slithered a few inches out of its hole into the light, he'd say an eel was a more accurate description. The wall-eel slowly opened its mouth to display its multi-toothed jaws and then hissed at him.

"Time to go," George muttered to himself. He immediately backed up out of the clearing, never taking his eyes off the wall-eel already slithering back into the depths of its den.

With his only other option being to backtrack to the grotto, he decided to press on down the stony path. As he did so, there was something about the headless body that still bothered him; -something about the man's hands.

Before he could figure it out, he heard the sound of a babbling brook emanating up ahead. This was a welcome change because the saltwater back in the grotto, compounded by the oversized blow dryer, had really dried him out. He was becoming increasingly thirsty.

George came upon another break in the jungle, only this time it was to the right of the pathway. The creepy wall-eel still at the forefront of his mind, he approached cautiously.

At first glance, this second clearing seemed harmless enough; in its center was simply a cone shaped rock with cool water bubbling out of it. The water was so fresh, he swore he could smell the crispness. He took a step toward it and froze.

Near the base of the fountain, lying face down, was a man dressed in a drab green army coat. The jacket reminded him of the one he and Maddie had discovered in the massive hanger.

I wonder if we shopped at the same place?

How the man had died didn't take nearly as much guesswork to figure out. Given his close proximity to the water fountain, and his hands clenched around his throat, the man had obviously been poisoned by the bubbling fountain.

Like the headless-knight, the man was pretty close to his height and weight. After double-checking for traps, George decided to search the dead body for weapons. He grabbed the corpse by the shoulder and began to flip him over. Even before turning him completely over, George knew, for the back of the man's head was so familiar.

It was him.

George threw his wrist up to his mouth and swallowed the bile gathering there. Even with the obvious states of decay, George could see the man once looked just like him.

Well, sort of.

That version of himself had more gray in his hair and wore a full beard that was almost stark white. George also noted the dead man had several scars that he himself didn't possess. So maybe it wasn't him.

A clone, maybe?

Whoever he was, he was wearing the same army coat, canteen, belt and holster he and Maddie had found on their first day. *Had this man come the same way we had? And why does he seem so much older than me?* George guessed the dead man to be at least ten years older. On a whim, he checked the corpse for dog tags and was surprised when he found them. They were labeled correctly but they were of the W.W. II variety and not like his modern pair.

Getting back to the task at hand, he shook the heebie-jeebies off and began searching W.W. II-George (as he had come to think of him) for weapons. The leather holster was empty and the canteen was too much of a risk. The only thing he found that was worth anything was three, half-spent magazines, which when combined, made two full ones. He decided to take them in the off chance he came across the missing pistol later.

He was about to leave, but before doing so, he took the time to lay the W.W. II version of himself out on his back with his hands across his chest.

George patted the dead man on the chest. “Sorry about this, buddy.” It was a terrible way to die.

As he got up, George recalled the man in the medieval garments who was also the exact same height and weight as himself. He particularly remembered the man’s hands.

I’m not sure how much more of this I can take.

The Gauntlet

George’s sanity slipped a little more with each dead version of himself he had found along the way. The last one had been a scuba diver dressed in modern dive gear, which had been a lot nicer gear than he had now. “Scuba-George” had obviously been mauled by some vicious animal that thus far, remained unseen.

Each George thereafter had been killed in some clever booby-trap with each body left behind in various states of decay, some possibly as much as decades. He found Cowboy-George, Space Smuggler-George, and Pirate-George among others. Regardless of which version, it didn’t make any difference, they were all dead-Georges now.

He was hardly comforted by the fact that if these other Georges hadn't tripped the booby-traps before his arrival, he more than likely would have.

Hopefully, the builders of this place ran out of traps before they ran out of Georges. Otherwise, he would most likely fall victim to the next trap. *Does that mean one day another version of me will come along and find my body?* He recalled the words of Mrs. Belle, or was it young Henry? Something about how he was the last.

As much as he had wanted to bypass each clearing he came across, he took the time to deduce how each version of George had died. He did this to possibly learn something that might keep him from sharing the same fate and to search for any much needed weapons. He also made a rule for himself before entering each clearing; if he didn't immediately spot a dead-George in residence, he would not go into that clearing for fear of triggering another trap.

As he pressed on to the next clearing, George found himself wondering why no one had thought to simply walk straight down the path and avoid the clearings altogether. Then again, perhaps a version of him had tried that and failed, because otherwise, why would he be here now.

Sadly, with each additional clearing, he found nothing useful and learned nothing more than that he was most likely going to die in some tragic way.

How long have I been at this? At some point I'm going to have to eat and drink something. He had to push aside this new feeling of dread as another clearing came into view.

Like those before, it was smallish and was surrounded by dense, impenetrable foliage. (He had tried to penetrate it but found it impossible to get through.) The only difference was this clearing included a fancy banquet table, like the kind a king would feast upon. The table was surrounded by high-backed chairs and encircled by a multitude of sparkling treasure chests spilling with gold doubloons and precious gems. As George came closer, he could see even the plates and dinnerware were made of solid gold.

George was suddenly assaulted by savory smells of baked turkey with all the fixings, and fresh baked breads. But when he scanned the table for their sources, he found the food had all spoiled and rotted away years ago, leaving black dust behind.

Was this some kind of aroma special effect?

All of these observations took place in a matter of seconds, and it didn't take long to find the next dead-George. This time, he was sitting at the head of the table, in a chair higher than the rest, like a throne. For some reason, this dead-George bothered him the most. He wasn't really sure why.

This George version was dressed like a jungle explorer, with khaki shorts, laced-up boots and an Australian bush hat folded up on one side. The way Jungle-George was sitting on his throne, it looked like he had too much to drink and simply dropped down into his chair, smiled, and died. Jungle-George had both elbows resting on the armrests of his throne. His left hand was holding a gem-encrusted goblet, while his right hand pointed to something across the clearing.

George turned toward the direction Jungle-George was pointing and noticed an out of place object. It was a full-length mirror standing upright all by itself. It was positioned near a rock wall and merely reflected the banquet table and jungle surrounding it.

In the end, George realized there was no point in sticking around here any longer. The cause of death for Jungle-George was also quickly apparent: two arrows sticking out of his chest, *or are they crossbow bolts*? Regardless, whatever trap had been here, it had already been tripped, so he decided to press on.

Then he spied the gun.

It was lying on the table within easy reach of Jungle-George.

His old pal Jimmy Stewart decided to weigh in. 'What if that gun is the trap, Georgie-Porgie? Hmmmm? What if the moment you reach for that gun, ole Jungle-George leaps up outta his throne, picks up that pistol and shoots you with it?'

Jimmy may have a point.

Still, if the gun was actually loaded, it might come in handy later on.

Images of Scuba-George shredded to pieces by some wild animal instantly came to mind. Without stepping any closer, George studied dead Jungle-George and weighed his options. As he studied the corpse, he realized exactly why he hated this version of himself so much. It was the fact that Jungle-George was smiling, even in death. Clearly, this man had an easy-going nature, loved to laugh and lived every day as though it were his last. You could see all of that right there on his face. This was a guy everybody liked, who seemed to cruise effortless through life and everybody wanted as a friend. It was the carefree version of himself he had always coveted, and often tried to be, but eventually that version of him had to be cast aside for family, duty and country.

George weighed the risk of grabbing the pistol some more. Was it even worth it? The pistol was a revolver, most likely a .38. The .45 caliber rounds in his pocket wouldn't even fit in the cylinder. George spied several more loads scattered on the table.

Pistol and ammo, were all within easy reach.

Okay, here it goes.

After a tense few moments, he lunged forward and snatched the pistol. As soon as he did, he flipped it expertly around in his hand and aimed it at the dead explorer.

Jungle-George merely continued to smile that big dopey grin of his. George cracked open the cylinder and found all but one cartridge spent. Using the plunger, he dumped all the ammo out into the palm of his hand and reloaded the one good cartridge into the pistol, so it was next in line to fire. Keeping the .38 trained on Jungle-George with one hand, he scooped the loose rounds up into his left hand. His eyes flicked over the table to see if he had missed any, but he had not. Stepping back, he quickly loaded the full rounds into the cylinder. He now had a total of five good bullets.

At least that's something.

Snapping the cylinder closed with a flick of his wrist, he found himself wondering what happened here. All he knew for certain was Jungle-George had fired five times, and at some point, had frantically dropped fresh ammo on the table. Before he could reload, he was shot in the chest by two crossbow bolts.

By whom, the Knight I saw earlier?

Whatever the case, he was now armed. Not that the pistol had helped Jungle-George all that much. He thought about removing the belt and holster too, but George knew his limitations. His nerves were fried, and it had been hard enough just absconding with the gun.

Leaving the clearing behind, he went back out to the pathway, and pressed on. He didn't get twenty-five yards before he came to another sheer rock face, with no way up or out.

A dead end. Did I miss something? Maybe something back at the banquet table?

A horrible thought came to mind. What if there was no way out? What if this was a prison for Georges, plural. What if all the Georges who had come before, killed each other? Realizing he couldn't stay at the wall forever, he double-backed to the clearing with Jungle-George sitting at the banquet table.

Studying the scene once more, he failed to discover anything new. The table, the treasure, dead Jungle-George were all exactly the way he had left them. There was nothing else here, except for the mirror.

He studied the mirror more closely. It didn't take him long, and he wondered why he didn't see it before, but he soon realized, he had *no reflection.* The mirror reflected the table and treasure perfectly, but he, and Jungle-George, were oddly absent from the reflection.

He stretched out his hand to touch the mirror, and his hand passed through its frame. He quickly pulled his hand back. *It's not a mirror! It's a doorway to another clearing that looks exactly like this one.* If he wanted to continue onward, he would have to step through the fake mirror to get to the next room.

George had no way of knowing he was being observed.

He also had no way of knowing this was exactly what the builders of this place wanted. Once he stepped halfway through the mirror, a razor-sharp guillotine could split him in half. Future Georges (if there were any) would sadly refer to him as Split-George.

But there would be no further Georges, for Mrs. Belle was right. He was the last, and he would fail.

Pistol held out in front of him, George raised his boot to step through.

Management, and everyone else watching, could not have been happier.

Chapter 27

Maddie, George and the Watcher

"Dad! Stop!"

It was a voice George knew as well as his own. It was his daughter, Maddie. *But why can't I see her?* He scanned the interior of the mirror room and then the clearing he had just left behind. Not seeing his daughter in either place, he cried, "Maddie! Where are you?"

His daughter's disembodied voice shouted back, "Dad, don't move! Don't take another step."

George had one foot through the fake mirror (the one that was really a doorway) and stood as stock still as a soldier standing on a landmine.

But what if the voice is a trick? he wondered. "How do I know it's you?" He purposely didn't say his daughter's name.

George heard a heavy sigh, "Dad, it's me. Mom's name is Tessa. Your best friend's name is Rick."

Anybody could know those things, he thought. Then she thought of something else.

"I had a cat named Lucy, but you called her Smelly Cat."

George heard himself exclaim, "Maddie!" He searched the area for his daughter again and asked, "Why can't I see you? Where are you?"

Half-crying, Maddie managed, "We're on the Dauntless, Dad. You've been gone for so long. I thought you were *dead*."

Hearing his daughter so distraught was beyond painful, and he felt his own cheeks moisten with tears. "I'm so sorry, Baby-girl. I've missed you. Are you alright? Who is with you?"

He heard Maddie sniff loudly before answering, "Everybody's here, Dad." She cleared her voice and added, "We found a watcher," she must've realized he wouldn't have understood and quickly explained, "He's a former park employee who can tap into all forms of surveillance systems. He helped us find you."

Something was wrong. Even distraught, her voice sounded so different, deeper somehow. "Maddie, why do you sound so... strange?"

There was a long pause. He thought he heard distant voices discussing something, then he heard Maddie's voice once more. "Dad, you've been missing for the last three years. Everyone thought you were dead."

"Three years? Maddie, you're fourteen?!"

She came back on, "None of that matters right now. We can talk about it later. All you need to know is that you're in incredible danger! The moment you step all the way into that room, a door is going to seal you up inside, and you will never be able to escape."

"Did this watcher tell you that?" George asked.

"Affirmative."

"Do you believe him."

(Another long pause)

"Yes. We rescued him from a band of Misfits, and we couldn't have found you without his help."

George nodded. It was a weird knowing they could see him, but he couldn't see them. He imagined Maddie sitting in the communications room aboard The Dauntless, a microphone to her lips with everyone crowded around her. "Okay, what do you want me to do? Talk me through it."

Maddie answered, "Carefully, back-out the way you came in."

George did as he was told and found himself back in the clearing. If Maddie could see the dead Jungle-George, she didn't mention it, and he wasn't about to bring it up.

"The watcher says, if you double back to some grotto, he thinks he can lead you out from there." Maddie was sounding hopeful.

George recalled the pool he had fallen into and said, "Copy that, I know the exact place." He reached the path and stopped.

Maddie must've seen him hesitate, for she asked, "Dad! What are you doing? I said, turn to your left and walk down the path."

George knew he couldn't go back without accomplishing the mission first.

"Dad, did you hear me? Turn to your *left* and head down the path."

"Maddie? Ask the watcher if anybody else is down here with me?"

(A pause)

"The watcher said you're the only living thing down there, Dad."

George thought about it some more. I must have missed something. A hidden room, something further underground. "Ask the watcher if I'm near any hidden rooms."

(Another pause, this one longer)

"He says there is a rock wall down the path to the *right* and something behind it, but he can't tell what it is."

George jogged back to the wall. *There has to be a secret door or something.*

"Dad, Uncle Rick and The Leftenant say they got a fix on your position. It will take a couple of days, but we're on our way to pick you up."

"That's great, honey," George said, studying the wall for clues.

Maddie observed her dad's actions closely on the monitor. "What are you doing, Dad? You have to go the other way now."

"Maddie, see if the watcher can open the door."

(Another pause, this one the longest yet.)

"Dad, the watcher said to *stand back*."

George did as he was told and not a second later, a vertical pool of water about the size and shape of a doorway appeared on the rock wall before him.

This has to be it!

George took a step closer to it, and Maddie panicked.

"Dad! Where are you going? Listen, the watcher says he has *no idea* what will happen if you step through there. It might even *kill you!*"

"Maddie, I'm sorry, but I don't have time to explain. I think this is the reason I was summoned down here." He left out the part about all the other dead-Georges who had failed to get far enough to find this watery doorway. Of course, this could just be another trap.

"No matter what happens, I love you."

"No Dad!" Maddie screamed. "NO! Go back to the grotto. I can't lose you again."

George bit his lip. "You... you won't lose me. Come get me, Baby-girl. I just have to do this thing first."

He could hear Maddie screaming-mad in the background when The Leftenant's proper English voice cut in, "We've got a fix on your location, sir. We're coming to pick you up."

"No, dad! NO!"

"I love you Baby-girl. See you soon."

The moment George stepped through, the connection was broken. Just before it was gone, he thought he heard Maddie scream three vile words.

"The Lamppost Man!"

Chapter 28

George & the Old Man

"Tessa!"

George was dreaming again.

(It was the one where Tessa was standing on the outside of the railing of the Dauntless in midflight at midnight.)

Tessa...

His wife pushes her hand through her hair, feels his presence, looks up, and smiles sweetly back at him.

A man is shouting. George is pretty sure it's himself. He lunges forward, his hands outstretched toward his wife, who even now is falling away from him.

"Tessssa!"

Automated words, "Bomb Detected," blare through loud-speakers repeatedly.

Two men (Michael and Doc, he thinks) are holding him tightly on each arm.

"Let me go. I have to save her."

Michael, "You can't."

Doc, "George, she's trying to save us, she's trying to save us all."

A massive explosion emanating from below, knocks them all backwards, away from the railing.

The love of his life is gone.

Engineer Rick pops out of a nearby hatch, stares at the abandoned deck where Tessa was standing only moments ago. Then he looks down at him and asks, "George, what have you done?"

The Prison

George opened his eyes.

No longer in a subterranean tropical paradise, he was now lying on his back inside an octagonal shaped room, heavy with concrete and absolutely nothing on the walls, floor or ceiling.

A prison cell?

If there was a door, George couldn't see it. He got to his feet and as he moved about the cell, more lights snapped on illuminating more blank walls and one very old man.

The man had to be in his eighties, perhaps even nineties. He was sitting against the wall with his lanky legs drawn up and his wrists resting on kneecaps. His stark white hair hung to his shoulders. Surprisingly, he was dressed in a tattered hip-length ringmaster's coat, his ratty top hat was lying next to him.

Is this man the reason I'm here?

"Hello, Sir," George began.

No response.

"Excuse me, my name is George Stapleton What's your name?

No answer.

"I think I'm supposed to rescue you now."

Nothing.

"Are you ok, sir?" Maybe he's deaf or dead.

George looked closer to see if the old man was still breathing. The guy's chest rose and fell, if only slightly. Kneeling down next to him, George waved a hand in front of the old man's open eyes to see if he was blind.

No response. *Or, was there a flicker in his eye just now? Was he hypnotized?*

He snapped his fingers. "Wake up. Hell-o… anybody home?"

George bobbed his head lower and tried to get the old timer to lift his eyes. "I'm talking to you, buddy. Wake up. We have to get going now." *What a big fat waste of time.*

The subdued old timer didn't move, except for the twitch of a single little finger.

It was as though he was turned off and now trying to re-boot.

Without warning, the old fellow whispered something.

"What?" George quickly asked. He tilted his better-hearing ear toward the old man's lips. "What did you say, Mister?"

The man wheezed in the effort and in a reedy voice asked, "What generation are you?"

What generation am I? Is this important?

Then, remembering earlier conversations he had with Sophia Davenport and The Leftenant about clones, he realized the old man wanted to know if he was a biological. After seeing all the other-Georges back there, he wasn't entirely sure anymore, and didn't know how to answer him.

The old man lifted his eyes to meet his. The eyes were a faded light blue, but there was a history behind those eyes, a long one.

The old man took in another wheezy breath, but deeper and stronger than before.

"Do you know your serial number?" George squinted and shook his head.

He watched as the man stared deeper into his eyes and gazed upon his soul. George held his stare as the old man's eyes suddenly widened, as if in recognition of an old friend.

"Oh my, you're an original, aren't you? Not a biological, nor even a clone... but a real live human being." The old man tore his gaze away, for which George was grateful.

He smiled then coughed, shook his head and croaked, "Boy, they must really be getting desperate to send an original down here to me."

George considered the fact that he wasn't a clone (like all the other dead-Georges back there) by allowing it to sink in for a moment. He nodded his head slightly in approval.

The old man, growing stronger by the second, rose to his feet.

Still a little doubtful, George asked, "How do... how do you know I'm not a clone?"

The old man, now studying the wall, seemed annoyed by the distraction of the question and answered George without looking at him, "Trust me. You're not a clone."

It simply wasn't good enough. Not after all the things he had seen. "Yes, I believe you. But how do you *know*?"

The old man pursed his lips, turned toward him and asked impatiently, "What color is your shirt?"

George shook his head. "What?"

The old man exhaled, this time without wheezing. Irritably, he asked George again, "What color is your shirt? Tell me."

Great. I've rescued a lunatic.

When George didn't answer quickly enough, the old man asked grumpily, "Do you want to know if you're a clone or don't you?"

"Fine. Blue," George blurted out. Suddenly, realizing the importance of his answer, he held his lucky over-shirt between a thumb and forefinger and added, "dark blue."

Tessa would be so proud.

The old man held his palms out to him, "Ya see, you're not a clone." He returned to studying the wall again.

"What's that prove?" George questioned. Shaking his head, he said, "That doesn't prove anything."

Like an inmate in an insane asylum, the old man began pushing invisible buttons in the air. "Why sure it does. Clones are color blind. We build them that way on purpose."

The old man turned a non-existent dial and flicked an equally invisible switch. "Ah, there we go." He punched a final invisible button, and a section of the wall magically slid into the floor, vanishing as though it never existed in the first place.

George's felt his face flush with rage, "If you could open the door all this time, why did you wait until now?"

The old man peeked his head out of the doorway like a woodland creature about to leave the safety of its den. Still studying the outside without actually stepping into it, he responded, "Opening it was easy, but I needed someone to unlock it from the outside first." He smiled to himself, gazed back at George and said, "Thank you for that by the way, my friend."

You're not welcome George thought to himself, as he gave him a fake smile and a couple half-hearted nods.

There were so many questions George wanted to ask, maybe now was his chance. Which one first? He settled for asking, "Who are you?" The old man waved him off with a weathered hand.

"No time for that now. We've got to get out of here before it's too late."

The old timer went to step into the hallway, but George caught him by the crook of his arm and held him fast. "A lot of people died trying to spring you out of here. I think the least you can do is tell me your name."

The old man jerked his arm out of George's grasp. *Pretty spry for an old man.* To his surprise, the old timer held his gaze for a moment longer and said, “My name’s Henry. Henry Stranger. I built this god-forsaken place. Now quit asking so many fool questions and start moving so we can get out of here.”

George followed him into a corridor he didn’t remember coming into. “Why are you here? That is to say, I mean, who locked you up down here?”

The old man’s face soured. “No one locked me in here. I locked myself up in here.”

Incredulous, George repeated, “You locked yourself in on purpose?”

Henry stopped walking, stared at him again, “Are you sure you’re not a biological? You seem pret-ty slow on the uptake.”

George gave him a curt, forced laugh. “Hey! You have no idea what I’ve been through getting down here. But, let’s just say it’s been a very long day.”

The old man sighed in frustration and said, “Very well, but if we get caught, I’ll blame you.”

George raised his eyebrows at him and said, “I’ll risk it.”

“Very well, George. I knew it was only a matter of time before management was going to kill me. I knew there was no place on the planet I would be safe.”

“So, you locked yourself in the basement?”

The old man patted his chest two times. "You think this old husk is really me?" When George didn't answer he continued, "No. The real Henry Stranger was in fact, murdered a long, long time ago. This," patting himself again, "this is merely a simple facsimile; a mere shadow of my former self."

"I know the feeling," George mumbled, but if old man Henry heard him, he didn't show it. Catching up with him, George took notice of the old man's clothes and asked, "Your clothes, they're just like the Lamppost Man's getup."

"What's your point?" the old man asked grumpily.

What was his point? Are the two related? Or was there a big sale on ringmaster coats at the gift shop?

One thing was for certain, the Lamppost Man was no friend of his. At least he didn't think so. On the other hand, the Lamppost Man did give him a couple piles of nicely folded clothing when he had none. He also made sure he had that multi-tool which allowed them to escape the zombie-pirate-king's dungeon that time. He may be a jerk, but he did spell SORRY in the sky once. (As if that made up for the raft incident)

Continuing to walk briskly, Henry must have sensed George's conflicting thoughts for he reluctantly explained, "I created the Lamppost Man Program to serve management while subverting it at the same time."

"Why would you do that? Why would you want to destroy management?" George asked.

Henry scoffed so hard he started choking on his own spit. "Why destroy management? Who do you think killed off the human race?"

"Huh? I was told we killed each other."

Henry gave him a swift glance, but never broke stride. "Who told you that? No wait, someone who works for the company? Some midlevel-to-upper management, maybe?"

George never really knew Dr. Sophia Davenport's rank, but it was obvious she was someone important. *Sophia said we had killed ourselves off, didn't she? Maybe that was a guess, either that or maybe she was lying.* He doubted the latter. George didn't give Henry the benefit of an answer so instead he asked, "If management was as bad as you say, why not just destroy them?"

"Even a man from the 21st century must have some semblance of an idea of how massive Stranger World is."

George didn't feel as though he did. The underground tunnels alone were immense, but he still thought of this place as being isolated, like in a desert or on an island. *Didn't Sophia say something about in her time, there had been dozens of domed theme parks the size of cities? And, this was centuries after that.*

"Without management, there would be total chaos. I needed a surgical tool that would cut out the cancer in management without killing it off completely. I reprogrammed the Lamppost Man for that very purpose."

"Isn't the Lamppost Man evil?"

"When I *first* created the Lamppost Man, he was little more than a weapon, a complex virus if you will." He stopped, studied George for a moment and asked, "In your time, you had computer viruses, yes?"

George flashed him a dirty look. "Yes, of course."

"Hey, don't get so offended; I can't remember everything. Where was I anyway? Oh yes, the Lamppost Man. I believed I wasn't going to be around much longer. So, I made a snap judgement and made the mistake of giving ole' Lampy his independence, the ability to learn and even to perpetuate himself. Once I did that, he evolved and kept on evolving. So, the Lamppost Man is about as good and evil as any other self-replicating species."

George's eyes narrowed as he recalled all the pain and suffering that imp had cost him and his family. "Oh trust me. He's evil. And, that's why he has to be destroyed."

Old Henry grabbed him by his elbow and stopped. "I agree completely. He's grown totally out of control. But not before the two of you, together, destroy the cancer that is within management. It's the only possible way." Henry let that sink in.

"However, I need you to be very clear on something. The only thing keeping the Lamppost Man in check and from becoming totally omnipotent is management. You take that away, and ole' Lampy becomes a god."

That's not good, thought George. Henry continued.

"So, the moment upper management is disabled, you have to kill the Lamppost Man, or he will unleash a reign of madness and terror that makes all this seem like a Sunday-school carnival by comparison."

If he wasn't feeling it before, he was beginning to feel very overwhelmed now. George let out a calming breath. "Okay, I hear you. But how about we focus on one thing at a time. Before we take on a planet-sized theme park. Why don't we just focus on finding a way out of here first?"

Old man Henry leaned on a cleverly disguised crash-bar, cracked the door open and replied, "After you, my good man," and tipped his hat.

Chapter 29

Kelpi & the Goons

"Will you at least try to keep up?" old man Henry grumped.

Henry seems pretty spry for an octogenarian who has been locked up (or powered down) for a few centuries.

Old Henry's prison cell emptied onto the trail near the banquet table. When Henry spied Jungle-George slouched at the table, he uttered, "Oh no."

George's grip on his pistol grew tighter, but he failed to see any attackers.

"What? What is it?" He remembered the animal-ravaged Scuba-George and suddenly became very mindful of the fact he only had *five* bullets.

Henry nodded toward the jungle explorer. "Oh my, poor, poor Jungle-George. I always liked him best. It's such a shame he didn't make it."

Feeling a tad bit offended, George said, "Maybe you'd like to keep waiting for him back in your prison cell?"

Henry didn't hear the jibe, or he simply chose to ignore it. Instead, he began patting down Jungle-George's pockets. When he didn't find what he was looking for, he asked, "Did you find the knife?"

George only recalled finding the pistol. Hefting it for Henry to see he said, "Nope. No knife this time, only the gun."

Henry sighed heavily. "It's not an *actual* knife," and becoming more irritable (were that possible) he added, "I told you before, you have to find the knife. When you were in the jungle, you didn't find it? I hid it in the cave for you." When George didn't answer quickly enough, Henry bawled, "You had *one* job."

Oh boy...the cranky old man's clearly off his rocker.

"You never told me about any knife, and I have never been in any jungle in Stranger World," George explained matter-of-factly, then added, more to himself, "At least not in one I remember, anyway."

The old fella heard him this time for he said, "Oh, you'd remember *this* jungle. That I guarantee."

George's patience was beginning to wear thin, but he managed, "I'm sorry, but we never had any conversation about a hidden knife."

Henry pounded the table causing the china to clatter. "We did too! We talked about all of this already. The knife is the only thing that can kill him."

"Kill who?"

Henry flashed him a look that clearly said he thought he was speaking to an imbecile. "The Lamppost Man of course. What have we been talking about this whole time?" Without looking back at him, he said, "You'll have to go back to the jungle for it. It's in a cave."

The old timer was working himself up so much that George was worried he might keel over from a heart attack. "All right. I promise to go back to the jungle and find the..." but before he could even finish his sentence, Henry strode purposefully over to him and tapped him on the forehead with one forefinger and said, "Boop."

George couldn't explain it exactly, but it was as though Henry had put something inside of his brain. Rubbing his forehead profusely, and remembering that the Lamppost Man had implanted a multi-tool in his stomach, he inquired with a bit of rage, "What did you just do to me?"

Old Henry waved him away, and responded, "Don't worry about it, you'll find out later," and strode out of the clearing. Calling back from the trail, he hollered, "C'mon, we've to get topside."

Henry led him through another hidden door and into an elevator shaped like a bathysphere with thick-paned windows. In the time it took George to explain how he had gotten down to the prison in the first place (the dive, the town and subterranean maze) they had arrived back in the Welcome Center.

Exiting the bathysphere George grumbled, "Ya know, you could have let Kelpi tell me about the express elevator down to the prison."

Henry flashed him a cynical smile. "Now where's the fun in that?"

Kelpi, the Helpful Mermaid, swished through the air to greet them. "Yay!" she said clapping her hands enthusiastically, "You found him, George. Congratulations! I'm so proud of you." Then to Henry she said formerly, "Welcome back Mr. Stranger. We've been waiting for your return for a very long time, sir."

Henry surveyed all the recent damage in the Welcome Center. To no one in particular he breathed, "Has it really gotten as bad as all this?"

Seeing Henry's pain-stricken face, Kelpi offered, "Cheer up, Mr. Stranger, nothing a little paint and good ole fashion elbow grease can't fix."

"Well, it's about time!"

George, Old-Man Henry, and Kelpi all lifted their gaze to see stocky Sven from the submarine approaching them. Nearly a dozen of his submarine crew came in behind him.

Seeing this too, Henry rolled his eyes, "Oh right, I almost forgot." Turning to Kelpi he asked, "Why does there always have to be goons involved?"

Kelpi clasped her hands and shrugged her shoulders. "Makes life more interesting, I guess."

Sven and his goons crossed over and formed a wide circle around them. Whatever it was they wanted, it was clear from their body language, they were willing to take it by force. Most of the goons were dressed like submarine crew-man, but one of them was dressed like the bounty hunters he had seen on the Fantasy River. George was pretty sure another goon was a zombie pirate. Sven, himself, was what George liked to call, *a real lady's man*: sweaty, bald head, crooked nose and protuberant eyes. George didn't see the Italian woman from the sub anywhere.

Studying Henry, but speaking about him as though he wasn't there, Sven said, "Do you know how long we've been waiting for one of you to free the old man? Do you have any idea?" He turned toward Kelpi. "How long we been waiting, mermaid?"

Ever helpful (even to villains) she answered, "Two hundred years, thirty-eight days, twelve hours, sixteen minutes and forty-eight seconds."

Hearing this, Sven raised his bushy-unkempt eyebrows and said to his crew, "Did you all get that?" Sven moved closer to George, withdrew a long knife and began tapping it on George's chest. "What makes you so special, anyway, huh Georgie?" Raising his voice louder for the rest of his crew to hear, "Ya know, My money had been on the Jungle-George. I liked that one the best...I really thought he was gonna go all the way."

Old Henry flashed George a toothy smile, "See what I mean? I'm not the only one."

George shook his head. Henry obviously didn't realize the gravity of the situation. They may have escaped from prison, but in a few moments, Sven was going to knife him in the gut and cut Henry's *short*-lived freedom *very short*."

George feigned boredom. What do you want with us, Sven?"

"You? Nothing." Raising his knife toward Henry he said, "It's Mr. Henry Stranger we want. You're looking at the most wanted man on the planet. Management's got a huge bounty on him that will set us all up like kings for centuries."

Turning his gaze back toward George he added, "We'll be taking him now, but there's no reason for us to kill you too. In fact, if you just step aside, there might even be a little reward in it for ya. Whaddya say?"

George hated bullies. His first fight in elementary school had been over a bully pushing down a young girl named Julie Cash. In fact, most of his fights had been about defending the defenseless against bullies.

In answer, he wiped the sweat from his brow on the back of his arm, "You know, as much as I'd like to let you guys take my new cranky friend here off my hands, I went through a lot of trouble to get him. In fact, I counted at least 12 versions of George down there in that labyrinth who died just to get him out. I don't know what's so important about this old timer, but I'd be remiss to let you just have him after so much trouble."

This didn't go over well with Sven, but he managed to keep his composure. "George, you've already died so many times. You don't have to do it again. You can go live your life.

"Stranger World," pointing to Henry for emphasis, "his world, is a dangerous and scary place, but it also can be a lovely one. There are so many places you could go. Reunite with your family. Live out your life in a cottage on a hill somewhere. I've seen people do it. They find a little corner somewhere, live out their lives, nobody bothers them, and everyone is happy."

George flicked his eyes over to the bounty hunter, "Like the ransacked village on the Fantasy River? Or the sunflowers with human faces? Or what about all those people who were killed by the leviathan on the sub?" He shook his head and continued.

"I haven't known this man for very long, but I don't think this world was what this man intended. This madness, what this place has become? If the little bit of humanity left is going to survive, it has to stop. And I'm not sure, but this man just might be the key. You could be part of that change, Sven. You don't have to serve Management anymore. You don't have to be a part of it. You could join us. You could join the fight."

CLAP...CLAP...CLAP...

Sven, tucked his knife in his armpit, and slow-clapped his hands sardonically. "That was... terrific." Casting a glance at Kelpi, he asked, "Don't you think that was terrific?"

Kelpi nodded enthusiastically. "Most impressive." She pouted her lips. "I'm sorry I didn't warn you, George. I couldn't."

Sven grabbed his knife again by the handle. Gesturing toward George with it, he said, "You know, I was wrong about you. I can see why the Lamppost Man chose you. You are one single-minded, stubborn-headed mule. You set your mind to something and that's it. You're a soldier, alright. Well, you know the old saying, 'There are old men, and there are heroes, but there are never old heroes." Sven raised his knife and began to lunge with it.

A single shot rang out. Sven stood up ramrod straight, and fell over with a smoking bullet hole in his forehead.

George fired four more times and four more submarine crewmen permanently hit the deck. Not realizing he was out of ammo, a few of the submariners dove for cover, but the zombie shuffled toward him. George flipped the pistol up into the air, caught it by its scalding barrel and clubbed him over the head with it. Skull crushed, the zombie fell to the floor with the pistol still imbedded in its head.

Having lost his gun, George picked up Sven's knife and tossed it to Henry, handle first. It bounced off old Henry's chest and hit the ground.

Seeing this George asked, "What are you doing? Pick up the knife."

Henry calmly explained, "Wrong knife."

George sighed in disgust. *I guess I'm on my own,* was what George was thinking when the two bounty hunters dog-piled onto him, knocking all three of them over a display wall. As he used various undersea displays to smash into his attackers (a starfish, a spent spear gun and swordfish), he spied Henry.

"Hey! I could use a little help over here." When the old man didn't move, George took another blow to the face. George flipped his attacker over the wall and shouted to Henry, "I wouldn't want you to strain your old self."

Two more crewmen crept from their hiding places and, after seeing George was preoccupied with the bounty hunters, they began pursuing Henry.

Seeing this too, Kelpi took several swipes at them, "Stay back you brigands. Don't make me angry," but being a hologram, her fists and tail merely passed through them.

As soon as the cowering crewmen realized she was powerless, they stalked their original target once more, dollar signs returning to their eyes.

George began climbing back over the partition, but the bounty hunters recovered from their attack and each took a leg of his, and pulled.

Hands holding onto the partition wall, and stretched out like Superman in midflight, George screamed, "Run Henry, run!"

Despite Kelpi's best efforts, the two submariner henchmen backed Henry all the way up into a nearby corridor. Before they could nab him however, Henry opened a panel where none existed before. He touched a few buttons and sprinklers dropped down from the ceiling and began soaking the two men with very cold water.

"That is it?" one of them asked. Shrugging his shoulders, he stepped forward again.

As the brigand approached him, Henry touched another button and a cabinet door opened so violently against the attacker's face, it knocked him out and onto his back.

Kelpi clapped her hands. "Oh, that was simply wonderful, just wonderful." She turned to Henry expectantly. "Do something else."

Old Henry waggled his eyebrows, turned back to the console and punched in more code.

Kelpi looked around expectantly, waiting for something to transpire and when it didn't, she said, "Ahh, nothing happened."

Henry smiled a toothy smile. "Try hitting one of them."

"Okay, but..." Kelpi swam off toward the second brigand and when close enough, with a violent twist of her body, she swatted him with her tail.

The man might as well have been hit by a city bus, for he went flying feet-over-head and landed upside-down thirty feet away.

Smiling devilishly back at Henry she said, "Oh, we're going to have some fun now." She immediately swished back out into the open area and wreaked havoc on the remaining submariners. All the while, she kept chanting things like, "Hi there, I'm Kelpi the Helpful Mermaid," TWACK! and "Here at

Stranger World, we like to offer service with a smile," THWOCK! Even the two bounty hunters, who were busy pummeling George, were soon field kicked over the nearest aquarium.

Seeing them land and not move, Kelpi exclaimed to George, "Wow, that was incredibly fun." Realizing she had dispatched all the evil submariners she pouted her lips and said, "Awww... no more baddies."

Henry helped George to his feet. "You alright young man?"

Feeling far from it, George grumped, "What are you talking about? I had them right where I wanted them." Then spying Kelpi, he added, "Thanks for the assist, Helpful Mermaid."

Kelpi clasped her hands in front of her and shrugged her shoulders. "You're most welcome, George."

Henry studied the Welcome Center once more, "Now that's out of the way, we need to get you to the surface."

One eye swollen shut and his lip still bleeding, George responded. "I don't see how. Even if we didn't have to worry about that dino-fish out there, I used the last of the dive equipment. There's no way for us to swim back up."

"Swim?" the old man asked incredibly. "Why would wouldn't you just take the elevator?"

"Elevator?" George repeated. He gritted his teeth while shaking his head, "That might've been nice to know on the way down here."

Kelpi shrugged, "Sorry, rules are rules."

Unlike the round-shaped bathysphere, this elevator was shaped like a flying disc. After it shot out of the ocean like a UFO, the walls cracked open like a blooming water lily, revealing fresh open air. The platform continued upwards on a telescoping pylon until they were about 70 feet above the ocean surface. George felt the wind on his face and through his hair. It felt good to be out in fresh air again.

He noted Henry at a control station, and how the old man grimaced when he moved. It was clear Henry was in a lot of pain and most likely dying. Kelpi continued to swim around the elevator's edges, marveling at the beauty surrounding them.

George watched him check his controls. "I've set up a homing signal for your friends. They're already on their way to pick you up."

Hearing this, George tilted his head to the side, "You mean to pick us up?"

Henry shook his head. "No, I'm not going with you. There's too much for me to do." The old man seemed to regard him for a moment as though flattered he had asked.

"But you're hurt. We've got a doctor who can help you."

"What, this body?" Henry clapped his chest. "This is nothing. Besides if you think I'm going to let a goofball like Dr. Bob operate on me, you've got another thing coming." The way he said it, George could tell they were old friends. Henry confirmed this when he said, "Tell Bob I said 'hi' by the way, when you see him."

Then, as though it had only just occurred to him, Henry said, "Oh, that reminds me, one more thing." Henry removed an ornate silver key dangling from a chain around his neck. "Give this to my son when you see him. He's the only one who can use it."

"Your son? You mean the Lamppost Man?"

Henry frowned. "No. Not that abomination. He is not my son." He pointed a gnarled finger at him. "You'd be wise to steer clear of him until you find that knife."

"I know, I know, the knife in the jungle, it's the only thing that can stop him."

Henry smiled at this, turning to Kelpi he said, "And, you said he couldn't be taught."

Kelpi only shrugged her shoulders in response.

"If the Lamppost Man isn't your son, then who is? How will I know him when I see him?"

"Don't you worry; he'll know what this is when he sees it. He's the only one who can use it so don't even bother trying to use it yourself."

Henry tapped another button and a circular hole, about the width of his shoulders appeared next to the console.

"When will I see you again?"

"When you are meant to. Until then..."

Old man Henry jumped up into the air over the hole, slammed his arms to his side like a penguin, dropped down into the abyss feet first, and was gone.

Kelpi began to follow.

"Wait, Kelpi, you can come with us?"

Kelpi stopped her retreat and gazed back at him for a moment. "That's sweet of you to ask, George." She gazed down the hole, and then back at him one last time. "But Henry's weak. Until he regains his strength he's going to need me. But don't worry, I'm sure we'll see each other again very soon." She swam closer to the hole, was about to dive in head-first, but then stopped and looked at him one last time. "I'm glad you made it, George." With that said, she too had vanished.

Were it not for the key, George would have found himself wondering if Henry Stranger and Kelpi had ever existed in the first place.

George was alone once more. As he waited for the Dauntless to arrive, he sat down on the edge of the elevator's platform. Letting his legs dangle over the side, he swung them back and forth in open air and his thoughts drifted toward his wife.

Tessa, I miss you.

Staring out over the vast ocean, he thought he could almost detect her presence. It was as though if he turned around right now, she would be there. He decided not to turn around and enjoy the feeling for a bit longer. Instead he focused on the shrinking sun.

You would have enjoyed this.

It was the most beautiful sunset he had ever seen.

Chapter 30

The Lamppost Man Cometh!

"Come with me and no one has to die."

Maddie pulled on the raggedy man's white gloved hand. "Let me go," then remembered, *Wait a minute, the raggedy-man wasn't wearing gloves earlier.* Peering up at him she saw the raggedy man no longer existed. In his place was the one her parents had warned her about, the man everyone steered clear of, and talked about only in hushed nervous tones... the Lamppost Man. *That's right, I remember now. He was in the communications room. Why am I so confused? How did we get to the back of the ship?*

They were now aft, above deck and in the open air. The gilded elevators were in their stables. She guessed that's where they were headed. *That'd be a big mistake*, she thought. Maddie knew that even if the Lamppost Man could override the safety measures in place and lower one of the elevators, it would be suicide to do so, while traveling over the ocean waves as fast as they were now. Which was why he surprised her by dragging her past the elevators and over to the railing on the starboard side of the ship. He threw her roughly to the deck, took out his pocket watch and frowned when he checked the time. Tsking to himself he muttered, "Late, late, late. Always late." He snapped the lid closed between a thumb and forefinger and replaced the pocket watch in his vest.

Staring up at him, Maddie cried, "Why are you doing this?"

The Lamppost Man seemed startled for a moment; as though he forgot she was there. Whether this was an act or not, she had no way of knowing. He answered her, "We're going on a little adventure, you and me. With your parents no longer in the picture, I think you'll quite enjoy it."

Maddie's fear was replaced with a rush of anger. "You shut up about my parents. My dad is alive, and he's coming for me!"

The Lamppost Man, rolling his eyes, cut her off by saying, "Yes, yes, yes, we've all heard this before." Mocking the way she spoke, he said, "My name is Maddie, and my dad is going to beat you up, blah-blah-blah." He purposefully stuck his tongue out on the last blah.

Resuming his countenance once more, he gazed across the distant ocean, and said, "Trust me, my dear Maddikins, by the time The Dauntless reaches your dad, we'll be long gone. After a time, you won't care about him anymore." Turning toward her, and leering his face in front of hers, he asked, "Won't that be nice? Hmmm?"

Maddie refused to give up hope, not when she was so close to seeing her Dad again. She grabbed the railing and pulled herself up slowly. She pretended being weak long enough to throw the Lamppost Man off guard, spun around violently with fist clenched and...

THWOCK!

The Lamppost Man actually stumbled back a few steps holding his nose. Pinching it, he asked in a nasally voice, "My, my. I think you broke my nose. Where in the world did you ever learn to punch like that young lady?"

Sticking her chin out at him and fists still clenched, Maddie shot back, "My dad taught me."

The Lamppost Man released his nose and checked his gloved hand for blood. Finding a few droplets, he sneered as he said, "Oh... George." He dusted off his gloved hands and Maddie was pretty sure the blood was now gone. "Well, I'm going to show you how to hurt people in a lot more interesting ways than clubbing them with your fists like some barbarian."

Maddie shook her head. "I'll never join you."

The Lamppost Man's eyebrow arched high. "I can see I'm going to have to teach you a bit of manners first." The imp pushed up his sleeves, flashed her a menacing look, and took a step toward her.

Frightened, Maddie tripped on her own feet dodging backwards and fell against the railing for support.

"Come-come now, Maddiekins. Time to take your medicine like a good girl."

Maddie shook her head. Scanning the deck for a place to retreat, she only saw the gilded elevators behind her, and they were too far.

She was trapped.

"Step away from the girl." The loud baritone voice echoed above the wind.

Maddie lifted her eyes to see Uncle Rick, Henry, and several other members of the crew coming toward them with weapons in their hands.

The Lamppost Man seemed amused, when he asked, "Are those metal guns?"

"Yeah, and wait until you see what's in them," Rick growled back. Spotting Maddie behind him, Rick asked her, "Maddie, are you okay?"

She nodded that she was, but even as she did this, the Lamppost Man removed a ridiculously large magnet from his coat.

First Rick's gun flew out of his hand, and then the rest of the crews' weapons did as well. The magnet became so heavy and overloaded with guns that the Lamppost Man could only hold it up for a few seconds more before it fell to the deck with a loud crash.

Bent over the magnet, the Lamppost muttered, "Well this is embarrassing."

When the imp released the giant magnet with the attached weapons, the pile skittered across the deck with loud scraping noises and slammed into the metal hull. One of the Dauntless crew tried to pull a rifle from the magnet, but the magnet and guns were stuck fast.

The Lamppost Man checked his pocket watch again, frowned, and then returned it to his vest. Realizing everyone was staring at him he asked, "Alright, who's next?"

A beefy oiler named Franco stepped forward. Rolling up his sleeves he growled, "My turn."

Rick shouted out a warning but Franco ignored him.

"Ahhhh... fisticuffs." The Lamppost Man said cheerily. "It's been awhile, but have at me, knave." The imp held his fists out in front of him the way prizefighters from the 19th century did. Franco immediately jabbed the imp twice in the face.

At first the imp stumbled about dazed and confused, but after playing the part of a beaten prize fighter, he came up smiling. “Ohhh... you’re quite good, Mr. Franco.”

Franco nodded enthusiastically, “Navy, two-time champion...”

The oiler never finished the last sentence of his life. The Lamppost Man struck Franco in the chest with an open palm so hard that the oiler’s body flew backwards twelve feet and slammed into the ship’s hull, shattering every single bone in his body, and killing him instantly.

Seeing the oiler’s body slump to the ground, the Lamppost Man made a disgusted face and said, “Ewwww... that was unpleasant,” and dusted off his hands. Spying the rest of the crew, he asked, “Anyone else?”

Despite what everyone had seen happen to Franco, Uncle Rick stepped forward. “Everyone, stay back.”

“No, Uncle Rick,” Maddie pleaded. “I don’t want anyone else to die.” To the Lamppost Man, she said, “I’ll go with you. You don’t have to hurt anybody else.”

The imp tilted his head to the side and sighed. “Awww... see? Is there any doubt as to why I want *you* to become my apprentice?”

The Lamppost Man did an odd gesture with his hand, one that almost resembled a salute. The hatches immediately opened behind all the crewmen on deck. The Lamppost Man swiftly brought his hand down and a great wind came out of nowhere. It violently whisked everyone, except Maddie, back inside. The hatches slammed shut, and Maddie could see where the frames were now melting.

On the other side of the sealed doors, Maddie could hear the muffled shouts of Uncle Rick screaming her name, but she knew nothing could stop this madman, and resigned herself to her fate.

If only Dad were here.

BANG!

Several more gunshots rang out in rapid succession.

The Lamppost Man recoiled from each round that slammed into him.

Finally recovering, with a confused look he asked, “How?”

The Leftenant stepped out of the shadows and into the light. Smoke curled out of the barrel of the pistol she was holding. “Before you try anything else, you should probably know that *my* firearm isn’t made of metal.”

One by one, the Lamppost Man plucked the fresh slugs from his body.

“Leftenant,” he snarled, “Always an *unwelcome* surprise.”

Seeing her opportunity for escape, Maddie ran over to The Leftenant.

The Leftenant pulled Maddie behind her protectively. “As are you, Lampy.”

Dropping another spent slug to the deck the Lamppost Man said, "Did you really think a mere hologram could stop me?"

Undeterred, The Leftenant took a step toward him, leveled her pistol at the imp's head and said, "Let's find out, shall we?"

The Lamppost Man smiled sadly, as though a hunter putting down a great specimen he would much rather leave alive. "Now, go away."

With a wave of his hand, Maddie was surprised when The Leftenant simply vanished. Maddie stared up at the imp, who was smiling down at her.

"Now that we're done with that nonsense," he began.

"What did you do to her? You jerk."

The imp smiled devilishly, shrugged his shoulders, and answered, "I sent her away. In fact, I sent her far... far away. I seriously doubt she will ever bother you in your mayfly existence ever again."

The Lamppost Man took another step toward Maddie and...

BANG!

Another shot rang out. This time the Lamppost Man's head recoiled from the round that had struck him in the head.

"Hello..."

Flabbergasted, the Lamppost Man scanned the immediate area for his attacker.

Maddie lifted her gaze to a railing on a deck overhead. The Leftenant was once more standing there, with her smoking pistol held firmly in her hand.

The imp's eyes were wide. "How did you...?" he began, "But I sent you...?"

The Leftenant waggled her eyebrows (almost perfectly this time), "My, aren't we at a loss for words this evening."

The Lamppost Man shook his head, "But I sent you away." The imp pursed his lips and waved her away again.

BANG!

A second later, The Leftenant reappeared near the gilded elevators. The Lamppost Man feebly waved her away, but she reappeared again and shot him five more times.

"Stop it!" the Lamppost Man cried.

The Leftenant gave the imp a little shake of her head, "I think not. Dare I say it, but I do believe I could do this all day." Before the imp could raise his hand to wave her away once more, she shot him five more times.

Maddie watched as the Lamppost Man fell to his hands and knees in defeat. The Leftenant took a step toward him and leveled her pistol at his head.

Breathing hard, the Lamppost Man held his hand up in defeat and managed, “You know, I wonder if there’s still some part of little Lisa inside of you.”

Finger tense on the trigger, The Leftenant went to fire again, but this time, found that she could not.

Maddie couldn’t believe what she was seeing. The Leftenant had the imp right where she wanted him. “What are you waiting for? Shoot him!” Studying her face, it was the first time Maddie had ever seen The Leftenant have a moment of fear.

The Leftenant feebly asked, “What are you doing?”

The Lamppost Man, using the railing to pull himself to his feet, asked, “You remember *Lisa,* don’t you? After all, she’s the one who created you.”

Maddie watched The Leftenant take a step backward. It was as though he had incapacitated her with his words somehow. She noted how he put heavy emphasis on the word, Lisa. *Maybe that’s how he’s controlling her.* The Leftenant’s hand, the one holding the pistol, fell down by her side.

“There’s a good girl,” he said, regaining his feet most unnaturally.

Seeing this, The Leftenant tried to raise her gun once more. Hand shaking profusely, her pistol slowly began to rise, but the Lamppost Man clenched his fist and asked, “Tell me, what was the name of that young beau, *Lisa* had? Some sort of architect fellow." The Imp put fist to chin and frowned as though in deep thought. "For the life of me, I can't recall his name. Josh... Joshua?" The Lamppost Man's face lit up in recollection. Snapping his fingers, he cried, "Oh yes, I remember now, Joshua Dawson."

Hearing the name, The Leftenant's pistol hand immediately dropped back down to her side, and a moment later, the gun clattered to the floor, and vanished.

Maddie shrank away as the Lamppost Man took a step closer to The Leftenant. He was so close to her now that he was able to cup his hand around The Leftenant's cheek. He patted it two times and asked, "Any last words?"

The Leftenant, fighting merely to speak, responded, "None for you, demon."

The Lamppost Man took a step back. "As you wish then."

GazIng down upon Maddie one last time with a look of sadness, The Leftenant whispered, "There now, little one. Chin up."

With a wave of his hand, the Lamppost Man commanded solemnly, "Be gone, spirit."

This time, when The Leftenant was gone, it was soon apparent she was not coming back.

Seeing this, Maddie screamed, "What have you done?!"

"Cheer up Maddiekins," the Lamppost Man responded jovially, although Maddie could tell there was some pain behind that smile. "That mean ole nursemaid won't be bothering you ever again." Withdrawing a white linen handkerchief, the Lamppost Man turned away, and Maddie thought she observed him wipe away a single tear.

Chapter 31

Mad-Maddie

"You're lying!" Maddie shot back.

"Oh, I'm afraid not. The Leftenant really is quite dead. I have suffered her infuriating interference for far too long. I not only deleted her, but I deleted her from *everywhere*."

Leaping from his hiding place, Henry grabbed Maddie by the hand and led her back to the sealed doors. "C'mon, Maddie."

This action caused the Lamppost Man to chuckle, "Where are you going?" He chortled again. It was a sickening thing. "I've fused all the hatches shut. There's no escape. Like it or not young lady, you're coming with me."

Henry tugged on the hatch with all his might, but Maddie could see the Lamppost Man had ruined everything. There really was no escape.

Refusing to give in, Young Henry wrenched a steel pipe from the railing and held it like a club. “Maddie, stay behind me,” he shouted, nearly knocking her out with his backswing.

Maddie lurched forward. “No, Henry. He’ll kill you.”

To their surprise, the Lamppost Man tucked his cane under his armpit (*Did he have that before*?) and started clapping. “Oh bravo! Bravo maestro. Playing the part right to the end.”

“Stay back! You come one step closer, and I’ll brain you good.” Henry took a swing at the Lamppost Man as he approached. The imp dodged nimbly back, surprised, and thoroughly entertained.

“Oh come-come-come now, Henry. Your mission has been accomplished. You needn’t pretend anymore.”

Maddie, shaking her head, “What are you talking about?” Turning toward Henry she asked, “What’s he talking about?”

The Lamppost Man smiled and sighed at the same time before answering. As though explaining to a small child he said, “Who do you think sabotaged The Dauntless?” Raising his eyebrows he added, “Hmmmm?”

Maddie’s eyes narrowed. “What are you saying?”

“Don’t listen to him, Maddie,” Henry said. “He’s lying. I would *never* betray you, or Traxx.” He swung the pipe again at the Lamppost Man for emphasis.

Again the Lamppost Man leapt nimbly out of the way. Maddie suspected he could have dispatched Henry easily with a wave of his hand, as he did the others, so it was no small secret she was beginning to wonder why he didn't do just that.

To Henry he said, "Think about it dear boy, all the black-outs? Waking up in usual places? Places you have no right being?"

Maddie took a few tentative steps away from Henry and heard herself ask, "Is this true, Henry?"

Not willing to tear his eyes from the Lamppost Man, Henry shot back, "No!" and then risking a glance at Maddie and seeing her face for the first time he answered, "At least I don't think it is."

If Maddie wasn't close to tears before, she certainly was now. People she had sworn herself to protect had been killed. The Leftenant... and now Henry... a saboteur! Softly she weeped, "Oh Henry. Say it isn't true."

The Lamppost Man nodded enthusiastically. "It is true. It's very true. Every word of it."

Defeated, Henry dropped the pipe to the deck. He stood there in shock as the Lamppost Man pushed him aside without even a glance at him.

"Wait," Maddie said, causing the advancing Lamppost Man to skid to a halt. "Was all this drama just to kidnap me?"

The Lamppost Man put his gloved fists on his waist, bent forward slightly and responded, "My, my, aren't we a tad self-centered." Putting the back of his hand to the side of his mouth and speaking across it he said, "Newsflash, the world doesn't revolve around you, Maddikins."

They both heard a clucking rooster sound emanating from the Lamppost Man's vest. "Oh my," he said, patting his vest. "Well, it's about time." Finally locating his pocket watch, he removed it from his coat and jerked comically at the sight of the time. "Oh, we've taken much too long." He moved back over to the railing and gazed into the storm. "Why our ride is nearly here." He clapped briskly a few times and gestured for her to come join him. "Come, come. No time to doddle now."

Beyond the Lamppost Man, Maddie saw a brief flash of light. In seconds an egg-shaped vessel, one that reminded her of an angry hover drone, flew out of the clouds and over to hover beside the Dauntless, matching its speed perfectly.

Staring at the egg-shaped vessel, Maddie was suddenly reminded of the children's nursery rhyme, *Humpty-dumpty sat on the wall. Humpty-dumpty had a great fall.* The hovering egg-ship cracked open, revealing a cockpit barely large enough for two passengers.

The Lamppost Man seemed quite pleased with himself. Still gripping the handrail, he turned back toward her and said, “Oh, I think you’re going to enjoy this.” Seeing Maddie shake her head no, he said, “Come now, Maddie. We really *do* have to be going.”

Maddie shouted back, “I’m not going anywhere with you!” She looked to Henry, but he still stood on the deck with his arms slumped down by his sides, in stupefied shock.

The Lamppost Man dropped his smile and stared at her evenly. “Oh, but I think you are,” he said with a venom in his voice she had not heard before.

The Lamppost Man began to cross over to her.

There was nowhere else for her to go.

Chapter 32

Traxx

"C'mon, there's no time!"

Traxx saw the sheer power of the Lamppost Man when he killed Franco. Not daring to waste another second, he quickly retreated to into The Dauntless to find the one person who might have a chance at stopping malevolent imp.

Gazing down at them from an upper balcony, Traxx now saw that only the Lamppost Man, and Maddie remained. *Did the Lamppost Man kill everyone else*? *Am I too late?* Movement caught his eye and Traxx spied the older boy hiding behind the elevators. *No wait, Henry is there too.*

Stepping up beside Traxx was a worrisome gargoyle. Lisp heavy as ever, he asked, "What is it Masthter Traxx? Did you find my kit-ton?"

Before Traxx could answer, Cheeves noticed the Lamppost Man below. The kidnapping imp lunged forward, grabbed Maddie by the wrist and began dragging her fighting form across the deck. The gargoyle's eyes narrowed, and he immediately begin unbuttoning his cufflinks and rolling up his sleeves. "You were wise to call me, Master Traxx."

Although Traxx's attention was divided with the scene unveiling below, he thought he detected a change in the gargoyle's voice. It was the way Cheeves now spoke, as though he were an actor who suddenly ceased playing his role in a play.

In a very calm, human-like manner, Cheeves began unbuttoning his vest. As he did so, he asked, "Do you want to know a secret, Master Traxx?"

"Not now, Cheeves," the boy replied, but again, there was something about the gargoyle's voice. It was no longer his usual jovial, childlike self

"The truth of the matter really is..." Cheeves turned to face him, "I don't really eat cats. It's only part of my backstory. I could never actually harm another animal, and personally, I think felines are simply wonderful creatures."

Despite the dire circumstances below, Traxx asked reflexively, "Yeah, what about balloons?"

The gargoyle's eyes grew wide. "Oh, balloons are another matter entirely." Realizing he was out of time, Cheeves gave up trying to unbutton his vest all the way and tore his it from his body. He dropped to all fours and leapt over the balcony, all the while screaming… "I LOVE BALLOONS!!!"

Traxx couldn't explain how he knew this, but he was suddenly aware that he would never see his friend ever again.

Chapter 33

Cheeves

"I LOVE BALLOONS!!!!"

Maddie heard the familiar cry and noticed a shadow cast over the Lamppost Man was growing larger by the second.

The gargoyle struck the Lamppost Man like a well-placed cannonball striking the mast of a pirate ship. The Lamppost Man catapulted backwards and slammed so hard into the steel railing his body left an outline behind in the metal.

Cheeves, already on his feet, appeared wild-eyed, and his normally smiling face had been replaced by one of pure animalistic rage and sharp teeth.

"Now, Cheeves," the Lamppost Man said, stumbling to his feet. "Now Cheeves… I demand you stop this behavior at once."

With a jerk of his wrists, Cheeves extended his claws several inches. With the roar of an enraged lion, he leapt onto the Lamppost Man and began shredding him to pieces.

The Lamppost Man cried out in pain and at one point during the mauling, Maddie saw his top hat fly off his head and go rolling across the deck.

Just when it looked like the fight was nearly over, Maddie heard a loud yelp of pain uttered by Cheeves.

The gargoyle stumbled backwards and held a clawed hand to the gaping wound in his side. Maddie didn't even know the gargoyle could bleed for she had never seen anything capable of penetrating his skin.

The Lamppost Man's clothes were completely ripped into strips, and she could see claw marks all over his face, neck and arms. His hair, now visible, was askew. In his hands, he was holding his cane like a spear; a steely blade was sticking out the end of it.

Through clenched teeth he growled, "Alright monster. Let's go again."

It was clearly a standoff between two titans with Maddie's life hanging in the balance.

Cheeves, seriously injured, stumbled a few steps into a pillar and was about to leap again. It was Maddie's plea that stopped him.

"Cheeves, no," Maddie cried. "I can't lose you too."

Hearing this, the gargoyle turned toward her and with a sweet but sad look on his face he said, "It's okay, Maddie. I have to do this."

Maddie, full on crying now, managed to ask, "Why? Why must you die too."

The gargoyle shrugged slightly. She thought he was going to say what he always said, how he loved balloons, in the most exuberant voice possible. That was why he surprised her when he said softly, "Because Cheeves loves you *more* than he loves balloons."

With his last ounce of strength, Cheeves lunged at the Lamppost Man one final time.

Lampy cried, "Cheeves, stop!"

But the gargoyle ignored this final plea and tackled the Lampost Man about his waist. This time, Cheeves hit the Lamppost Man so hard that their bodies smashed right through the steel railing. The gargoyle and imp slipped from the heavens and fell to their deaths seventy feet below. "Nooooo!" Maddie ran over to the broken railing, and stared over it. Both gargoyle and imp had already slipped beneath the waves.

Overcome with grief, Maddie would have fallen to the deck had not Henry walked up behind her and caught her in his arms. She would have thanked him, but Henry placed a white handkerchief over her mouth. Her eyes grew wide and she tried to say, “Henry, what are you doing?” but her vision blurred as he said to her, “I’m sorry. I’m so-so sorry.”

She felt Henry scoop her up into his arms and could only watch helplessly as he carried her into the egg-shaped vessel. The last thing she saw before drifting off to Never-Never Land and blacking out completely was Henry’s face.

Her last thought was simply…

Why is Henry wearing a stupid top hat?

"We hope you have enjoyed your return visit to Stranger World and come back real soon."

-The Lamppost Man

And now, for a sneak peek of your next adventure...

Stranger Desert

-A Stranger World Story-

Chapter 1

Finding The Dauntless

A battered, barely-functioning, Hopper crested the ridge and ground to a halt at the edge of a precipice overlooking a vast desert far below.

Once the driver inside switched off the loudly chugging engine, the all-terrain desert vehicle coughed and sputtered a few more times, belched out a cloud of black smoke, and finally died.

Seconds later, the sound of metal unlatching was heard and a circular hatch over the rectangular-shaped cab lifted upward. A man wearing a desert cap and a drab-green, field-army coat popped out like a gopher on Groundhog Day.

Lifting his dirt-caked goggles onto the brim of his cap, he surveyed the wasteland below.

From this height, the desert floor appeared to be a dried-up lakebed, tan and orange in color, cracked in most places. Monstrously large, it stretched without end, like a sand-swept version of the sky.

Despite the miserable heat, the driver pulled down the scarf from over his mouth and inhaled.

Fresh air.

This was no bio dome. Most couldn't tell anymore, but for him, it wasn't the perfectly replicated sky that glitched on occasion that gave it away. It was always the smell. No recycled air here, no sir. For better or worse, this was the *real* outside.

Some days it was hard to believe places like this still existed outside the giant domes that peppered the earth's surface like a leper's sores.

The driver reached down to grab something inside the cockpit and banged his head on the hatch's edge. Biting back a curse, he couldn't help but rub the ouchiness out of his forehead with his palm. Bending down again (a bit more carefully this time) he grabbed a clunky, box-shaped device affixed to a loose-hanging leather strap. Like the ramshackle vehicle, the metallic box had also seen better days. Studying the archaic gauges, he soon realized nothing was happening.

So... he did what any self-respecting vagabond would do in his situation and banged on the side of it, with his palm. Despite his awesome display of technical prowess, still nothing happened.

He then began sweeping it back and forth in slow moving arcs. Finally, the stupid thing began to beep. Slow and intermittent to the north, and the same to the south, but due west (into an approaching sandstorm -naturally, of course, why would it be anywhere else) the signal began to beep steadily.

After four years of searching, Colonel George Stapleton had finally found her.

"The Dauntless..." he breathed.

Four years. Has it really been so long?

During his original timeline, the same trek across the United States would've only been a twelve-hour flight, with maybe a slight layover. However, such amenities were no longer afforded to today's would-be traveler, at least not to the non-corporate folk.

From Henry's tower in the middle of the Atlantic, he had to cross nearly half an ocean just to reach the mainland. He was pretty sure he'd landed on the east coast of Florida, but it was difficult to tell anymore without GPS systems and having to use only provincial Kingdom maps to guide him.

After spending nearly a year in the Elvin dungeons of the Aurora Ice Mountains, he finally managed to pick up the Dauntless's transponder signal again. Tracking it forty-five degrees northwest, he crossed thousands of miles of terrain, filled with every manner of creature anyone could possibly imagine. The journey had taken every survival skill he possessed.

He wasted another year getting caught up in a useless kingdom war. The outcome changed little more than thinning out both sides, which he was pretty sure Corporate's intention all along.

The journey wasn't all bad, though. He'd made many a friend along the way. Sadly, most were soon lost.

As far as to what state of the union he currently occupied, he hadn't the foggiest. Certainly, west of the Mississippi river, but it didn't matter anymore, for the United States no longer existed. If what he had learned was true, it hadn't for nearly the two centuries he had slumbered as a corpse.

"Better check my tail."

Summoning what little energy he still possessed, he climbed the rest of the way out of the cockpit. Crossing over the uneven roof of the Hopper to the back, he used a pair of binoculars he'd absconded from a W.W. II tank commander to survey the road from which he came.

Staring through the lens, about half-a-day's journey down the mountain, he saw sunlight reflecting off a windshield.

Yep. They were still following him.

The lead truck was gray in color and called a half-track (on account of the heavy-duty knobby tires in the front, and tank-treads in the back). A massive swastika painted the door on the side. At least seven Nazi stormtroopers rode in back. The man leading the Nazi parade George knew well.

Franz Goober, a Colonel in the Faceless Nazi Army. Only (unlike his men) Franz did have a face, one that was always painted in a permanent sneer, cold and icy.

For the record, Franz Goober wasn't his actual name. It was a play on the name of the nemesis of one of his all-time-favorite movies, *Die Hard.*

Focusing the binoculars, George could see Franz clear as day. Like many times before, Franz seemed unscathed from their previous encounters. Either the Colonel was able to re-generate or Corporate had been replacing him with a fresh model after every encounter. In Stranger World, both were possible.

For two years, Franz had been trailing him. George didn't know why he was so surprised, Corporate still had a hefty bounty on his head.

Last time Franz had caught up with him, it was in the Madlands. George had thinned out Franz's men pretty well.

He'd also stuck his knife in the Nazi-biological's right eye. In exchange, George absconded with Franz's Mauser. It was the same pistol currently occupying the worn leather holster on his right thigh.

Undoubtedly, ole Franz Goober wasn't happy about the trade.

Sorry, Franz. No backsies, George thought, then figured, *How about I give it back to you one bullet at a time? Yeah, that* might make for a better comeback. He imagined his long-deceased wife, Tessa, rolling her eyes at him and telling him what a cheeseball he was. Gosh how he missed her.

Besides, he didn't know why Franz was so sore. While floating down the Emerald river, one of Franz's snipers had put a slug into his shoulder. George would've died were it not for an Elfin princess who took pity on him. She had plucked the slug out and healed him up. *What was her name again? Oh yeah, Asha. She communicated through moving art tattooed on her arms, hands and face.*

Even after cutting down half his troopers, Franz still pursued him. *Dogged-determination, that's what Tessa would have called it.* He supposed in that way, he and the Franz were a lot alike.

Taking one last look through the binocs, he saw the newest addition to Team Goober. A bounty hunter dressed as Maji, who even now was pounding on the side of the truck with his palm, signaling for the driver to stop. Once halted, the magi deftly dismounted over the side (his robes snapping in the wind like a superhero's cape). He unslung his rifle from his shoulder even before his boots touched the desert floor.

Dang, I must've been spotted too.

As the magi bounty hunter focused in on him through the scope of his long rifle, George thought, *He's probably wondering if he could get off a shot. Good luck buddy, that's got to be at least a two mile...*

George heard the distant report from the magi's rifle and thought nothing of it until...

KA-CHUNK!

"Geez," he cried out, instinctively picking up his foot after the bullet had chunked into the back of the Hopper just below him. Calling up one of Rick's more crass colloquialisms, he thought, *Well, shut my mouth and slap my Grandma, he nearly got me!*

He imagined the magi sniper smiling in satisfaction in response to his reaction, but George would never know because he wasn't about to give the maji a second shot. Jogging back across the roof of the Hopper, he put both palms to either side of the hatch and lowered himself back down into the cockpit. Standing on the short ladder, he pulled the hatch closed behind him like a submariner about to dive.

Flicking on switches even as he was finding his seat, he thought, *It took me nearly half a day to get up to this ridge, it'll take them a lot longer in that half-track.*

Turning the ignition switch, he smiled and said, "So long, Franz."

And... nothing happened.

Sure... why not?

He tried the ignition again.

Still, the engine didn't respond.

According to the tracker, the Dauntless was only 4.8 miles away.

"Oh, C'mon! Just one more time."

Nothing.

"Give me a break!" he roared, slamming his combat boot into the control panel.

A second later the console lit up like a Christmas tree, sparked in a few places and then, in an awesome crescendo of noises, the engine sputtered to life.

Gritting his teeth, George said, "Last time, ole girl," and shoved the throttle forward.

On command, the broken Hopper lurched forward.

It descended to the desert floor in only a fraction of the time it had taken to climb to the top of the mountain. Unfortunately, the strain of getting up and over was too much for the old girl because it hadn't even gone a full mile on the desert floor when the engine started clanking. George knew from personal experience it wouldn't be long before engine seized up entirely.

A quarter mile later, it did just that.

Even if he had the parts, he knew he'd never get the chance to effect repairs. Not with Franz and company so close to his tail.

I suppose I should be grateful it didn't break down sooner.

Angry black and grey smoke began filling the engine compartment. With little options, George pulled over and abandoned ship. It's wasn't like there was a lot to take. Nearly all his fuel and provisions were used up getting here.

Still...

The portable tracker was as much a necessity as the German pistol. With any luck, he wouldn't need either. According to the tracker, the Dauntless was less than two miles from where he now stood.

Besides, even if the Hopper's engine hadn't seized up, the fuel tank was practically on fumes. Another spark caused him to jump. Most people thought a full tank was the more volatile, but George knew the opposite was actually true. In a full tank, there's no room for oxygen. However, in a nearly empty one, well sir, that's the tank you want to watch out for; plenty of fumes mixing with lots of oxygen equals high chance of boom-boom. Thinking about this gave him an idea, maybe a little surprise for Franz and his goons. As he took the time to rig up the trip wires to an ignition source, he thought with a chuckle, *wow, these guys must really hate me.*

Gathering up a few remaining things, and donning his army coat laden with compass, flashlight and survival gear, he carefully stepped over the trip wire. Before leaping from the cargo door, he took one last look inside. His bunkbed, the collectibles, and every little piece of junk inside had a story behind it. It was a shame he had to leave it all behind.

Worth it, if it helps me get the last few miles back to the Dauntless... and back to Maddie.

Tightening his coat around his shoulders for warmth (it was surprisingly cold in the desert), he leaned into the buffeting winds and started to trek.

After a mile-or-so, he encountered an oversized propeller sticking up out of the sand like a grave marker. He recognized it immediately... it belonged to the Dauntless. It was one of her guidance props.

What's it doing down here?

Farther on, he found a massive sheet of hull plating submerged in the sand. It was scorched, most likely due to an explosion.

The wind died down a little, revealing a massive wide-open area for only a few seconds. In that time, George saw enough wreckage to fill a junkyard. Whatever happened, must have been bad.

Standing on the largest sheet of metal, he kicked sand away with his boot and then, as urgency set in, he fell to his knees and cleared more off with his hands. The pit in his stomach grew with each letter he revealed.

D… A… U…

Please… no…

"Dauntless…"

Walking fast, then jogging, he broke into a run. Stopping only long enough to inspect more pieces of wreckage, he began to piece together the crash in his mind. The vast debris field must have been the P.O.I. (point of impact), and what was left of the ship began breaking apart. As the wounded vessel sojourned mightily onward, it left behind a trail of wreckage in its wake.

It's like they were hit by a massive rocket or something, dropping pieces off as they soldiered on.

As the wind picked up in intensity, he shielded his face with his hand and plodded forward, tying his scarf tighter over his mouth and nose.

This went on for the last two miles.

Then, the edge of the sandstorm finally ended and gently swept over him as a curtain revealing a scene on a stage.

Even the wind had grown tranquil, as though in reverence as to what lay before him.

The Dauntless...at least what was left of her, had belly landed, and broke mid-beam. She was left abandoned, little more than a ruined hulk of her former self.

"Oh no."

What had he been expecting? A welcome home party? A cake? Everybody to yell, 'Welcome Home George! We missed you!'.

How could I have been so absurd?

His first clue should have been the locator transponder. It had showed her position as fixed for the last two years.

I've sacrificed so much, and for what?

He had gambled everything on getting here, and lost.

Chapter 2

Dead Survivor

"I have to know..."

George knew getting inside the wrecked ship wouldn't be a problem. The hull had more holes than a kitchen colander.

Working his way beneath the aft section with its tail sticking up in the air, he passed beneath the payload area (where they normally kept the Hoppers and salvage).

Hearing loud creaking noises from the loose-hanging bay door above him, he quickened his pace.

Clearing the squash-zone, he thought, *That certainly would have been an anti-climactic ending,* and imagined the inscription on his tombstone to read: 'Flattened by Door.'

Climbing a mangled section of deck plating, he clasped the handle of the first hatch he came too. The moment he did, it fell the rest of the way off its hinges and clanked to the deck, nearly crushing him.

I have to slow down, be more careful.

He took a deep calming breath, in through his nostrils, held it for a few seconds, and then let it out, slowly. Only then, did he venture inside.

Stepping over the hatch's threshold, George felt a chill of recognition. Even after a four-year absence, the smooth, riveted steel hull, the wood planking underfoot, especially the smell of metal and mahogany -it all took him back.

The outer hull may have been peppered with holes, but the interior walls were relatively intact. The only problem with that was the inside was either bathed in shadow or completely dark.

In the pitch-black areas, he activated his trusty army-surplus, L-shaped flashlight affixed to his belt.

"Hello?" he called out and immediately felt foolish for thinking anyone would answer. It was obvious the ship had been a ghost ship for years. Despite this, he tried, "Leftenant?" and was rewarded with only the echo of his own voice.

Exploring the lower decks first, he headed for the bridge. It didn't take long to see that most of the floor had crumpled inward on impact and was now filled halfway up to the ceiling with sand.

I hope everybody made it out okay.

Thoughts of his friends, Rick, Dr. Bob, Mike and Sue immediately came to mind... then...

Maddie.

As he made his way back to his daughter's room, it was apparent the shipwreck had been ravaged by scavengers.

In many places, even the hull plating had been removed post-crash. More than a few bodies were strewn about, most too badly burned or mangled from the crash to be recognizable. One thing that was for certain, there were far too few. So most of the crew had managed to abandon ship.

But what about Maddie?

Until reaching his daughter's quarters, he had moved steadily and methodically throughout the corridors. Once he got to Maddie's berth though, he hesitated. George kept imagining the worst things he might find inside. Realizing he couldn't stand in the hallway forever; he ventured inside.

Thankfully, his daughter's corpse wasn't forthcoming, only a few meager trappings the scavengers hadn't deemed worthy enough to steal. Seeing Maddie's hand-drawn maps all over her wall, he realized, *That little girl never gave up on finding me.*

He unslung his portable tracker device and put it on Maddie's workbench. He couldn't help but admire all the drawings and mathematical equations etched into her table.

That's my baby-girl.

Sitting on her bed, he ran his hand over one of her hand-drawn maps taped to the wall. Removing his favorite (the one with all the little red X's on it and doodles in the margins), he studied it a moment longer. A tear slid his cheek, but he didn't bother to wipe it away. Too much time lost. So much so that he struggled to recall how long they'd actually been apart.

The last time he'd heard her voice was nearly four years ago, and even that was in only the briefest of transmissions. At the time, he had been so focused on his mission, he'd barely said hello. That mission seemed foolhardy now. He should have realized then that only his family and friends truly mattered. Nothing else should have ever come before them. After that short communique, he hadn't received anything further from her or the Dauntless. He'd assumed the worst, but promised himself he wouldn't stop searching until he knew for certain.

He was never one to give up, but seeing all the devastation around him, he was fairly certain this time would be his final resting place.

It wasn't like he had a choice. He'd used the last of his currency on the fuel and provisions getting here and passed the point of no return days ago. He was counting on the hopes of finding the Dauntless and her crew, but there was obviously nobody here and certainly nothing left behind that could help him get out of the desert, the scavengers had seen to that. If the lack of provisions didn't get him, Franz and his buddies surely would.

The wreckage of the Dauntless. A fitting tomb I suppose.

As though in answer, his portable tracker began softly beeping. Brow furrowed, he folded Maddie's map into his shirt pocket, got up from her bed and checked the instrumentation still situated on the desk. Moving the device about the room, he homed in on the signal. It *was* a power source, and judging by the distance, it was coming from inside the ship, somewhere around... officers' quarters.

Tracking the power signature through the ship, George began to wonder, *How could any part of the ship still have power? It's a ruined hulk.* Even if there was any power left, the scavengers would've detected it too. *Why hadn't they taken it?* More theories ran through his head, after all, the Dauntless was never short on secrets, hidden rooms or surprises.

The power signature led him past the library, through the galley and all the way to the Leftenant's quarters. It was no surprise to him that her door was locked, and clearly impenetrable. The blast marks on the hatch from where scavengers had used every manner of explosive to gain entry was proof of that.

George palmed the plate by the door and a tiny lid lifted. Although the panel wasn't very big, the display field was bright enough to lighten up the darkened hallway.

Hmmmm... judging by the six blank fields, it is a six-digit code.

George pressed the first blank field and the letter 'A' popped up. *Oh, it's not a numbered code but one of letters.* He knew that the Leftenant was the most state-of-the-art intelligence on the planet. She could have easily programmed a very difficult non-existent word in the English language, or any language for that matter. But George knew better. First, the Leftenant would have planned for the contingency that someone else (most likely someone dear to her) would need to gain access. Second, the Leftenant may have been created in a lab, but at heart, she had the soul of a seafaring poet.

He started with the most obvious choices...

D-A-U-N-T-L... *Duh, Dauntless has nine letters, not six.*

M-A-D-D-I-E... *Shoot, I would've thought that would've been it.*

He went through the ship's manifest and plugged in as many of the crew's six-lettered names (first and last) he could remember.

No joy.

On a whim, he tried one last name. It was a long shot. He was surprised he even remembered the man's name to begin with, but it had to work, because he had no other ideas.

D-A-W-S-O-N...

Nothing happened... until it did.

BEEP-CLICK.

As the hatch to the Leftenant's quarters slowly swung open, it occurred to him that he had never actually been inside her room before. Of course, as ship's Captain, he knew she had one.

Surprisingly, she had quite the collection of trappings. Some he recognized, like the sword and scabbard from one of the crew of the Zombie-Pirate-King, and Lady Wellington's porcelain mask was easy enough to identify. But many other things were a mystery to him, like a safari-looking knife in a boxed case and an old-framed photograph of a human male dressed as the Lamppost Man. Squinting at it, he wondered, *Is that Henry?*

The crown jewel of her collection was a bell-shaped, glass shell covering, housing something on a Roman pedestal. It appeared to be some kind of futuristic metal wrist band like he'd never seen before.

Turning back to inspect the knife further, he realized too late that one of the carabiners on his belt snagged the cloth handkerchief on the pedestal. As he turned, the cloth, glass dome, and contents came with him.

He jumped slightly when the glass covering shattered upon the deck plates.

Brushing away the broken glass with a gloved hand, he picked up the metallic bracelet.

After fiddling with it only for a second, the genie within the bracelet made herself known.

He immediately recognized the woman wearing the black knee-high boots, off-white trousers, and royal-blue nautical long coat.

Speaking with an equally familiar crisp British accent, she said, "Oh, hello there. I am the Leftenant, 2nd in command of Her Majesty's Airship Dauntless." She took a moment to adjust the black leather pistol belt ensnaring her small waist, then asked, "Who, pray tell, might you be?"

Huh, she doesn't recognize me. I wonder if she's malfunctioning.

Before he could answer, the Leftenant observed her surroundings, and blurted out, "Please tell me, why in heaven's name are you in my personal quarters?"

"Leftenant, it's me, George." When the Leftenant raised a quizzical eyebrow at him, he added, *"George Stapleton?"*

Her facial expression shifted from one of mistrust to recognition. "Oh, I remember you now. You're young Maddie's father." Leaning over and looking past him with a quizzical eyebrow, she asked, "Where is the young scamp by the way?"

"Oh good, for a second there I was beginning to worry," he began, but she cut him off.

"Ah yes, I recall everything now, perfectly. It was you who assisted me in my return to the Dauntless."

Huh, I don't think she remembers everything.

"Leftenant, we've been friends for nearly ten years."

"Hhmmm..." she said, and then looped into one of her many stalling techniques that he hadn't seen her do in quite a while. This one was the one where she was about to say something but took a moment to blow an errant strand of blond hair out of her face first. It would promptly fall back down. Raising one eyebrow, she would exhale again, repeating the procedure as many times as needed.

Allowing her time to process, he clumsily clipped the high-tech bracelet to his wrist. *I wonder what the range of this thing is?*

"Right then. If what you say is true, clearly I am having some sort of mal-function." The Leftenant then took another survey of her room. "Oh my... what an awful mess." Using the side of her shiny black boot as a broom, she casually slid the broken glass beneath her desk.

"Leftenant, we have a lot of catching up to do."

"Quite..."

With steadfast determination, she raised her petite nose in the air, marched out of her room and into the corridor. Stopping in the hallway outside her door, the Leftenant surveyed first one way, and then the other. Slamming her small fists into her waistline, and taking in a very deep breath, she exclaimed, "What have you done to my ship?! Whatever hasn't been nicked is in bloody shambles! Who is responsible for this? I demand to know immediately."

"Leftenant, we really need to talk about..."

She held up the palm of her hand toward him, "Not now, Mr. Stapleton. I don't have time for your ramblings as I must take this up with the current Captain, posthaste." And with that said, she marched off toward the bridge.

Great, George thought, and jogged after her before she could vanish out of the emitter's range. Despite her obvious memory loss, seeing her again provoked a little smile.

As the last echoes of their footfalls died on the Leftenant's walls, George had failed to see the miniature gold nameplate on the dumbbell's shard of broken glass.

It read only one word.

"Sister"

For those of you curious of how it all began,

Stranger Origins

-How it All Began-

The White Rabbit put on his spectacles. "Where shall I begin, please your Majesty?" he asked.

"Begin at the beginning," the King said very gravely, "and go on till you come to the end: then stop."

–LEWIS CAROLL, *ALICE IN WONDERLAND*

Prologue

Lisa Burton

"Would you please hold still?"

"I will not."

"You don't want me to carve your face off by accident, do you?"

Senior hologram-engineer, Lisa Burton, activated her hydrostatic-scalpel once more and resumed re-crafting the nose of her most favored creation. Just as the blade was about to reach its target, her subject abruptly turned her face to the side... for the fifth time.

Lisa sighed, and switched off the scalpel. Removing her safety glasses, she asked, "Now what?"

In a crisp British accent, she replied matter-of-factly, "I dare say, I quite like my nose right the way it is."

Lisa hopped down from her high stool and said, "Well, there's been some uh," Lisa coughed into her fist, "...complaints."

The woman before her wore black knee-high boots, off-white trousers, and a navy-blue, nautical jacket. A black leather pistol belt with spare pouches ensnared her narrow waist. The taller woman arched a high eyebrow down at her and asked cynically, with only the slightest hint of curiosity, "Complaints you say, what sort of complaints?"

Not sure exactly how to respond, Lisa settled for saying, "*The guests* say that you think you're better than them."

Her subject adjusted her naval coat slightly, "I am a Leftenant in Her Majesty's Navy and second in command of Her Majesty's Airship, *Dauntless.* So, one would think that those sniveling, puerile infants would mind their betters and be grateful every time I bring them back in one piece from another harrowing expedition."

She thought about this some more. "Furthermore, I fail to see what any of that nonsense has to do with the shape of my nose."

Lisa knew she could easily have shut down the Leftenant's programming to perform the cosmetic surgery, but in truth, she quite liked these little bouts of banter with the

Leftenant. In fact, if an outside observer didn't know she was a hologram, they might even say the two of them were best friends.

Without warning, a man with a contentious mound of bright-orange hair and a face with more freckles than skin popped up from behind the partition wall and announced, "Hey, Nerd-a-Saurus-Rex, the boss's-boss's-boss wants to see you."

The carrot-top's name was Cliff Munson, or as the gene slicers down on seventh called him, *Cliff Munchin'*. The latter was usually the more accurate of the two, as Cliff's dumpy frame was hardly undersized, and he was always eating potato chips or some other vending machine related snack.

Normally, Lisa's work and rank afforded her a minimum of no less than three floors, but due to last month's attacks, she had been forced to share her office space with some of the other designers and creationeers.

If that wasn't bad enough, Cliff Munson was easily her least favorite co-worker. Like most things in Stranger World, Cliff was a perfect dichotomy in that his work was as brilliant as his lab was an untidy dung heap. He had several degrees from M.I.T., but he gave off the impression of a slovenly dimwit trapped inside the body of an overweight man nearing forty. Cliff had an almost childlike enthusiasm, yet also an incredible mean streak. He was like the neighbor's kid who liked to fry ants under a magnifying glass, all the while laughing about it.

Still, why would Corporate want to see me? she wondered. Typically, when a creationeer was called upstairs, it was for a swift termination. *What could I have possibly done?* She realized Cliff was still watching her with a bemused look upon his face.

Refusing to let *him* see her sweat, but failing to keep her voice from wavering, she asked, "Do you know what they want?"

Cliff must have picked up on her non-verbal cue, because he appeared more tickled than ever when he answered, "Dunno, lab-rat. They didn't say."

Numbly, Lisa nodded. "Okay, thank you."

Cliff was always calling her names like that: bookworm, lab-rat, Vampira. Unfortunately, most of them were fairly accurate. She almost never saw the sun, usually arrived at work long before everyone else, and left long after the sun went down. Also, she had taken her current employment straight out of college eight years ago. The j-o-b was so demanding, she rarely had time for a social life.

Cliff shuffled around the partition dividing their workstations in his ridiculous foam slippers. "I don't know what you did, but it must be pretty bad for you to get called *upstairs*."

Munch-MUNch-MUNCH...

As usual, Cliff was loudly snacking away and leaving behind enough crumbs to fill a pastry shop. Deep down, what she wanted to say was, *Hey Cliff, in case you can't read the ka-bizillion signs, this entire floor is clearly designated as a clean and sterilized area. So, here's an idea, whaddya say, now and forever, you leave your germy crumbs out of the tissue sequencer?* But, because she had worked with Cliff long enough to know it would be only wasted breath, she chose to avoid confrontation, and settled for saying, "Okay, Cliff, thanks for letting me know."

The Leftenant would've socked him a good one, she thought, *and* even now the Leftenant was arching an eyebrow toward her as if to ask why she wasn't doing that very thing.

Lisa whispered to her creation, in reproach, "Not you, too."

The Leftenant straightened her nautical coat with a firm swift tug, stuck her untouched nose into the air, and responded in equal volume. "I have no idea what you're talking about. I didn't say so much as a word."

MUNCH-CRUNCH-MUNCH...

Cliff swallowed noisily, nearly choking, and said, "Hey, I've been meaning to ask you something."

Oh goodie, look who's still here, the Leftenant managed to communicate to her with only the merest of glances.

Cliff must've missed it for he asked, "Why Leftenant? That doesn't even make sense."

As Lisa returned the scalpel to its proper place, along with all the other tools in her tool tray lined up at precise right angles, she fought down a sigh and explained. "The word *Leftenant* is an archaic spelling of *Lieutenant,* which is actually derived from the Latin words, *locum tenens*. When literally translated, it means, *taking the place of*."

MUNCH-MUNCH-CRUNCH.

"Yeah... if that's the case, then how come that's not the way we spell it now?"

As Lisa removed her gloves and disposed of them properly, she replied, "The only reason we spell it wrong is Charles Merriam and Noah Webster, of Merriam and Webster Dictionary, chose the spelling that *sounded* more correct over the actual, original French word."

"Oh, alright, alright," Cliff said, and continued munching away like a dim-witted dolt.

Thinking about the V.P. waiting for her, she began switching off her work station, and thought, *I really don't have time for this.*

Tossing his reddish curls toward the Leftenant, Cliff asked, "So how come she looks like you?"

This was preposterous of course. Lisa was well aware of how many creationeers would build biologicals in their own image, but Lisa refused to stoop down to such narcissistic levels. Firing back, she said, "What are you talking about? She doesn't look a thing like me."

Cliff was about to inhale another chip, froze, smiled and said, "Sure she does, she might be a little taller, a bit thinner, have perfect skin and corn silk hair, but in the end, she's still you."

Cliff was being absurd, and judging by the Leftenant's face, she thought so too. The Leftenant was 5'7," while she was a mere 5'3." The Leftenant had long silky fibers of serene yellow hair, whereas hers was an ordinary dirty blond.

Lisa smiled politely and rose from her chair. "You're being ridiculous."

Cliff inhaled another handful of chips, and laughed, spewing crumbs everywhere. "Whatever you say, Lab-ra-doodle." He brushed the crumbs off his hoodie and onto the floor. Disappearing around the cubicle wall, she saw he left behind another trail of crumbs in his wake.

Ugh. Where's my mini-vac?

Realizing she didn't have time to clean up after Cliff now, she finished powering down her lab. After verifying that she had saved her work, Lisa turned off her primary monitor and on cue, the Leftenant also vanished.

She was about to leave her station entirely when she noticed a framed black-and-white photograph hanging on her wall that was slightly out of place. The photo depicted the famous jungle explorer (and distant ancestor, thank you very much), Sir Richard Francis Burton. Sir Richard Francis had been a member of Britain's prestigious Royal Geographical Society. He had spoken no less than 29 languages, and was predominantly known for exploring Asia, Africa and the Americas in the mid-nineteenth century.

Straightening out the tilted photo with one forefinger, Lisa glanced below the frame at the antique knife displayed in a handsome glass case. The dull silver blade was about the size and length of a common English carving knife. It had a cylindrical-brown wooden handle, with a metal cross-guard to protect the user's hand.

"Better shake a leg, Lab-monkey," came Cliff's disembodied voice from his workstation. "Hell hath no fury like a V.P. kept waiting."

As much as she hated to admit it, Cliff was right; she needed to get moving. It wasn't every day a senior manager wanted to have a little chat. Passing Cliff's workstation on her way out, she noticed he was performing another touch up on one of the *Fairy Maze* monarchs. "Hey, didn't you just give that model a refresh last week?"

Cliff snorted, "Yeah I did, but her Ladyship here thought she could use a little touch up. Can you imagine that? She actually found her way down here, and when security nabbed her on twelve, she demanded a..." he changed his accent to a haughty woman with a Scottish accent, "bit o' sprucing up, post haste."

Lisa studied the monarch sitting there poised and holding up one of those creepy porcelain masks at the end of a thin rod. The analytics in Lisa's bi-optics displayed the biological's designator in floating white letters over her head: LADY WELLINGTON. The way Cliff was always fawning all over her Ladyship, he might as well have been her personal manservant.

Still, Lisa was hardly surprised by her Ladyship's behavior. Lady Wellington was a top-of-the-line TK-12 series, and by design, she was programmed to be as narcissistic as she was cunning. "Yep. Lady Wellington is a wagonload of mischief-makers," she managed.

See Lucifer, I can mix it up, she thought inwardly.

Lucifer was Lisa's cat.

He was so named for two reasons. The first being, he seemed to go out of his way to make her life a living *torment:* peeing on (and subsequently killing) all of her plants, shredding the curtains, scratching up the sofa and anything else he could get his wrathful claws into. The second reason Lucifer was so named, was because he didn't even like her, only allowing himself to be petted on the rarest of occasions.

Snapping her out of her daydream, Cliff complained, "They say it won't be long before these things are ruling the world. I say they're practically doing it right now."

At this, Lady Wellington's eyes opened abruptly, flicked over Cliff for a moment, as though processing what he had just said, and then, realizing she was being watched, immediately screwed them shut tight again.

Cliff, busy with his paints, had been none the wiser.

Seeing Her Ladyship's behavior, Lisa thought, *That was kinda weird.* Of course, she had bigger things to worry about than an eavesdropping biological. *Maybe I'll do a diagnostic on her learning behavior program when I get back.*

Lisa was about to ponder the incident further until she realized she had no idea where she was going. The V.P. responsible for overseeing her work was well known for almost never being in his office. "Do you happen to know where *he* is?"

Cliff smiled. It didn't look good on him, more like a dopey grin on an evil, yellow- toothed chimp. "I dunno. *He* didn't say. The usual place I suspect."

Why'd I even bother even asking? She tapped the control device placed inside the bracelet on her wrist. A map of all the park lands soon appeared in front of her. Of course, no one other than the wearer of her glasses could see the translucent map hovering before her. "Show me, Mark McCormick."

The ear implant in her ear commanded, "Please specify title."

Lisa pursed her lips. This automated request was obviously something Mark had programmed himself. He had been recently promoted to V.P. and no one could locate him by his name unless they specified his new title first. "Please locate Senior Vice-President, Mark McCormick."

Even before she completed her sentence a flashing yellow star appeared on the map.

Of course, he'd be there.

As she departed, Cliff sang, "Good luck, Burton."

Leaving Cliff, and his eavesdropping Ladyship behind, Lisa took the L-Tube beneath several lands, including Arctic Adventures, the town of Havenport, and the Zombie Apocalypse.

While traveling on the train, never once did she gaze up from her holographic data pad and notice any of the other passengers around her. The interior of the tube car could've been filled to the brim or totally empty, and she would've never been any the wiser. If the other passengers could see her holographic schematic (which they couldn't), they would see she was busy working on integrating the Leftenant into the newly upgraded airship, *the Dauntless*.

Without actually hearing the stop announcement, she automatically departed the tube car and headed for the elevators, which would take her topside. She would have preferred to take the tunnels *all* the way to Mark's location, but after last week's terrorist attack, a large section of tunnels was still under repair. So, she had to cross through some of the park and navigate through throngs of park guests.

Glancing up from her holographic display with only merest of glances, she reached the elevator just in time to see it enclose a bunch of suits inside. Before the elevator doors closed completely, a slender man out in front (who liked to give his hair a little flip over to one side) mouthed the word, 'Sorry.'

"Thanks a lot, pal," she grumped aloud.

Spotting a stairwell nearby, she ascended it (in heels no less) and lightly pushed on the crash-bar that would transport her to the outside world.

The blinding daylight outside washed over her, melting her eyes out of their sockets and consumed her human flesh right down to her very soul.

Cliff's right. I really do need to get out more.

Chapter 1

Welcome to Atlantis

Oh, pooper-scooper.

Unfortunately, the particular door Lisa chose opened up into an Atlantean bathhouse. It was filled with elderly, half-naked men loafing around in bath towels, having a good steamy soak. As she made her way past the sweltering baths, she averted her eyes from their unmentionables. Unfortunately, when she did, her eyes came to rest on the *extremely* inappropriate reliefs on the walls, based on actual renderings found in the similar ill-fated city of Santorini.

Gross.

One of the hairest patrons (a sweaty middle-aged man growing a roundish belly and ridiculous goat-tee) tapped his thigh loudly and bellowed, "Hey, slave girl, I think I need a *massage.*" As she passed him, he sluggishly reached out to grab her, but she simply increased her pace slightly and avoided his meaty grasp.

I really do loathe park guests; I absolutely do.

Of course, Corporate was always eager to point out that without them, she (along with everyone else) would be out of a job.

Laying a hand over her souring stomach, she briskly exited the disgusting bathhouse of elderly half-naked men, in dire need of an eye-wash station.

Fluroantimonic acid wouldn't be enough.

Outside on the streets of Atlantis, Lisa's eyes were re-adjusting to the harsh sunlight when a wagon piled high with barrels of salt and fish nearly ran her over. As she leapt nimbly out of the way, the wagon's driver cursed in Atlantean, "Make way for your betters." The made-up language was a combination of Greek and Italian, only simplified phonetically so guests could learn and assimilate it more quickly.

Traveling in the opposite direction was a passing patrol of Atlantean soldiers, who nearly trampled her beneath their sandaled feet. Dodging out of the patrol's way, she almost tripped over a brood of chickens that appeared out of nowhere, clucking at her feet. *Do chickens cluck when they're not laying eggs?*

Moving further into the street of the busy little seaside town, she encountered the smells of fresh bread and searing meats permeating the air. Her eyes drank in the vast array of richly-colored fabrics: brightly dyed togas and cleverly-painted curtains hanging over merchants' tables. Exquisite tapestries adorned every wall.

The last time she had been inside the new park was a week before its official grand opening. Lisa had purposely avoided the opening months, knowing full well it would be crowded with only the wealthiest and most influential people on the planet, all of whom acted as such and demanded only the highest level of attention and service.

But now that she was completely immersed in this fully-functional world, brimming with the most cutting-edge biologicals (like the aged beggar on the street corner collecting alms or the dozens of merchants yelling for passing patrons to buy their wares), even she had to admit, it was easy to get caught up in the excitement of it all.

Atlantis, of all the places we could have built. I guess Corporate was incapable of coming up with an original idea.

This was true. The creationeers had exhausted every mythology and fairy tale ever written. *That's what happens when you have a theme park littering every city, continent, and body of water on the planet.* Point-of-fact, Stranger World owned more surface of the moon than all the other lunar property holders combined. Even though Lisa had never actually been to any of the theme parks on the moon, her work certainly had. So, with all that in mind, it was no surprise to Lisa that they had to *dig up* the ancient story of the doomed city, *pun intended.* Lisa smiled at her own joke.

Contrary to myth, the town was laid out in a traditional grid pattern, with the overall architecture being a mix of Mesoamerican and Greco-Roman. Themed houses, restaurants and shops lined both sides of the street. Marble statues of Olympian deities decorated every street corner, with lots of sea inspired motifs like seahorse fountains and dolphin statues scattered nearly everywhere.

It was easy to become lost in, and because Atlantis was the newest Stranger World theme park on the planet, the streets were so crowded with park guests, she could barely see the polygonal stone paved streets beneath their feet.

Fortunately, she had seen it all long before the first guests arrived to Stranger World's newest attraction; for she had personally known one of the senior architects (he always did loathe the designator "creationeer"). Even now, as she weaved her way through the town's bustling streets, it was easy for her to imagine him walking by her side, as he often did, regaling her with the island's infamous past.

"According to the Greek philosopher Plato, the fabled kingdom of Atlantis was supposedly a continent somewhere in the mid-Atlantic. It was home to an advanced civilization and struck by a cataclysmic event that sank the entire island beneath the sea in a single day and night."

During those years of the Atlantis creation, Lisa didn't mind all the scaffolding and busy work crews as they explored the large villas adorned with countless splendors and works of art. In a lot of ways, those years had been the happiest of her life, namely because of said handsome young architect.

Lisa slowed her walk as she passed the restaurant where they used to meet for lunch with their bagged lunches (as the restaurant had not yet opened). She then passed the Minotaur's maze that he had personally designed and was so proud of. The entrance was framed by two colossal statues of minotaurs, and the marquis overhead read, "The Minotaur's Labyrinth of DEATH!" Lisa knew she was far too timid to attempt such an attraction.

Even backstage, during the testing phases, the Minotaur biological was far beyond terrifying. She never did understand people's desire to have the beejezus scared out of them. When quickening her pace past the second Minotaur statue, she spied something farther up ahead that made her heart ache a little. It was the magnificently alive, ornately sculpted water fountain...where he proposed.

Nope. Stop it! her maternal inner-voice chided her. *Don't do this to yourself, Lisa. This is why you don't come up here anymore. This is why you've buried yourself in your work and haven't walked these streets, not since...*

Lisa still tried to shake herself free of the past. *Besides, it's not like you were ever really interested in this place.* She really wasn't sure why so many people seemed to LOVE Atlantis. Of course, the tourists do partake in a lot more than marriage proposals.

Atlantis was a fascinating legend, on that she could agree, but archeologists had never found any evidence of an actual city with this name. She chalked it up to being in the same category as Bigfoot, the Loch Ness Monster, and aliens crashing in Roswell, New Mexico. Atlantis wasn't real. It was just a story told to a guy (named Solon she thinks), by a band of Egyptians, who told a guy, who told another guy, who happened to be a philosopher named Plato.

What Lisa did find fascinating, however, were facts. The fact was, many scientists now believed the source behind the legend was the remnants of a doomed little island named Santorini. In approximately 1620 BC, this tiny island in the Aegean Sea was devastated by the second largest volcano in history. Just like the Atlantis legend's cataclysmic demise, the major seaport town on Santorini (home of a thriving Minoan civilization) succumbed to the most powerful explosive event ever witnessed. The eruption ejected up to four times as much ash fall as the well-recorded eruption by Krakatoa by in 1883.

As though reading her thoughts, a slight tremor rippled through the streets, nearly knocking her off her feet.

Oh fudge. Is it Friday already?

In the distance, a massive volcano loomed over the condemned city like an Atlantean Titan. Corporate had decided it was a Friday when the *real* Minoan eruption occurred for purposes of increasing weekend profits. Creationeers produced all the ideas for it, including when several million tons of lava to go spewing over the doomed denizens of Santorini, enveloping the bodies of nearly every last inhabitant, forever petrifying them.

Lisa quickly checked the courtyard calendar where the days of the week were listed: Moon, Mars, Mercury, Jupiter, Venus, Saturn and Sun. *Yikes, today is Venus, The Day of Reckoning.*

Her fiancée's ghost reappeared beside her wearing his lopsided grin and saying, "Better shake a leg, darling. You *don't* want to be topside when that thing goes off." She smiled inwardly at the recollection of other visitations. He was always saying goofy little colloquialisms like that.

Joshua's ghost soon vanished again. Funny, how she had been seeing him around the different parks more and more lately. It was as if he was just keeping his eye on her. She had hoped the worst of her grieving was behind her.

Maybe it's not.

The attraction of Atlantis was designed to be a great deal more than simply visiting and living amongst the doomed citizens of the Atlantean colony. No, it was crazy more.

For the maximum experience, guests paid for the entire week, selecting one of several fees. How high their station in their faux life would be depended on how much money they wanted to spend. Lisa had to keep in mind this was the newest park, so prices were at an all-time record high. For example, for $42,000.00, a man, or woman, could spend their week as a slave, a shop keeper or even an Atlantean soldier. They were expected to do menial chores and serve their masters, whether they were human guests, or biological characters.

At the opposite end of the price list, for a quarter of a million dollars, guests could spend the week as a senator, Atlantean General or some other high-ranking official. For a cool million, a person could be worshipped as a god.

When she had first heard about the prices, she thought surely no one would pay such ludicrous amounts. She was shocked to learn the waiting list had already surpassed five years out.

Still, that wasn't the main point of the experience that everybody was talking about. The original idea was based on Dr. Elizabeth Meadow's famous theory that if you study a person for one week you can pretty much predict how they are going to live their entire lives. The goal was to examine your life in the six short days you have left to you in Atlantis and flourish and prosper as much as possible. Those who did their best and rose in rank, or collected the most money, or saved the most lives, were awarded prizes in the form of credits that could be redeemed at any resort, restaurant, or gift shop. Corporate had even come up with a nifty slogan: *"Our Theme Parks aren't just Themed. They're Therapeutic!"*

On the final day of each weekly guest's visit, instead of drowning park guests beneath a tsunami of waves, it was decided that a giant volcano would erupt and shroud the citizens of the entire town in hot molten lava and petrify them perfectly in place. This of course was an illusion created with special foam that hardened for only a few seconds. Before it dissolved, the guest's petrified form was scanned by multiple camera angles, so each visitor could go home with an extremely detailed replica of their own petrified corpse. Depending on their budget, they could purchase their petrified corpses in miniature, or all the way up to a life-size statue, or any size in-between. That way, they could stare at their statue on their desk, or in the corner of their house or garden, and reflect on how they felt and what they had learned.

After being open for only three weeks, rich moguls and movie stars were already telling the world how their guest experience at Atlantis and impacted their lives forever. Of course, most of these claims were paid indorsements arranged by Corporate.

Lisa had never actually been topside during any of the eruptions, as all rehearsals had been conducted behind closed walls, and were strictly off limits to unessential personnel. Her understanding was that the special effects (FX) were quite good and most convincing. Ever since the new section opened, she stayed away and wanted nothing more to do with it for her own personal reasons.

"You there!"

Lisa lifted her gaze from the polygonal stoned street to an oafish merchant whose robes did little to conceal his girth. "Whence thou came?" *he slurred.*

Lisa didn't need the optic scanners built into her glasses to know that the portly man before her was a human guest and not an engineered denizen of the city; his horrible Atlantean accent was more than proof enough for that. Lisa also didn't need her optical-identifiers to know that the extremely beautiful and well-endowed servant girl hanging off his arm was a biological. *5th Generation. Hmmm... That's pretty low* *given that this is our newest park*, she thought. *Must've been a rush job to meet the demand.*

In perfect, classic Atlantean the woman asked, "What strange attire is it that you are wearing?"

Lisa gazed down and examined her own clothes. *Oh, farfegnugen! I forgot to change into a costume down in the tunnels.* As if she weren't in enough trouble already, walking around a themed land *not* in costume was about as serious offense as any employee could make.

"Excuse me," she said pushing past them, and then remembered the word for excuse me in Atlantean too late. Talking out of character was equally frowned upon. All employees were strictly forbidden from entering any land that they didn't have at least a rudimentary grasp of the language, even made up ones.

Checking her holographic map out in front of her glasses, she spotted Mark's location. Naturally, he'd be at the town's most important building, The Temple of Poseidon.

In a fusion of Greek and Atlantean architectural ideas, the temple itself was on a high podium surrounded on all four sides by a wide series of grooved columns. To gain entrance one had to ascend an imposing set of steps that ensnared a white marble altar on a travertine base that supported an impressive golden sundial.

Checking the time, Lisa thought, *Is it really 4 pm? Why did it take me so long to get here?*

As she climbed the steps, she heard herself huffing and puffing with exertion and thought, *I really need to work out more than three times a week.*

Reaching the top, she was forced to slide to a stop because a biological dressed as an Atlantean guard blocked the entrance. Spotting her, he fiercely commanded, "You there, halt!"

According to the script in such cases, Lisa had three choices before her: Bribe the guards with earned coinage, outwit them (which took too much time), or fight them.

Short on time, and checking to see no one was watching, Lisa field kicked the Atlantean sentry between the legs, and the man went down. Two other Atlantean guards stepped from the shadows, already drawing their swords.

Lisa immediately recognized the soldier's advance as stunt choreography programed by Billy Colter (the stunt coordinator assigned to Atlantis). Billy used to let her spar with the biologicals to work out any bugs in the fight scenes. For someone who had trouble finding time to hit the gym, it was not only great exercise, but it was also a wonderful diversion from work.

Remembering the fight choreography, and without even gazing up from her data pad, she easily stepped to the side of the guard's thrusting sword. She then squatted down and ducked under a second brigand's blade swinging over her head from behind. When the first solider went to shove his sword through her stomach a second time, she dodged nimbly out of the way, again without even looking up, causing the first guard to skewer his fellow soldier.

The optics in her glasses for the safety protocols were in place, but for some weird reason, they were set at the highest level (meaning the guards could still break her arm or stab her in a non-vital area of the body; all of which could be fixed in minutes with modern medical technology.) Lisa knew each guest could select their preferred threat level, which ranged from a rated yellow experience (no pain or physical injury), all the way to a rated purple experience (intense pain, and susceptible to an injury that could put a guest in the hospital for weeks).

Despite the higher combat level setting, Lisa wasn't afraid. She started to circle around the mortally wounded guard, when to her surprise, the stabbing soldier planted one foot on his dead companion's pelvic bone and pulled his sword back out of his abdomen. Blood now painting his blade, he came at her again.

That's new, she thought, but dodged a series of sword swipes that were another familiar combination. As she did so, she noticed the first sentry, down with a field kick, was now climbing to his feet. *I really don't have time for this.*

As both soldiers encircled her again, she uttered the word, "Turducken," and both soldiers immediately froze into place. This was a stop-command the technicians had decided amongst themselves to program. More than any other reason, it was for saving time when moving across the parks. The *stop-word* only lasted a few minutes, so she quickly squeezed past them.

As she ducked under the angry-faced guard's outstretched sword, she said politely, "Excuse me," even though they couldn't hear her, and she remembered the words in Atlantean again too late. The guard, a bulbous-nosed fellow with a wicked glare, seemed none too happy about not being able to move more than his eyes at her.

Shuddering involuntarily, she thought*, Wow. That's a little too real, even for me.* Spotting the entrance to the temple, she steadied her nerves and*, Now, to find Mr. McCormick.*

She wasn't looking forward to the meeting. Unlike Mark McCormick, her last boss had been a great man, and an even greater mentor. He had personally taken her under his wing for the first seven years of her employment and helped her initiate the Leftenant Program when no one else believed a young intern like her could accomplish such a daunting task. But like all the other good men, he had been drafted, and like all good soldiers, he had been killed in the stupid, stupid war that had already claimed over thirty-million lives world-wide.

Chapter 2

Temple of Mark

Inside the Temple of Poseidon, it took a few moments for her eyes to adjust to the light. When they finally did, Lisa beheld an elongated courtyard with colorful peristyle gardens, open to the sky. The sound of a gurgling fountain drew her eyes to the marble and bronze statues set amongst the plants.

Her clicking heels echoed off the stone walls as she traversed the long, deserted corridor. With the throngs of people outside, it was weird not seeing anybody. About halfway to the inner chamber, she heard a splashing sound. This was followed by the sound of a man moaning. She rounded another grooved pillar and located its source.

Just shy of the reception room, a bubbling pool of excrement was being used as some kind of sick torture device. A man in a non-themed business suit was tied to a great disc about the size of a wagon wheel. As the Atlantean slaves turned the handle, the wheel would dunk under the sewage, cycle under, and then pop out again on the other side of the pool. Written in Latin, above the man, she saw words, *Computantis Monitum, (Accountants Be Warned).* Lisa didn't see a designator above the victim's head indicating what level biological he was. *Huh, my glasses must be malfunctioning.*

She had a hard time puzzling out the purpose of that scene. *Was this something Mark added? It didn't exactly match the whole Atlantis motif.* It was almost as though Mark was torturing a human accountant. *If so, why?* The word *embezzlement* came to mind. *No, surely Mark isn't disciplining any living employee in such a manner. Human Resources would never stand for it. Then again, Mark was a senior V.P. in the company. Is there really anything they can't do?* As a shiver ran down her spine, a large, beefy Centurion, much bigger than the others outside, spotted her and commanded gruffly, "Andare avanti."

Lisa needed no translation to, 'move along.'

As she turned on her heel to do just that, the accountant groaned once more, took a quick breath and went under for another dunking.

There's no way that's real. You're just being silly.

Lisa quickened her pace to her meeting.

Stepping inside the lavishly decorated throne room, enhanced by colorful murals and intricate mosaics, it didn't take Lisa long to locate Mark. He was sitting on a white marble couch in front of a giant golden statue of the Greek god, Poseidon. He was sculpted riding a chariot pulled by six beautiful winged horses.

Mark was dressed in elaborate traditional Atlantean garb (a violet tunic) and was surrounded by scantily dressed slave women who were attending to his every need. One woman was pouring a pitcher of steaming water into the atrium pool at his sandaled feet, while two others sponged his bare shoulders and legs. A fifth woman was fanning him with a long and colorful feather that belonged to a peacock that probably never existed. By the pool, a trio of women, all as beautiful as they were exotic, played soothing music on their lyres. Lisa's optics scanned all the occupants. There wasn't a single human within.

Save Mark.

One of Mark's eyes lazily opened. He drank her in, and before speaking, he sighed with contentment. "You haven't lived until you've had a warm sponge bath." Another slave girl poured steaming water over his head and Mark exhaled with even greater pleasure.

Mark was what the other park *cast members* called a *full-timer*, meaning he never actually went home. The parks were his home now. Besides, why would you want to drive home (even in the most luxurious limo) just to be another regular Joe in rush hour traffic? When instead, you could stay here and be worshiped as a living god, twenty-four hours a day, seven-days a week. For some managers, turning full-time was too much for them to handle, but Mark made the transition seamlessly. Probably because prior to making V.P., he already thought of himself as a god.

As his eyes washed over her, she thought she detected a lingering glance, but Lisa knew there was nothing to it. It was well known amongst cast members that Mark preferred the company of flawless bioengineered women to the aging real thing.

It wasn't enough for him to be a high-ranking Atlantean senator either, or even the emperor himself. No. Mark McCormick had to be the Sun God Apollo, the biggest ladies' man of all the deities. To look the part, he had chest, calf and bicep implants surgically installed. Of course, not a single muscle on him had been earned in a gym. Unfortunately for Mark, it was obvious to everyone but him. The human tissue between the muscles was as fleshy and lumpy as before. Mark's physique in its entirety reminded Lisa of a late Van Gogh painting.

"Ah," he said snapping his fingers two times. "Uhmm… Lisa… uh, Burton, isn't it?"

He hadn't forgotten her name. They had started with the company at roughly the same time; he had gone into sales, and she, engineering. It was all part of how he made everyone feel inferior.

"Hello, sir. I came as soon as I was summoned."

He held up his chin and gazed down his nose at her. Holding up three fingers he said, "Three things... there are three things I, the sun god Apollo, wish to discuss with you."

Lisa was fairly certain Mark didn't really believe he was an actual deity; he thought much higher of himself than that. Unsure of what to say, she only nodded that she understood.

"The first, is... excellent work."

Whew. She hadn't realized she'd been holding her breath until she let it out.

"To be more precise, excellent work on the Leftenant Project." Mark put his fingers to his lips, kissed them and pulled them away like a French Chef who just created a masterpiece. "Absolutely first-rate work on the A.I. The eggheads tell me that it is the most advanced state-of-the-art artificial intelligence they'd ever seen."

He frowned, leaned forward, and squinted his eyes down at her. He quickly changed the subject and asked, "Who put you in holographics, anyway? Who did that?" Sitting back up, he said, "No. We need to put your skills to better use and put you on the bio-log-i-cals."

Waving his hand in dismissal, "Holograms are a thing of the past." Mark noticed the young pitcher-girl proactively staring at him with a slender finger touching her pouting lips. "People want things they can feel," he gently caressed the girl's cheek, "and touch."

Well, touch and feel are actually the same thing, she thought inwardly. What she said was, "Sir, I'm perfectly happy working on The Dauntless Project."

This got his attention. "Oh, right. The Dauntless Project. Man, are we ever over-budget on that monster." Mark stopped and studied her as though seeing her for the first time. Frowning, he asked, "Wait a second. Why aren't you in costume?"

Before she could answer he said, "Larissa, what is our job here?" Again, not giving her time to answer, he answered for her, "To create fantasies, right? And, those fantasies break down when some dunder-head walks around ancient Atlantis in a white lab coat, glasses and high-heels."

She didn't bring up the fact the tunnels had collapsed and are still being remodeled. Mark flashed a sidelong glance at the scribe, who also doubled as Mark's administrative assistant in real life. The scribe, a high-functioning TK-11, read and understood his master's look.

Seeing the brief exchange, Lisa thought, *My paycheck's going to be a little short this week*. Not that she needed it.

She never went anywhere. She had more than enough money. Stranger World was her life now.

Oh, fudder-dudder, does that make me a full-timer too?

"Now what was I saying?" Mark asked the scribe. The scribe opened his mouth to speak and Mark waved him off, "Never mind, I got it-I got it."

"Number two, we love everything you're doing. So, with The Leftenant Program, I want you to replicate her and put a copy of her on every Exploratory Air Ship in the world. And, it is my understanding that you already refused this request?"

"Sir?" Lisa asked.

This is unacceptable. It was bad enough the Dauntless had already been replicated. Originally, Her Majesty's Air Ship (H.M.A.S.) was built to take guests on harrowing expeditions through differently-themed, steampunk storylines. However, since the Victorian airship proved so popular among the guests, Corporate (in their infinite wisdom) decided to build a fleet of poor facsimiles which could fly guests from port to port all over the planet like some common shuttle bus.

Now they want to duplicate the Leftenant? No way!

Mark crisply shook his head. "What part don't you understand?"

If we replicate the Leftenant, it will only cheapen her, she wanted to say. No, she wanted to scream it. What she ended up saying was, "I was told that each airship would have her own exclusive signature crew, thereby making everyone's experience unique from everyone else's."

"Yeah-yeah-yeah. That's all well and good. Maybe it's a great idea, but I'm the poor shmuck who has to worry about crunching the numbers."

Under his breath, and yet loud enough for her to hear, he mumbled, "I'm beginning to see why you're still in holographics." He went to rise from his throne but feeling it would take more energy than he wished to expel at the moment, he sat back down.

Realizing she was still in the room, he added, "Look, don't blame me. Thank the war. Thanks to the military constantly stealing our best engineers, biologicals and technology, we are overworked and over budget."

Lisa thought this last bit might have had more impact if a slave girl hadn't been feeding him individual grapes while he said it.

The irony was lost on Mark.

Mouth still full with grapes, he managed, "So, instead of having a different crew on every air ship in the park, I want the same crew, with the *your* Leftenant on every air ship.

"Yes sir," was what she said. *Over my dead body* was what she thought.

Mark sighed, "Ah, great then. Good." He cast a sidelong glance at the scribe and muttered, "And, *you* said she was going to be difficult." He then clapped his hands together and exhaled, "Oh, wonderful, just wonderful."

Lisa thought Mark was referring to their conversation, but then realized he was gazing past her at three, tall, provocatively-dressed women gliding into the room. Lisa didn't need her optics. They were far too beautiful to be human. In fact, they were probably the most beautiful women she had seen in her life. Technically, park cast members fraternizing with biologicals was strictly against Standard Operating Procedure (S.O.P.), but company policy never seemed to deter Mark. It was well known that, *Mark gets what Mark wants.*

His attention was obviously divided between the three women and their meeting. Still gazing upon them, he snapped his fingers to his scribe and asked, "What was the other thing?"

The scribe opened his mouth to speak again, but he waved him off, "No, no, no. I got it-I got it. The last thing. No more joy rides in *the Dauntless*." He tore his eyes from the beautiful slave girls and leered down at her, "And, don't raise your eyebrows over big Bambi eyes at me and say, 'Sir?' You know exactly what I'm talking about. I read your time card. In fact, I read all of your reports. The joyrides are *not* for research and development. Just because the original, track-free prototype can still go up and down and isn't locked onto a fixed track yet, doesn't mean you can go joy riding whenever the mood strikes you. No. *No...more...joyrides.* Am I making myself perfectly clear?"

One of the beautiful slave women walked up behind him, leaned over and put her lips to his ear lobe while the other began fondling his hair. "Now if you'll excuse me, I have a very important meeting I must to attend to." As the slave women helped him to his feet and led him away, he said over his shoulder, "I feel like we got a lot done here today. When you leave, make sure you use the tunnels. Or, for Neptune's sake, get a costume. I don't care which." He was speaking faster and faster now. "Remember, Fulfilling Fantasies is our mission." As the sultry slave woman led him off to a private chamber, he said over his shoulder, "Thank you, Teresa, good talk."

The scribe raised a hand toward a side entrance and under his watchful gaze she was forced to retreat through it. To the outside observer, it actually appeared as though she had walked through a wall and vanished.

'What a farfegnugen'.

"...afterwards there occurred violent earthquakes and floods; and in a single day and night of misfortune, all your warlike men in a body sank into the earth, and the island of Atlantis in like manner disappeared in the depths of the sea."

-Plato, 360 B.C.

Chapter 3

Day of Reckoning

Great.

To Lisa's dismay, the side door didn't lead to the tunnels or even backstage. Instead, she found herself back outside, on the streets, amongst the throngs of people milling about and going on with their daily lives. A brief rumbling under her feet was a harsh reminder that the end was nigh. *I best get downstairs before the fireworks show starts.*

Still mulling over her meeting with Mark, and trying to sort out what was said, she spotted everyone's beloved gargoyle, dressed in Atlantis attire and making balloon animals for the kids. Lisa couldn't help but smile. The Leftenant aside, Cheeves always had been her favorite and was one of the "Big Five" major Stranger World characters that guests had expected to meet and greet in every park, regardless of theme.

As she made her way toward the nearest tunnel entrance, she spotted another theme park-staple. As usual, he was perched on his lamppost, only this lamppost and been traded for a torch-bearing pillar and his ringmaster's outfit was swapped out for a toga.

Normally, the extremely popular Lamppost Man was far too busy with park guests to ever take notice of her. Maybe it was because she was out of costume, but their eyes locked, and for a full ten seconds, they just stood there like that, simply staring at one another. Surprisingly, it was the Lamppost Man who blinked first. He smiled knowingly, tilted his head to the side and then pointed toward a distant Titan, who even now was beginning to awaken from his week-long slumber.

As Lisa turned to cast her eyes toward the massive volcano in the distance, the *Great Destroyer* belched violently. In a matter of seconds, the top of the mountain blasted off. In its place was a raging plume of fire, and lava began spewing from its maw. She could only watch as a black and dreadful cloud, embroiled with flames and lightning, filled the sky and enveloped the town in sudden darkness.

Everyone tilted their heads back to watch the awesome spectacle of man-made nature. One guest began laughing nervously, and now another couple began backing away. Echoing her own thoughts, an oafish merchant next to her said in a thick New Jersey accent, "I didn't expect it to look so... real."

It did look real, and majestic, also breathtaking and terrifying all at the same time. *Wow, the creationeers did quite a convincing job.* So good in fact, she found herself backpedaling away from it without even realizing it. She glanced around at the other park guests to see if they were as intimidated as she was. The guests were also backing away. She found herself staring at the fat merchant with the beautiful, biological slave. When he saw her looking at him he asked her in a wavering voice, "This is normal, right?"

Lisa felt herself nod.

"I mean, I heard it looked real, but I never expected anything like this."

Lisa was about to reassure the frightened park guest that everything was going to be alright, when the sound of missiles soaring through the air caused her to lift her eyes skyward once more. As she did, an endless downpour of glowing volcanic rock, some no bigger than pennies, others fist sized, descended down upon them; one of which, bounced off her shoulder. *Ow, that really hurt. I don't think it's supposed to hurt anyone.*

Another tremor shifted the stone tiles beneath their feet. With a stupendous crack, the city street opened up and a fresh chasm swallowed up several terrified citizens.

This can't be right. Confirming this thought, a woman near Lisa kept shouting, "Something's wrong, something's gone very wrong!"

The fiery hailstorm increased, and now everyone was covering their heads with seat cushions, silver platters, and anything else they could find. Even the biologicals were playing their parts (or were genuinely frightened) and seemed frantic to get away. The merchant's curvaceous wife kept screaming in character, "The sky is falling, the sky is falling!"

Amidst the pandemonium, only the Lamppost Man, perched high upon his torch pillar, seemed unaffected and unafraid. If anything, he appeared thoroughly amused by all the chaos happening around them. Smirking, he adjusted his toga over his striped pants and boots.

More missiles of lava rock rained down upon them. Several lamps shattered, spilling their oil and fueling numerous fires. Within minutes, the roof of the theater collapsed. The destruction of other buildings soon followed.

Something is definitely wrong!

Only a mere few minutes ago, the nearby waters in the bay were glistening off a sun in a cloudless sky, and the streets had been alive with commerce and friendly banter.

The taverns and the shops were brimming with inhabitants enjoying the vast amenities Atlantis had to offer. Yet, now, the sun was blocked out by ominous clouds and those same happy citizens were shrieking for someone to save them. She had never actually experienced the Atlantis *Day of Reckoning* before, but this couldn't possibly be going as planned.

The shrieking woman was right, something had gone wrong; people were getting hurt and dying all around her.

Lisa snatched up a basket, emptied out its contents and used it as a helmet to protect her head. As she sought cover, a myriad of theories ran through her head; *technical malfunction, corporate sabotage, a terrorist attack?* She became increasingly frightened. Man-made or not, the volcano was trying to kill her, and every last person within the park. It had happened before, *only not on such a large scale as this!*

Surprising even herself, Lisa shouted, "Everyone, stay calm!" but she was ignored when a giant boulder of red hot magma came hurtling down upon them and impacted the area like a mortar round. Several victims were blown sky high into the air.

Then, almost as quickly as it had begun, the hailstorm of fire began to decrease.

Oh, thank you, Lord.

Just when she thought the worst of it was over, she witnessed a massive tidal wave of hot molten-ash, accompanied by a continuous roar, sweeping down the street toward them. The mob saw it too and formed a human wave of flesh that began trampling toward her.

In an instant, Lisa went from professional park employee trying to calm everyone down to just another panicked soul, desperate to outrun a monstrous black river of crushing, burning debris.

Out of the corner of her eye, Lisa saw the wave of bubbling molten ash overtake the grinning Lamppost Man first. It would happen to her too, only a second later.

Choking on the poisonous gas, Lisa made one final dash for the stairwell that would take her to the safety of the tunnels below. She didn't get more than a few feet before the hot cloud of volcanic ash enveloped her body, searing her flesh instantly. Ash filling her lungs, she was already beginning to feel the effects of petrification as she was rendered immobile.

There was a brief moment of disembodiment. She couldn't see, hear, or even breathe, -it was more horrible than she could have ever imagined.

As her body became forever entombed, adding to the necropolis of the dead all around her, for all eternity, Lisa's last thought was simply...

We finally went too far.

AFTERWORD

Most Stranger World stories are inspired by one or two particulars. For *Stranger World* it was decades of experience working at major theme parks and the love for my sick daughter. For *Stranger Realm* it was my time as an Alaskan Tour Guide, every week, getting to take an eclectic group of passengers across a landscape as dangerous as it was majestic. *Stranger Tides* is unique in that it was inspired by several themes. Here's the top three: The Ocean, Twilight Zone and my crazy Kids.

First, I love the Ocean.

More specifically, I love humanity's exploration of the ocean. Most likely this had a lot to do with growing up in Florida and spending more time on, in or under the water than on good ole terra firma. As a kid, I still remember fantasizing about being that tiny antique diver exploring the far reaches of my dad's oversized fish tank. This fascination only grew as my friends and I would often to pretend to be Captain Nemo's crew, exploring new underwater worlds and mysterious islands.

Then, as a working adult in the theme park industry, I was privy to a lot of amazing plans still on the drawing boards. You wouldn't believe all the stuff that is on the horizon for underwater theme parks! These not only inspired much of the futuristic leisure palaces mentioned in this book, but they're not as far off as you might think.

Twilight Zone: I seriously doubt this will come as a shock to any of you, but the original, black-and-white Twilight Zone was a serious impact on my childhood. Back then, you couldn't simply download a movie or show just by speaking its name into the Genie that is today's television. No. Back then, when I was about ten-years-old, if I wanted to watch it, I had to set my alarm clock to wake me up at 11:30pm (the only time it would air), sneak out into the living room, and keep the volume low so as not to wake my parents. Every episode, I'd sit on the floor in my pajamas close to the Tv, mesmerized by some pretty terrifying episodes.

I think what interested me the most about Rod Serling's masterpiece was it was the one show that I couldn't predict the outcome. You never knew what the main characters were going to find behind the next door, in the diner, or... on the wing of a plane. This is not only a theme for the book, but easily one of my favorite themes for the whole series.

Finally, ***my Kids***. Every day I am amazed to learn the things they are capable of and how they are not so much children as they are miniature adults with only a little bit of life experience. Their constant unpredictability surprises me as much as any Twilight Zone episode ever could. It was important to me to address Mad-Maddie and Traxx and what it might be like for them to grow up in this mixed-up, upside-down world.

I also really wanted to show the Leftenant in her most maternal form and how she interacted with the kids. Believe me when I say this, when she didn't make it, *no one* was more shocked and upset as I was. Well, almost no one. The moment the beta readers learned of her demise, they ripped off the front door off my house and I had to change zip codes.

Speaking to the last, I can only quote one of our dearly departed friends when I say, "Chin up little one," and have faith.

Until our next adventure together,

-Jack

ABOUT THE AUTHOR

Jack Castle's novels have been consistently ranked in the Top 100 Bestselling books on Amazon and are available worldwide in e-book, print, iTunes, Kobo, and Barnes and Noble.

He has been labeled by the Coeur D'Alene Press as the "Man of Adventures!" and traveled the globe as a professional stuntman for stage, film, and television. While working as a stuntman for Universal Studios, he met Cinderella at Walt Disney World, and they were soon married.

After moving to Alaska, he worked as a tour guide, police officer, and Criminal Justice professor. He has been stationed on a remote island in the Aleutians as a Response Team Commander, and his last job in the Arctic Circle was protecting engineers from ravenous polar bears.

Moving his family to North Idaho, for the past decade, Jack Castle has been crafting thrilling, award-winning, adventures for Silverwood Theme Park and guiding millions of guests through them. He also enjoys helping others get published by teaching writing classes at North Idaho College.

www.JackCastlebooks.com

CPSIA information can be obtained
at www.ICGtesting.com
Printed in the USA
LVHW082346170120
644096LV00012B/281

9 781087 858715